P9-CRQ-236

INTRODUCTION

Minifigures bring the LEGO *Star Wars* galaxy to life—whether they are celebrated heroes like Obi-Wan Kenobi and Luke Skywalker, humble droids, or virtually identical clone troopers. They may be small figures, but they have many LEGO® elements that make them fascinating and highly collectible.

How to use this book:
The book is divided into eight *Star Wars* sections—Episodes I through VI, the Clone Wars, and the Expanded Universe. The minifigures are ordered according to the *Star Wars* property in which they first appeared or mostly featured. Tabs at the top of each page indicate every *Star Wars* property in which a minifigure appears (see above)*. As most *Star Wars* characters appear in the Expanded Universe, that tab is highlighted only if a minifigure appears in an EU set. The book distinguishes between "versions" of minifigures and "variants." Versions are separate minifigures in their own right—so each version has its own page. Variants are the same version of a minifigure but with modifications. For example, there are ten versions of Luke Skywalker in this book; one of those is X-wing pilot Luke, and that minifigure has been released in five different variations or variants. Like Luke, some minifigures have lots of variants, though, sadly, not all of them can fit in this book. The most significant ones, however, are shown in a "star variant" picture box. Data boxes on every page detail a minifigure's most recent set number and name, the year that set was released, the number of LEGO pieces from which the minifigure is made, any equipment or weapons it carries, and its number of variants. An alphabetical index of minifigures at the end of the book lists all the LEGO *Star Wars* sets in which each minifigure has ever appeared, along with its page number.

*Note that if a character has both a Clone Wars minifigure and a classic minifigure, the Clone Wars tab is highlighted only on the Clone Wars version's page.

Contents
MEET THE MINIFIGURES

EPISODE V

EPISODE VI

CLONE WARS

EXPANDED UNIVERSE

Maverick Jedi Master Qui-Gon Jinn has appeared in seven LEGO *Star Wars* sets since 1999. There are four slightly different variants of Qui-Gon, but he always appears in his Jedi robe and tunic, ready to undertake a mission for the Jedi Order. Each variant has either his unique brown hair or a brown hood, which helps him to keep a low profile.

STAR VARIANT

Qui-Gon wrong
In the Republic Cruiser (set 7665), Qui-Gon has tan legs, a hood... and the wrong head! His head is Obi-Wan Kenobi's from General Grievous Chase (set 7255). It was later replaced with the correct head.

Qui-Gon Jinn
JEDI MASTER

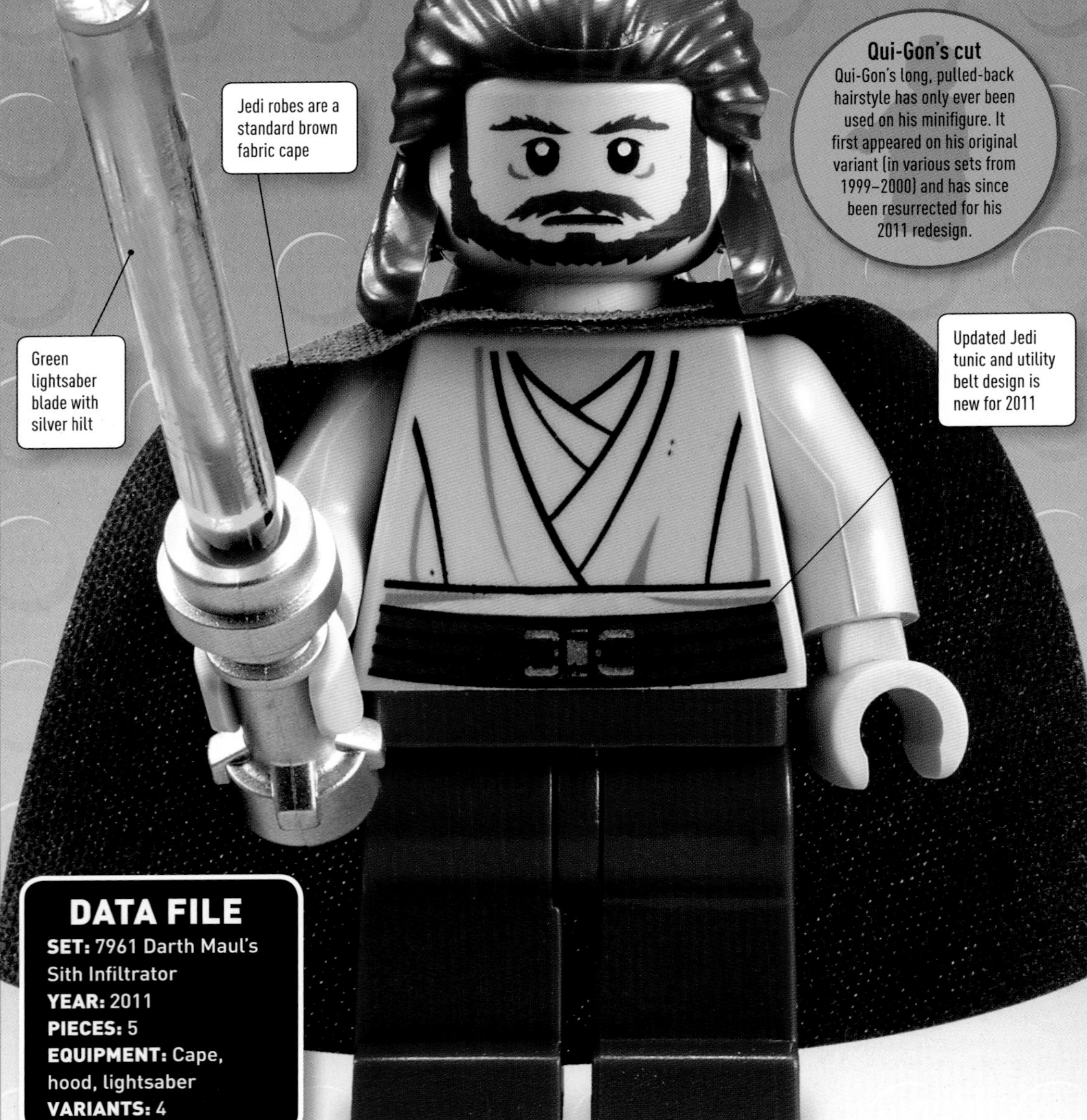

Jedi robes are a standard brown fabric cape
Green lightsaber blade with silver hilt
Updated Jedi tunic and utility belt design is new for 2011

Qui-Gon's cut
Qui-Gon's long, pulled-back hairstyle has only ever been used on his minifigure. It first appeared on his original variant (in various sets from 1999–2000) and has since been resurrected for his 2011 redesign.

DATA FILE

SET: 7961 Darth Maul's Sith Infiltrator
YEAR: 2011
PIECES: 5
EQUIPMENT: Cape, hood, lightsaber
VARIANTS: 4

Obi-Wan Kenobi
PADAWAN APPRENTICE

Young Padawan Obi-Wan Kenobi is apprentice to Jedi Master Qui-Gon Jinn, faithfully learning the ways of the Force. This version of Obi-Wan appears in four different sets and each minifigure has a slight variation. He is, however, always dressed in his Jedi apparel and is seldom without his blue lightsaber.

DATA FILE

SET: 7962 Anakin's and Sebulba's Podracers
YEAR: 2011
PIECES: 5
EQUIPMENT: Cape, lightsaber
VARIANTS: 4

STAR VARIANT

Padawan braid
Obi-Wan Kenobi has a Padawan braid over his right shoulder in Jedi Defense I (set 7203). The variant is unique to that set, and the torso piece is not used on any other minifigures.

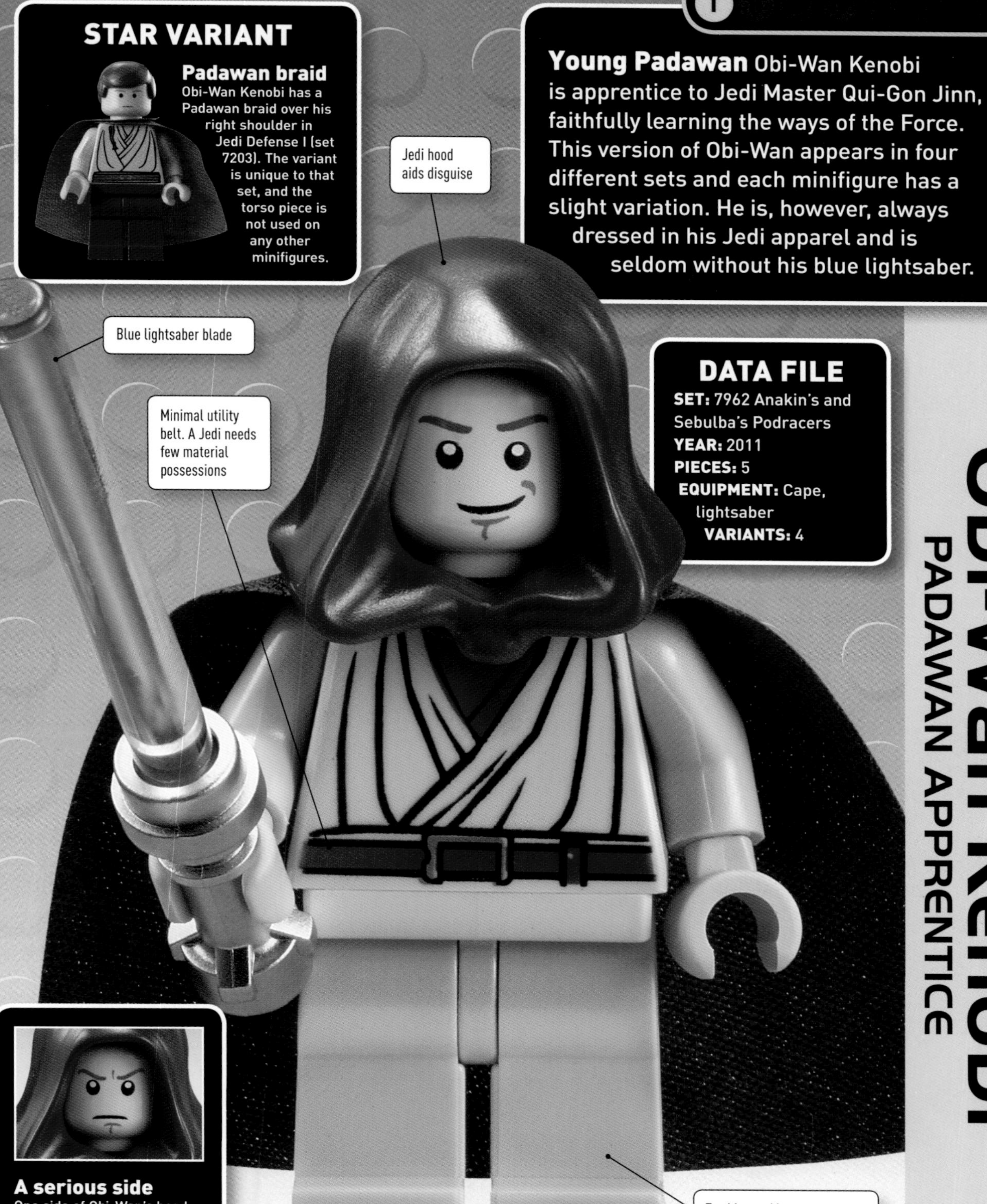

Jedi hood aids disguise
Blue lightsaber blade
Minimal utility belt. A Jedi needs few material possessions
Tan hips and legs are seen on the 2011 design and the variant found in the Republic Cruiser (set 7665)

A serious side
One side of Obi-Wan's head looks relaxed, with a slight smile, but the other is more serious and ready for action.

Jar Jar Binks

GOOFY GUNGAN

Bumbling Gungan Jar Jar Binks broke the LEGO mold as the first minifigure ever to have a unique head sculpt. He found his way into five Episode I sets in 1999–2000, and then made a comeback in the 2011 set The Battle of Naboo (7929). In 2011, Jar Jar's head-mold had printing added to it to give him a new look.

Flat eyes, painted yellow with black pupils

Mottled skin is good for camouflage

Jar Jar is an outcast from his people and lives alone in the swamps, so his clothing is dirty and ragged

Torso design is first seen on the 2011 design. The pattern continues on the back

This Jar Jar has flesh-colored arms and hands, while the original has lighter tan arms and hands

STAR VARIANT

Early Jar Jar
The first LEGO Jar Jar Binks has a very similar head-mold to the 2011 design except for one thing: his eye stalks are split to depict his eyes. On the 2011 design, Jar Jar's eye stalks are flat and he has painted eyes.

Amphibious ears
Jar Jar's distinct floppy ears are integrated into his head-mold and are printed with a mottled-skin pattern.

DATA FILE

SET: 7929 The Battle of Naboo
YEAR: 2011
PIECES: 3
EQUIPMENT: Energy balls
VARIANTS: 2

Padmé Naberrie
DISGUISED QUEEN OF NABOO

Don't tell anyone but Padmé Naberrie is actually Queen Amidala of Naboo in disguise! She is dressed as one of her handmaidens to avoid detection on the planet Tatooine. Padmé appears in this disguise in three LEGO *Star Wars* sets, in two variations, but she remains an enigma in the LEGO world—she has never been seen in her royal robes as Queen of Naboo.

STAR VARIANT

First Queen
The original Padmé Naberrie minifigure has yellow flesh, a unique wide-smiled head, and slightly different printing on her torso. She comes in two sets: Anakin's Podracer (set 7131) and Mos Espa Podrace (set 7171).

Two faces
One side of Padmé's face is smiling, but turn it around and the other side has a look of concern.

Padmé's long hair is braided at the top and flows down her back

Padmé is simply dressed in a gray vest and blue undershirt. This unique torso pattern continues on the back

Red-jeweled belt

Padmé carries a short blaster pistol to protect herself

DATA FILE

SET: 7961 Darth Maul's Sith Infiltrator
YEAR: 2011
PIECES: 4
EQUIPMENT: Blaster
VARIANTS: 2

Anakin Skywalker
PODRACING SLAVE BOY

Young slave Anakin Skywalker may be just a boy, but he can handle a Podracer like no one else! This minifigure made his Podracing debut in 1999 and has since sped into seven sets. The 2011 variant can change from ordinary slave boy to Podracing supremo, ready to ride in his redesigned Podracer.

Anakin's Podracer (set 7131)
Look out for Anakin's Podracer swooshing through the skies! Seated in the control pod of this 1999 set is the original Anakin, with regular (not short) legs and a gray helmet. Anakin's Podracer was updated in 2011.

DATA FILE
SET: 7962 Anakin's and Sebulba's Podracers
YEAR: 2011
PIECES: 4
EQUIPMENT: None
VARIANTS: 4

The variant in the Naboo Starfighter (set 7877) has a brown helmet and hair

Necklace given to Anakin by his mother

Anakin wears a simple slave tunic with a brown belt on Tatooine. His clothing can be seen on the back of his torso, too

The shorter LEGO legs do not have a moveable hip joint like regular legs

STAR VARIANT

Short stuff
The young Anakin minifigure was one of the first to try out shorter legs. The first variant seen with them is in the 2007 set Naboo N-1 Starfighter and Vulture Droid (7660).

Rare racer
This early variant is exclusive to the 1999 set Naboo Starfighter (7141). A similar variant with a gray helmet appears in three 1999–2000 sets.

Podrace face
This side of Anakin's face has goggles and a determined look. He is ready to Podrace!

R2-D2
ASTROMECH DROID

Brave astromech droid R2-D2 has ventured into 22 LEGO *Star Wars* sets to date, making him the most recurring minifigure in the LEGO line. R2-D2's head was redesigned in 2008, but the rest of him has remained the same since his release in 1999, with one exception: In Jabba's Sail Barge (set 6210), poor R2 is forced to carry drinks on a serving tray.

Jedi Starfighter (set 7256)

R2-D2's head piece alone appears in two sets: Jedi Starfighter (set 7256) and Ultimate Space Battle (set 7283). Only R2-D2's head is visible when he is in flight mode, navigating his owner safely through space aboard a Jedi Starfighter.

STAR VARIANT

Jabba's droid

R2-D2 is set to work serving Jabba the Hutt and his low-life friends in the 2006 set Jabba's Sail Barge (set 6210). He has a serving tray with drinks between his head and body pieces.

DATA FILE

SET: 7877 Naboo Starfighter
YEAR: 2011
PIECES: 4
EQUIPMENT: None
VARIANTS: 3

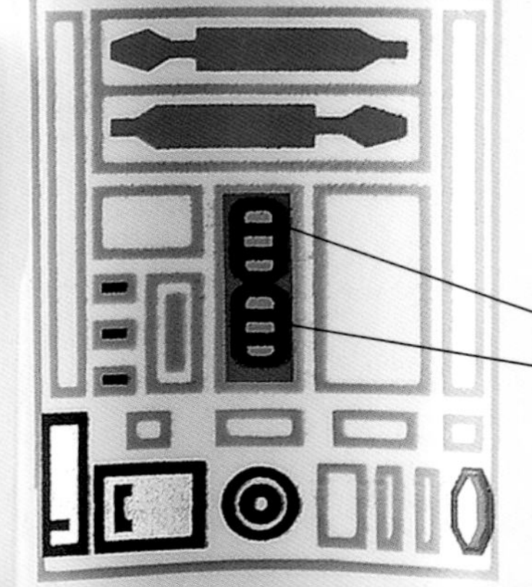

Camera eye records messages

Holoprojector transmits holographic images and acts as a spotlight

LEGO R2-D2 had a white head with silver and blue printing before his redesign in 2008, when he acquired this bluish-gray head

LEGO Technic pins join R2-D2's legs to his body

Acoustic signaler and ventilation point

Astromech

When R2-D2 was first released in 1999, his entire body was made from unique LEGO pieces. Since then, all LEGO *Star Wars* astromech droids have used the same pieces but with varying printing and colors.

Watto
JUNKYARD DEALER

This tricky Toydarian junk dealer is a tough minifigure to get hold of! Watto first appeared in a single set in 2001, Watto's Junkyard (set 7186), and was not seen again—until he resurfaced in 2011 with a new look. As he is constantly in flight, Watto's minifigure has a translucent stand to raise him above the dusty earth of Tatooine.

STAR VARIANT

Blue Watto

The original variant of winged Watto is not one for details—he has a plain blue head and torso piece with no printing on it. Underneath that is a plain tan torso piece. This variant is rare, appearing in only one 2001 set: Watto's Junkyard (set 7186).

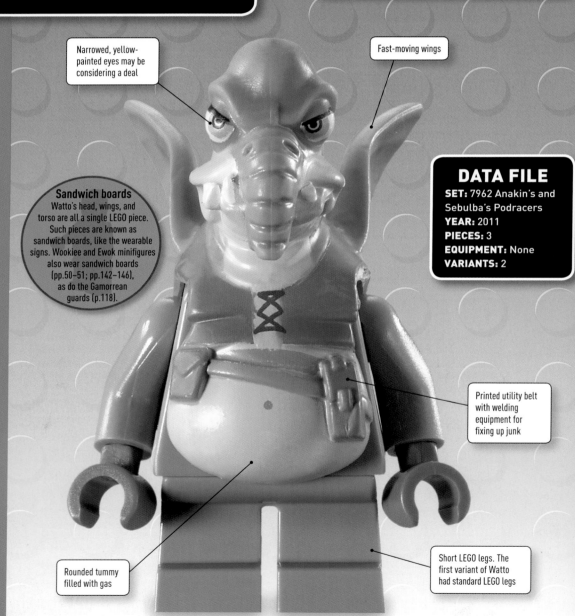

Narrowed, yellow-painted eyes may be considering a deal

Fast-moving wings

Sandwich boards

Watto's head, wings, and torso are all a single LEGO piece. Such pieces are known as sandwich boards, like the wearable signs. Wookiee and Ewok minifigures also wear sandwich boards (pp.50–51; pp.142–146), as do the Gamorrean guards (p.118).

DATA FILE

SET: 7962 Anakin's and Sebulba's Podracers
YEAR: 2011
PIECES: 3
EQUIPMENT: None
VARIANTS: 2

Printed utility belt with welding equipment for fixing up junk

Rounded tummy filled with gas

Short LEGO legs. The first variant of Watto had standard LEGO legs

Sebulba
PODRACER PILOT

Dangerous Dug Sebulba is the arch rival of Anakin Skywalker and one of the most successful Podracers on Tatooine—mostly through his ruthless rule-breaking. He made his minifigure debut in 1999 at the helm of his imposing orange Pod packed with deadly weapons, and reemerged in 2011 clad in a flashy leather race outfit.

Anakin's and Sebulba's Podracers (set 7962)
Sebulba's Podracer in the Anakin's and Sebulba's Podracers set is built to intimidate. Not only is it bigger than his opponents' Podracers, but it also has a bunch of illegal weapons—some hidden—for sabotage purposes during the race.

STAR VARIANT

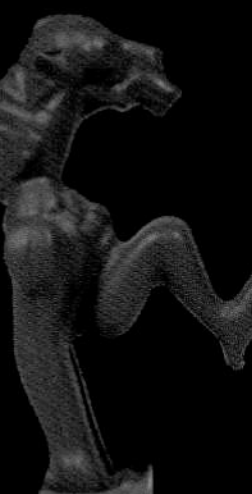

Static Sebulba
The original Sebulba is all one LEGO piece and has no movement capabilities, making it an unusual minifigure. This variant is rare—it is exclusive to the 2001 set, Mos Espa Podrace (set 7171).

Racing cap with goggles

Sebulba's head and body are one LEGO piece, but his arms are removeable

Sebulba has adapted his hind limbs to steer his Podracer

Sebulba walks on his arms. They are moveable on the 2011 redesign

Tight leg straps wind around Sebulba's hands

DATA FILE

SET: 7962 Anakin's and Sebulba's Podracers
YEAR: 2011
PIECES: 3
EQUIPMENT: None
VARIANTS: 2

Aldar Beedo
PODRACER PILOT

This mercenary minifigure has accepted payment for taking down his racing rival Sebulba during the Boonta Eve Classic Podrace. Can Aldar Beedo complete his task? His pretty impressive Podracer appears in the 2001 LEGO set Watto's Junkyard (set 7186) along with the latest variant of his lanky Glymphid minifigure.

Watto's Junkyard (set 7186)
The 2001 variant of Aldar Beedo is exclusively featured in Watto's Junkyard. His impressive Podracer is a *Mark IV* Flat-Twin Turbojet model with huge engines and afterburners. Beedo fits inside the pod.

This Podracer clearly isn't too worried about safety—he isn't wearing a flight helmet! But Beedo's original variant wears a brown helmet

STAR VARIANT

Older Aldar
This variant of Aldar Beedo appears in the *Star Wars* Podracing Bucket (set 7159), in a simplified version of Beedo's Podracer. The minifigure has no unique LEGO pieces and his body is mostly made up of parts from battle droid minifigures.

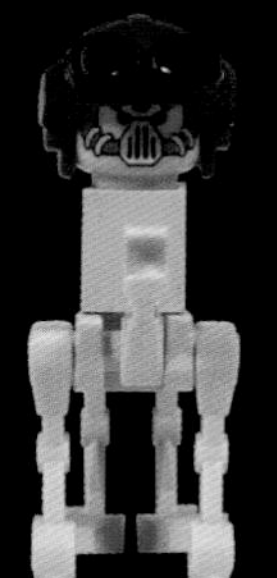

Elongated Glymphid snout

Glymphids have suction cups on their fingertips

DATA FILE

SET: 7186 Watto's Junkyard
YEAR: 2001
PIECES: 1
EQUIPMENT: None
VARIANTS: 2

The LEGO Group created Aldar Beedo's long, thin minifigure mold especially for him

One piece
Aldar Beedo is one of the few LEGO minifigures to be made from a single LEGO piece. The original variant of Beedo's Podracing rival Sebulba (p.11) is the only other single-piece minifigure in the LEGO *Star Wars* theme.

Stand fits into the cockpit of Beedo's Podracer. It is not removeable from his body

Gasgano
PODRACER PILOT

Multitasking minifigure Gasgano likes to keep his Podracing competitors at arm's length! He employs his many LEGO arms to pilot his Podracer at great speeds and takes second place in the Boonta Eve Classic. Blink and you will miss him, as the minifigure only appears in one LEGO *Star Wars* set.

Mos Espa Podrace (set 7171)
Watch out for Gasgano in this 1999 LEGO set—he is one of the fastest Podracers on the track! His exclusive minifigure can reach enormous speeds in his powerful LEGO Podracer thanks to anti-turbulence vanes that move as the craft races for the finish line of the Boonta Eve Classic.

This light gray LEGO helmet is popular on the Podracing circuit—young Podracer Anakin Skywalker (p.8) also wears it

Gasgano's arms
In Episode I, Gasgano has six arms, but his LEGO minifigure only has four! Two of Gasgano's arms work the foot pedals of his Podracer during a race and can't be seen—this may be why his minifigure has just four arms.

Gasgano's white head with large alien eyes and a driven stare is unique to his minifigure

These arm pieces feature on many droid minifigures in LEGO *Star Wars*

Gasgano is the only LEGO minifigure to feature this piece. It is often part of a chain saw tool in other sets

DATA FILE
SET: 7171 Mos Espa Podrace
YEAR: 1999
PIECES: 8
EQUIPMENT: None
VARIANTS: 1

W. Wald
RODIAN SLAVE

Young W. Wald is a slave on Tatooine. He is a Rodian minifigure—the third of the species to appear in LEGO bricks—and wears a simple slave tunic. W. Wald first appears alongside his friend Anakin Skywalker in the 2011 set Anakin's and Sebulba's Podracers (set 7962). He doubts his friend's Podracing skills, but maybe Anakin can change his mind in the Boonta Eve Classic!

Anakin's and Sebulba's Podracers (set 7962)
W. Wald makes his only LEGO *Star Wars* appearance to date in this 2011 set. The Rodian minifigure cheers on his friend, Anakin Skywalker, as he prepares to Podrace in the Boonta Eve Classic!

W. Wald's unique Rodian head has large, multifaceted eyes, rough green skin, and a protruding snout

Rodian
W. Wald is the third Rodian minifigure to appear in LEGO *Star Wars* sets—the first is bounty hunter Greedo (p.78). W. Wald's Rodian head is made from the same mold as Greedo's, but the color and printing is different.

Simple, hardwearing slave tunic. This torso design is unique to W. Wald's minifigure

W. Wald is a small Rodian child, so his minifigure has short, unposeable LEGO legs

DATA FILE
SET: 7962 Anakin's and Sebulba's Podracers
YEAR: 2011
PIECES: 3
EQUIPMENT: None
VARIANTS: 1

Pit Droid

PODRACER MECHANIC

Any Podracer problems are quickly fixed by the LEGO pit droid! There are three variants of the pit droid minifigure and all are present at the Mos Espa Podrace (set 7171). Each Podracer pilot included in the set—Anakin Skywalker, Sebulba, and Gasgano—has a dedicated pit droid. The pit droid is built to make speedy repairs, so its Podracer pilot won't be left waiting for long!

Mos Espa Podrace (set 7171)
This 1999 set contains all three variants of the pit droid. Each one has a repair station with a fully-stocked tool rack and race flags in its Podracer's racing colors. It looks like Sebulba's afterburner needs some attention!

STAR VARIANTS

Gasgano's droid
This pit droid is made from the same LEGO pieces as Anakin's pit droid but they are mostly white. It only appears in the 1999 set Mos Espa Podrace (set 7171).

Sebulba's droid
Sebulba is a shady character, so his pit droid is made up of dark-colored LEGO bricks! His mostly brown droid appears in Mos Espa Podrace (set 7171).

This head plate protects the pit droid from falling machinery

Single yellow photoreceptor

The pit droid's robotic arms handle various LEGO tools, including a circular saw and a power drill

This pit droid is dedicated to Anakin's Podracer

Wide feet steady the pit droid when it is working at fast speeds

DATA FILE

SET: 7131 Anakin's Podracer
YEAR: 1999
PIECES: 12
EQUIPMENT: Maintenance tools
VARIANTS: 3

Darth Maul
SITH APPRENTICE

Darth Maul is the terrifying Sith apprentice of Darth Sidious. Maul wears black robes and a hooded cape as he lurks in the shadows, waiting for his chance to attack the Jedi! Maul's minifigure appears in five LEGO *Star Wars* sets from 1999–2011. The 2011 variant has a unique Zabrak-horned head sculpt and new face and torso patterns.

The 2011 minifigure includes a new mold for Darth Maul's head. This detachable piece features the Zabrak horns that Maul usually hides under his hood

STAR VARIANT

The eyes have it
The early Maul minifigures have regular LEGO heads printed with Nightbrother tattoos and yellow eyes. This 2007 variant from Sith Infiltrator (set 7663) has black pupils in the eyes and different face patterns.

Darth Maul is a Nightbrother from Dathomir. His eyes have turned yellow from studying the dark side

Only one other minifigure wields a double-bladed lightsaber: Savage Opress (p.198)

Updated torso patterns

In the first set to include Darth Maul—Lightsaber Duel (set 7101)—Maul's lightsaber hilt came with only one blade

DATA FILE

SET: 7961 Darth Maul's Sith Infiltrator
YEAR: 2011
PIECES: 5
EQUIPMENT: Double-bladed lightsaber, cape, hood
VARIANTS: 3

Yoda
JEDI GRAND MASTER

As Grand Master of the Jedi Order, Yoda is the most respected Jedi in the LEGO *Star Wars* galaxy—despite his small size. Although Yoda's minifigure is dressed in the traditional tan robes of a Jedi, he is easily recognizable by his short legs, unique head sculpt, and green skin color.

An old Jedi
Yoda is over 900 years old! Although he can leap through the air during a lightsaber duel like a Jedi half his age, his minifigure also comes with a wooden walking stick in X-Wing Fighter (set 4502).

DATA FILE
SET: 7103 Jedi Duel
YEAR: 2002
PIECES: 3
EQUIPMENT: Lightsaber
VARIANTS: 1

Getting a head
Yoda's unique sand-green head with large, distinctive ears was designed specifically for his 2002 minifigure. It is a different mold from the Clone Wars version of Yoda (p.158), which was first released in 2009.

Yoda's head is made of rubber instead of the ABS plastic used for most LEGO pieces

Yoda's species has never been revealed

Yoda's tan and brown torso looks similar to those of other Jedi, but the patterns are unique to him

Yoda is smaller than most other Jedi, but his lightsaber is standard LEGO size

Yoda was the first LEGO minifigure to have short, unposeable legs

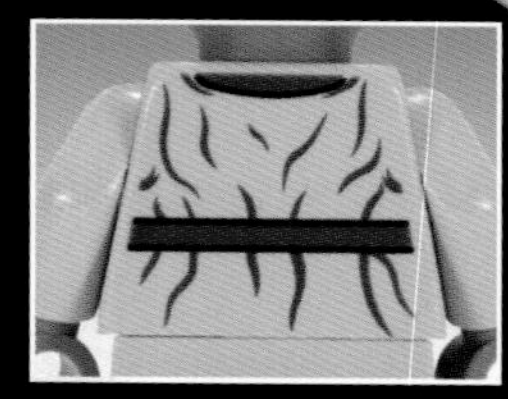

Front and back
Yoda is always on guard: His back is never turned. But his utility belt and Jedi robes pattern are printed on the back of his torso, too.

Mace Windu
LEGENDARY JEDI MASTER

Wise Jedi Master Mace Windu appears in brown Jedi robes and a blue-gray tunic in Clone Turbo Tank (set 7261). He is the only minifigure to wield a purple lightsaber, and in the 2005 release of the set, its powerful blade lights up to make it look even more impressive. A similar Mace with a non-light-up lightsaber appears in the 2006 reissue of the set.

Clone Turbo Tank (set 7261)
Mace Windu takes part in the Battle of Kashyyyk in Clone Turbo Tank. In the 2006 reissue of the set, Mace brandishes a normal lightsaber and has removeable parts.

Purple lightsaber blade is removeable from the hilt

Head button operates light-up lightsaber

DATA FILE
SET: 7261 Clone Turbo Tank
YEAR: 2005/6
PIECES: 1
EQUIPMENT: Cape, lightsaber
VARIANTS: 2

Mace has no right hand piece—his right arm extends into the lightsaber hilt

Light-up lightsaber
The head, torso, hips, right arm, and lightsaber hilt are not removeable on Light-up Lightsaber minifigures. This allows electric current to flow from a battery in the torso to an LED in the lightsaber hilt when the head button is pressed.

Reddish-brown cloth cape can't be removed

Republic Captain

CRUISER COMMANDER

The smartly dressed Republic captain minifigure appears in only one LEGO set, flying alongside the almost identical Republic pilot. As captain of the imposing Republic Cruiser (set 7665), the minifigure is charged with the mission of safely shuttling Jedi Obi-Wan Kenobi and Qui-Gon Jinn across the galaxy to Naboo.

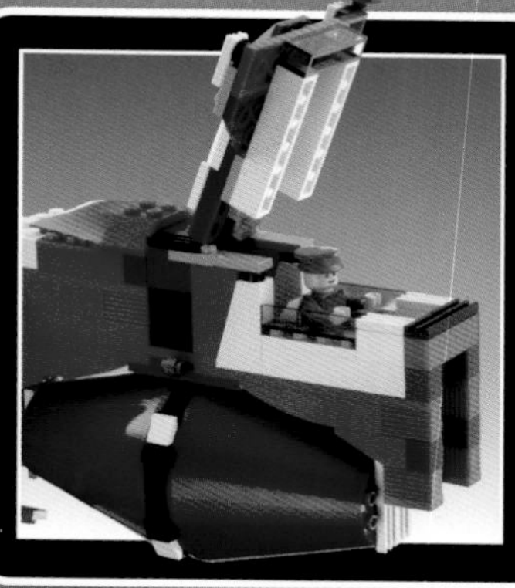

Republic Cruiser (set 7665)
The Republic captain is in command of the Republic Cruiser *Radiant VII*. He runs the starship from a control panel inside its middle section and leaves the job of flying it to the Republic pilot (pictured). The Republic pilot sits in the cockpit, which has room for just one minifigure.

Light flesh head with standard grin pattern

This blue crew uniform is unique to the Republic captain and pilot of the Republic Cruiser

Silver belt buckle

Dark-blue hips and legs

Republic Pilot
The Republic pilot is exactly the same minifigure as the Republic captain but he has a blue hat instead of hair.

Maoi Madakor?
The Republic captain minifigure may be the female captain of *Radiant VII* Maoi Madakor, as seen in Episode I —although it is not named as her by the LEGO Group. The Republic pilot may be her co-pilot Antidar Williams.

DATA FILE
SET: 7665 Republic Cruiser
YEAR: 2007
PIECES: 4
EQUIPMENT: None
VARIANTS: 1

R2-R7

GREEN ASTROMECH DROID

Working away behind the scenes on the Republic Cruiser (set 7665) is R2-R7. If you blink you might miss him, as this green astromech droid has only ever been seen in one LEGO set. He has a docking station aboard the starship from which he provides indispensible in-flight backup for the Republic captain and pilot minifigures.

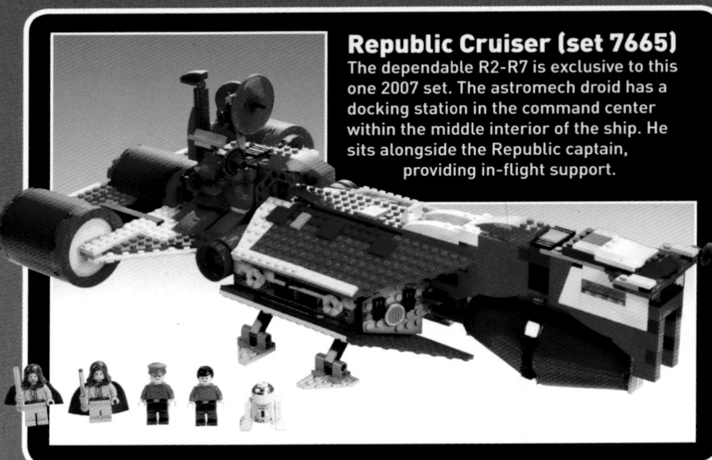

Republic Cruiser (set 7665)
The dependable R2-R7 is exclusive to this one 2007 set. The astromech droid has a docking station in the command center within the middle interior of the ship. He sits alongside the Republic captain, providing in-flight support.

DATA FILE
SET: 7665 Republic Cruiser
YEAR: 2007
PIECES: 4
EQUIPMENT: None
VARIANTS: 1

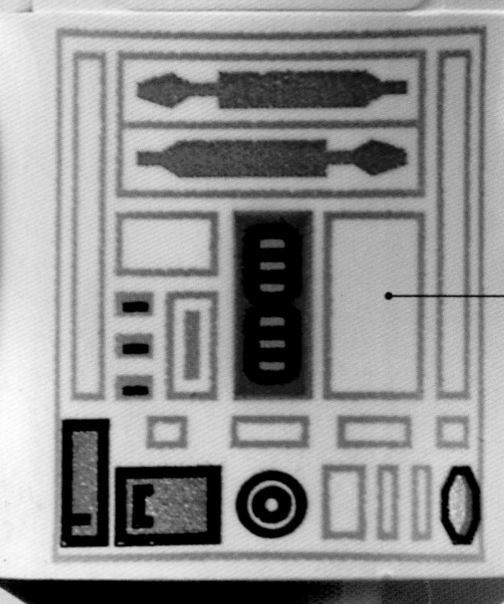

Radar eye tracks flight paths and scans for malfunctions

Silver and green printed head. The only other green astromech droid is R4-P44 (p.46)

R2-R7's legs are moveable because they are attached to his body piece with LEGO Technic pins

These compartments house tools and connectors that mean R2-R7 can fix just about anything

Protruding lower body stores a third leg for extra maneuverability

Ghost droid
R2-R7 was obviously very hard at work aboard the Republic Cruiser in Episode I because he was never actually seen in the movie! His role is to monitor flight performance and carry out repairs.

Gungan Soldier
AMPHIBIOUS FIGHTER

The Gungans are a peaceful people, but when Naboo is deluged by the Trade Federation's droid army, they are forced to wage war to protect it. The Gungan soldier has battled in two LEGO *Star Wars* sets, and due to a 2011 redesign, the minifigures in each set are different.

STAR VARIANT

Green Gungan
This was the first variant into battle in LEGO *Star Wars*. He is exclusive to the 2000 set Gungan Patrol (set 7115). His plain head is the same as that seen on the first Jar Jar Binks (p.6), and his uniform is green instead of brown.

This head-mold is the same as that on the Jar Jar Binks minifigure (p.6), with different printing

Combat eye mask

DATA FILE

SET: 7929 Battle of Naboo
YEAR: 2011
PIECES: 3
EQUIPMENT: Cesta and energy ball, energy shield
VARIANTS: 2

This cesta has an energy ball mounted on it, ready to be hurled at a battle droid

Brown uniform is first seen on the 2011 design. Many Gungan soldiers are part-time and provide their own uniforms—which might explain the difference in uniform on both variants

Unique energy shield protects the Gungan soldier from blaster fire

Gungan garb
The Gungan soldier's primitive Grand Army uniform and gold belt can be seen on the back of his torso as well as the front.

Battle Droid
SEPARATIST FOOT SOLDIER

The battle droid minifigure has been released in vast numbers in the LEGO *Star Wars* galaxy, appearing in 27 LEGO sets to date. The Separatist soldier relies on quantity, not skill, to defeat its enemy: It cannot think independently and its firing accuracy is poor—partly because the minifigure could not hold a blaster correctly until 2007!

This LEGO head piece was specially created for the battle droid minifigure

Armed arm
Two variants of the battle droid minifigure can't hold a blaster vertically. However, from 2007 sets onward, the battle droid has had one straight, or turned, arm so the minifigure can hold a gun correctly.

As with normal LEGO minifigures, the battle droid is only articulated at the shoulder, but his two arms are not identical

Regular infantry battle droids have plain tan torsos, but command officers have colored torsos to denote rank

SE-14 blaster pistol

The battle droid's feet and legs are one LEGO piece

STAR VARIANTS

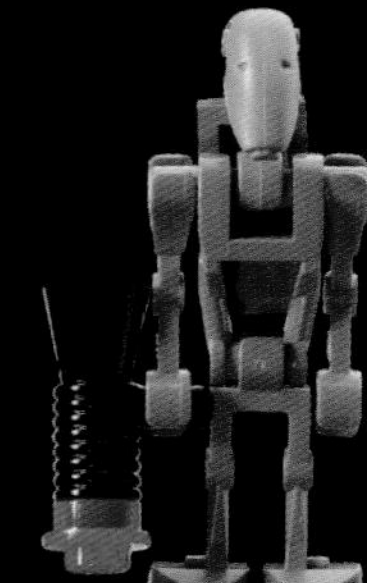

Geonosian
This variant of the battle droid minifigure appears in Geonosian Fighter (set 4478). It is sand-red instead of tan in color because it was produced on the planet of Geonosis.

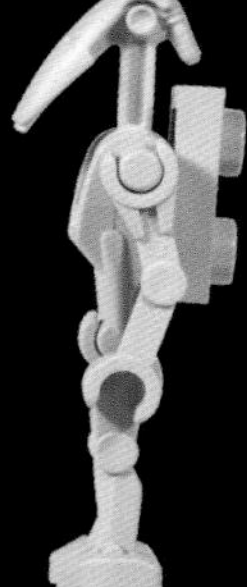

Backpack
Two 1999–2000 LEGO sets have included this battle droid with a backpack: Naboo Swamp (set 7121) and the *Star Wars* #4 Battle Droid Minifigure Pack (set 3343).

DATA FILE

SET: 7929 The Battle of Naboo
YEAR: 2011
PIECES: 5
EQUIPMENT: Blaster
VARIANTS: 5

Battle Droids
SPECIALISTS

Although all battle droids are structurally identical and made from the same LEGO pieces, specialist battle droids are fitted with a colored torso to identify their function. These droids are chosen for certain roles to increase the army's efficiency. They are found in a select few LEGO sets, where their specific skills are required.

DATA FILE
NAME: Security droid
SPECIALTY: Guard duty
SET: 7877 Naboo Starfighter
YEAR: 2011
PIECES: 5
EQUIPMENT: Blaster
VARIANTS: 3

Torso piece has dark red markings

The security battle droid has a red tip on the back of its head piece. This head detail is first seen on the 2011 design

Battle colors
Specialist battle droids have had varying amounts of color on their torsos since their first release. The earliest variants have mostly tan torsos with small patches of color, and other variants have full-color torsos.

The pilot droid is identified by blue markings

Straight arm holds a blaster vertically

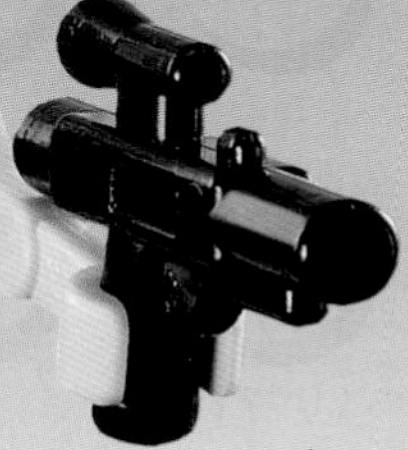

This variant of the droid commander has an all-yellow torso piece, but a previous variant (seen in two 2000–2002 sets) has a mostly tan torso with yellow markings

DATA FILE
NAME: Pilot droid
SPECIALTY: Vehicle handling
SET: 7929 The Battle of Naboo
YEAR: 2011
PIECES: 5
EQUIPMENT: Blaster
VARIANTS: 3

DATA FILE
NAME: Droid commander
SPECIALTY: Squad leader
SET: 7670 Hailfire Droid and Spider Droid
YEAR: 2008
PIECES: 5
EQUIPMENT: Blaster
VARIANTS: 2

Naboo Fighter Pilot
INFREQUENT FLIER

This pilot of peaceful Naboo is not used to conflict, but when the Trade Federation invades his planet, he must take action to defend it in his N-1 starfighter! The pacifist pilot minifigure never carries a weapon, but his 2011 redesign finds himself bound with handcuffs when he is captured by security battle droid minifigures.

Naboo Starfighter (set 7877)
The latest variant of the Naboo fighter pilot appears in this 2011 set. The minifigure can pilot a fast and agile N-1 starfighter—if young Anakin Skywalker's minifigure hasn't already taken off in it!

Reddish-brown flying helmet with removeable goggles

Unique torso features a safety harness, flying jacket and undershirt, and a red overcoat

Reddish-brown flying gloves

Full-length Space Fighter Corps overcoat

DATA FILE
SET: 7877 Naboo Starfighter
YEAR: 2011
PIECES: 5
EQUIPMENT: Handcuffs
VARIANTS: 2

STAR VARIANT

First look
The Naboo pilot in the Naboo N-1 Starfighter and Vulture Droid (set 7660) looks different to his 2011 counterpart. He wears a brown cap, tan flying jacket, and reddish-brown pants.

Captain Panaka

NABOO HEAD OF SECURITY

A great deal of responsibility rests on this minifigure's shoulders. Captain Panaka is Head of the Royal Naboo Security Forces. He is also solely responsible for the Queen's safety. Dressed in a distinctive Naboo High Officer uniform, the minifigure makes his first and only appearance in the Sith Infiltrator (set 7961).

Sith Infiltrator (set 7961)
Captain Panaka's minifigure is exclusive to this 2011 set. Deadly Sith apprentice Darth Maul is in pursuit of Captain Panaka and his charge, Queen Padmé Amidala, in his Sith Infiltrator. Can the minifigures escape Maul?

Unique gold and red LEGO helmet bears the Naboo Security crest

Captain Panaka has a unique LEGO head. His stern expression shows how seriously he takes his responsibilities as Head of Security

As a Naboo High Officer, Panaka wears a protective jerkin with inbuilt anti-blast armor plates

Protective reddish-brown gloves

DATA FILE
SET: 7961 Darth Maul's Sith Infiltrator
YEAR: 2011
PIECES: 4
EQUIPMENT: Blaster
VARIANTS: 1

Naboo Security Officer
INVADED INFANTRYMAN

This smiling security guard patrols the peaceful planet of Naboo. The minifigure is rarely called into combat, so he carries no weapons. When Naboo is invaded by the Trade Federation, he is forced to use his Flash Speeder (set 7124) in battle—but he might need to arm himself with more than his binoculars!

Flash Speeder (set 7124)
The Naboo security officer is exclusive to this 2000 set. He pilots the repulsorlift craft with a joystick and control panel. He places his electrobinoculars in a storage compartment during flight.

Brown guard cap

The Imperial officer (p.80), Dak Ralter (p.105), and the Imperial pilot (p.126) also have this yellow LEGO head

DATA FILE
SET: 7124 Flash Speeder
YEAR: 2000
PIECES: 4
EQUIPMENT: Electro-binoculars
VARIANTS: 1

Naboo security guards wear distinctive brown and tan uniforms

Protective gloves

Headgear
The Naboo security officer's hat is a popular one among LEGO minifigures, but only he wears it in brown. In LEGO *Star Wars*, the Imperial officer (p.80) wears the same headgear in gray and the Republic pilot (p.19) wears it in blue.

The Naboo security officer's torso piece is unique to him. It features resilient armor plates and a silver-buckled belt

Count Dooku

EVIL COUNT OF SERENNO

Enigmatic minifigure Count Dooku was once a Jedi Master, but he has fallen to the dark side. He now lurks in the shadows of the LEGO *Star Wars* galaxy, having remained exclusive to one LEGO set since 2002. As befits a man of Dooku's wealth and status, his minifigure wields a custom-made lightsaber and has a unique head and torso.

Jedi Duel (set 7103)
Crafty Count Dooku has only ever appeared in this 2002 LEGO set, and he is attempting to make a quick getaway! Dooku has an open-cockpit speeder bike to flee on, but he is forced to duel with Jedi Master Yoda first.

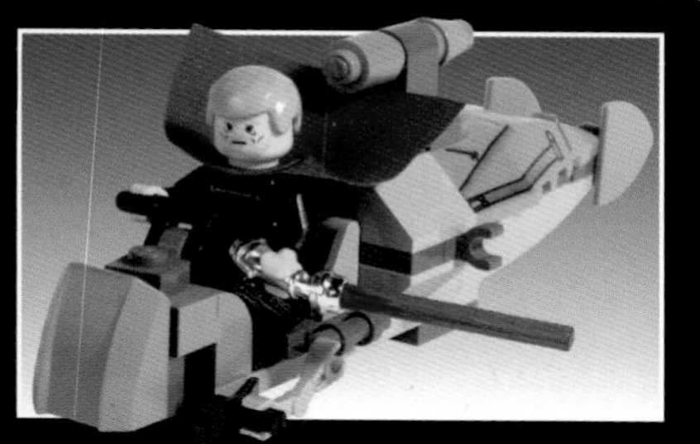

Curved lightsaber
Count Dooku wields a unique lightsaber with a curved metallic hilt. The piece is exclusive to Count Dooku and it also appears with Dooku's 2009 Clone Wars minifigure in Count Dooku's Solar Sailer (set 7752) (p.161).

Count Dooku's unique head has a gray beard, wrinkled skin, and a steely gaze

Only Count Dooku's minifigure has this torso, adorned with a cape clasp and brown belt

This is a standard LEGO minifigure cape, but it acts as a symbol of Dooku's prestige as Count of Serenno

Yellow tone
All minifigures in the Episode II LEGO *Star Wars* sets have yellow flesh, like Count Dooku. This is because they were all released prior to 2004, at which point the LEGO Group began to release minifigures with lighter flesh.

DATA FILE
SET: 7103 Jedi Duel
YEAR: 2002
PIECES: 5
EQUIPMENT: Cape, lightsaber
VARIANTS: 1

Obi-Wan Kenobi
JEDI KNIGHT

As a skilled Jedi Knight, Obi-Wan Kenobi is focused and controlled at a time of turmoil in the LEGO *Star Wars* galaxy. Two variants of his minifigure have starred in two sets; in both he faces dangerous challenges that require great judgment. He pursues bounty hunter Jango Fett in Jedi Starfighter (set 7143), and Zam Wesell in Bounty Hunter Pursuit (set 7133).

Jedi Starfighter (set 7143)

Jedi Master Obi-Wan Kenobi pilots a Delta-7 starfighter in this 2002 set—the only one to feature the Obi-Wan variant with a headset. The minifigure has binoculars and a lightsaber, but he has nowhere to store them when he zooms into flight mode.

DATA FILE

SET: 7143 Jedi Starfighter
YEAR: 2002
PIECES: 4
EQUIPMENT: Lightsaber, electrobinoculars
VARIANTS: 2

Most Jedi Knights wear their hair long

This minifigure has a neatly trimmed beard and wears a headset on his head. The variant in Bounty Hunter Pursuit (set 7133), is identical but without the headset

Utility belt for Jedi essentials

Obi-Wan shares his Jedi tunic torso with two minifigures: his old mentor Qui-Gon Jinn (p.4) and the young Padawn version of himself (p.5)

Knight flight

Obi-Wan Kenobi's long Jedi Knight hair is standard female LEGO hair. The hair piece in Obi-Wan's dark orange color is worn by only one other minifigure: a female airline passenger in the LEGO World City theme.

Anakin Skywalker

JEDI PADAWAN

Headstrong Padawan Anakin Skywalker is training under his more cautious mentor Obi-Wan Kenobi. The minifigure has broken away from Jedi tradition by wearing a torso piece with dark Jedi robes—this coupled with Anakin's half smiling face could suggest a darkness within him that he cannot control.

Bounty Hunter Pursuit (set 7133)
The Padawan Anakin minifigure is involved in a fast-paced pursuit in this 2002 set, which is the only one to feature this version of Anakin. He and Obi-Wan Kenobi are chasing changeling assassin Zam Wesell on Coruscant. The Jedi minifigures can store their lightsabers within a secret compartment in their airspeeder.

As is befitting of a unique Jedi like Anakin, his slight smile was designed specifically for his Padawan minifigure

Earth orange
Anakin's earth orange hair-color is unusual for a LEGO minifigure. Only three others have it: Uncle Vernon Dursley (who has the same hair piece as Anakin), and Ron and Ginny Weasley, all from the LEGO Harry Potter theme.

Padawan learner braid

Padawan Anakin wears a Jedi tunic with a protective black surcoat. His torso piece is unique to him

A variant of this minifigure appears in Tusken Raider Encounter (set 7113) and has a brown cape

DATA FILE
SET: 7133 Bounty Hunter Pursuit
YEAR: 2002
PIECES: 4
EQUIPMENT: Lightsaber
VARIANTS: 2

Jango Fett
BOUNTY HUNTER

Bounty hunter Jango Fett keeps a low profile in the LEGO *Star Wars* galaxy. He is exclusive to one 2002 set: Jango Fett's *Slave I* (set 7153). Jango is made up of many unique LEGO pieces that might make his minifigure as legendary as the man himself, including his two-sided head piece, and helmet with a J-12 jetpack.

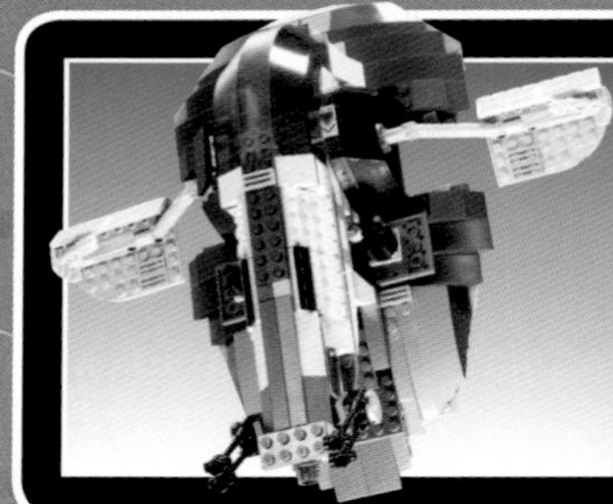

Jango Fett's *Slave I* (set 7153)
Jango Fett's *Slave I* has secret compartments and hidden weapons to aid Jango on his bounty-hunting missions. The ship even has a compartment where Jango's hair and blasters can be stored when he isn't using them.

Jango's head
One side of Jango's head has a yellow face with a headset and stubble. His black hair can't fit under his helmet.

Jango's black head is visible through the open T-visor of his blue-painted helmet

Torso piece with Mandalorian silver armor plates is unique to Jango

No other LEGO minifigure has these violet arms

Jango's custom-made WESTAR-34 blasters are LEGO revolvers

Like father...
Jango's J-12 jetpack and helmet are one piece. The adult Boba Fett minifigure wears the same piece in green (p.108).

DATA FILE
SET: 7153 Jango Fett's *Slave I*
YEAR: 2002
PIECES: 4
EQUIPMENT: Helmet and jetpack, twin blasters
VARIANTS: 1

Boba Fett
YOUNG CLONE

Jango Fett's *Slave I* (set 7153)
Young Boba Fett sits right behind his father, Jango, in the two-person cockpit of Jango Fett's *Slave I*. When the ship rotates 90 degrees from its horizontal stationary position to its vertical flight mode, the cockpit turns on LEGO Technic axles so the minifigures are always upright. Both young Boba and Jango Fett are exclusive to this 2002 set.

This determined young clone will one day become a great bounty hunter, but for now he is learning combat skills under the guardianship of his father, Jango. Young Boba's minifigure is equally as elusive as his father's, appearing in only one set. As he is a child, Boba has short LEGO legs to make him smaller than the Jango minifigure.

DATA FILE

SET: 7153 Jango Fett's *Slave I*
YEAR: 2002
PIECES: 4
EQUIPMENT: None
VARIANTS: 1

Lady locks
Young Boba's long black hair is typically used on female minifigures. Luke Skywalker (p.82) and Anakin Skywalker (p.42) have also been known to sport this hair in LEGO *Star Wars* sets, but only Boba wears it in black.

Boba's unique yellow face with sloping eyebrows and a straight mouth gives him a serious look

This torso piece was specially made for Boba. He wears a v-collared tunic with a drawstring belt

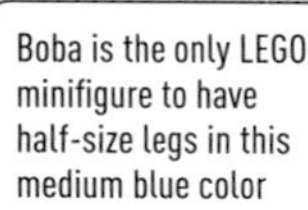

Boba is the only LEGO minifigure to have half-size legs in this medium blue color

Zam Wesell
BOUNTY HUNTER

This shady character has proven elusive in LEGO *Star Wars* and her minifigure is exclusive to one 2002 set. Zam Wesell is a bounty hunter with a special edge: She is a Clawdite shapeshifter who can alter her physical appearance as she chooses. Her minifigure head can change between her pretty human face and her natural Clawdite face!

DATA FILE

SET: 7133 Bounty Hunter Pursuit
YEAR: 2002
PIECES: 5
EQUIPMENT: Projectile rifle
VARIANTS: 1

Podracers Anakin Skywalker (p.8) and Gasgano (p.13) also wear these dark gray LEGO flying goggles

Bounty Hunter Pursuit (set 7133)
Zam flies her nimble airspeeder in just this one 2002 set. The speeder's cockpit has a small control panel for Zam's navigation.

Face veil disguises Zam's human identity

Internal comlink for communicating with associates, including Jango Fett

Zam's torso, hips and legs, printed with her specialized armor and equipment, are unique to her minifigure

Zam wears muted sand-purple and silver/gray tones so she can lurk in the shadows undetected

Grappling hook for scaling buildings

Changeling
Swiveling Zam's head around exposes her true Clawdite form. Zam was one of the first double-faced minifigures.

Heavy helmet
Zam's face-framing crash helmet is only seen on her minifigure in LEGO *Star Wars*, but it is also used as a heavy-duty helmet (in various colors) by miners in the LEGO themes Rock Raiders and Power Miners. Only Zam wears it in light gray.

Tusken Raider

DESERT DWELLER

This fearsome Tusken Raider is part of a fierce nomadic species native to Tatooine. The mysterious minifigure can move almost invisibly through dusty desert dunes dressed in his desert-colored sandshroud. His unique LEGO head and torso pieces are adapted to help him survive in intense heat.

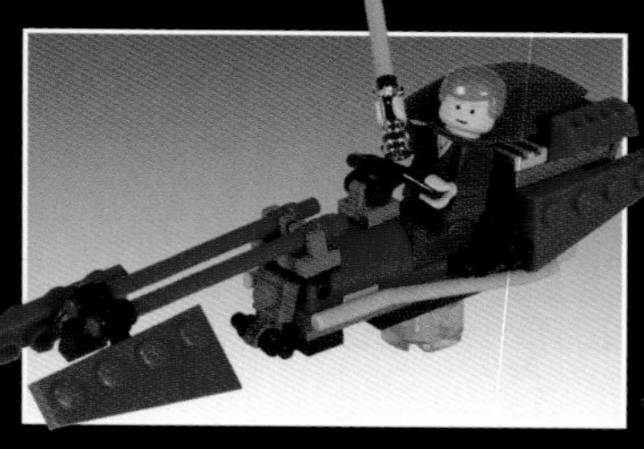

Tusken Raider Encounter (set 7113)
The Tusken Raider is exclusive to this set, which contains two of the minifigures. The Tuskens have captured Anakin's mother, Shmi. When an enraged Anakin discovers their primitive camp on his swoop bike, it can only mean trouble.

Eye goggles offer protection from the fierce desert sun

Bandaged face mask on this unique head piece has an open mouth to facilitate breathing

This moisture trap humidifies the dry desert air before the Tusken breathes it in

Desert details
The Tusken's sandshroud and crossed utility belt are also printed on the back of his unique torso piece.

The Tusken Raider's LEGO torso piece is unique. It is covered in rags to protect him from sand and conserve moisture

Some Tusken Raider minifigures have these tan hips, but most have appeared with gray hips

DATA FILE

SET: 7113 Tusken Raider Encounter
YEAR: 2002
PIECES: 3
EQUIPMENT: Projectile rifle
VARIANTS: 1

Jedi Knight
MYSTERY MAN

Do you know this mysterious minifigure? Not very much is known about the Jedi Knight, who appeared on the Republic Gunship (set 7163)—and has never been seen again. Some know him as "Jedi Bob." The hooded minifigure with a confident smile and a flowing cloak carries a green lightsaber, but he only uses it when forced to defend himself in battle.

Republic Gunship (set 7163)
The Jedi Knight minifigure flies into LEGO *Star Wars* on this Republic Gunship. The Low-Altitude Assault Transport/infanty (LAAT/i) deploys clone troopers as the Jedi Knight leads them into war against the Separatist army.

The Jedi Knight's smiling, bearded face is also found on a construction worker in the LEGO City theme, and Mac, the astronaut in LEGO Life on Mars

The Jedi Knight may be a generic Jedi, but he has a unique torso. He wears a gray Jedi tunic and a belt with a silver buckle

Jedi Bob
Named only "Jedi Knight" on the LEGO set box for the Republic Gunship (set 7163), the minifigure has become "Jedi Bob" to many LEGO *Star Wars* fans! He was first named this in DK's *LEGO* Star Wars: *The Visual Dictionary* (2009).

Brown cloak and hood help the Jedi Knight to remain anonymous

DATA FILE

SET: 7163 Republic Gunship
YEAR: 2002
PIECES: 5
EQUIPMENT: Cape, lightsaber
VARIANTS: 1

Clone Trooper
GENETICALLY MODIFIED SOLDIER

The Phase I clone trooper is part of a vast army that has been cloned from a single individual. Sealed in a heavy-duty shell of white armor, this minifigure is the first of its kind. During the Clone Wars, clone trooper armor is revised so it is lighter, stronger, and more adaptable.

AT-TE Walker (set 4482)
The AT-TE Walker comes with an army of four Phase I clone trooper minifigures, but it can carry up to seven. A gunner operates the swiveling cannon and a driver pilots the vehicle from inside a central cabin.

Blast from the past
The Phase I clone trooper's blaster is a LEGO loudhailer with a translucent blue round plate attached. LEGO *Star Wars* minifigures carried this blaster until bespoke LEGO *Star Wars* blasters were released in 2007.

Only Phase I clone troopers in Episode II sets wear these LEGO helmets

Stripes denote the clone trooper's rank

Blank Head
Phase I clone troopers do not have identities—they have faceless black heads under their LEGO helmets.

DC-15 blaster

Utility belt carries clone trooper survival gear

DATA FILE
SET: 4482 AT-TE Walker
YEAR: 2003
PIECES: 4
EQUIPMENT: Blaster
VARIANTS: 1

Destroyer Droid
ROLLING FIREPOWER

In 2002, the first destroyer droid rolled into the world of LEGO *Star Wars*. Also known as a droideka, this robotic ball of firepower is a key part of the Separatists' ground forces. With its distinctive curved spine, the droid posed a challenge to LEGO designers. Two versions were created, the second a more elaborate and complex design.

Trade Federation MTT (set 7662)
A destroyer droid is delivered in a hulking troop transport along with racks of unfolding battle droids in this 2007 set. It shows the formidable firepower of the Separatist ground forces!

These pieces are also used for battle droids' arms

Blaster energizer

A LEGO Technic piece evenly separates the three legs for stability

Arm section is an adapted hose nozzle piece

Foot piece is used in other LEGO sets as horns on Viking helmets

STAR VARIANT

Simple start
The original droideka figure has a much simpler design than the 2007 variant, but its 26 pieces still capture the droid's distinctive shape.

LEGO Technic
As well as two minifigures, the destroyer droid has been made as a 567-piece LEGO Technic model in 2000 (set 8002). When spun across the floor, the LEGO droid rolls and then unfurls itself into its attack position.

DATA FILE

SET: 7662 Trade Federation MTT
YEAR: 2007
PIECES: 35
EQUIPMENT: Two blaster energizers
VARIANTS: 2

Super Battle Droid

WALKING WEAPONRY

Bigger, bulkier, and more bullet-proof than standard battle droids, super battle droids are a force to be reckoned with. Not only are they physically stronger than their spindlier cousins, they also have more brainpower. Three variants of the hulking minifigure have been made—each more intimidating than the last.

Technical droid
Like the destroyer droid, the super battle droid has also gone beyond its minifigure beginnings and been created as a LEGO Technic set. The robotic figure, released in 2000, is made from 379 technical parts.

Specially molded head-and-body piece is used for all three variants of the super battle droid

Arms clip to shoulder pieces with same grip as minifigures' hands

Pearlized, dark gray body

Hands can grasp LEGO blaster .weapons

Thin legs create a small target for enemy fire

Leg piece is unique to LEGO *Star Wars*. It is also found on the MagnaGuard (p.163) and TX-20 tactical droid (p.196) minifigures

STAR VARIANTS

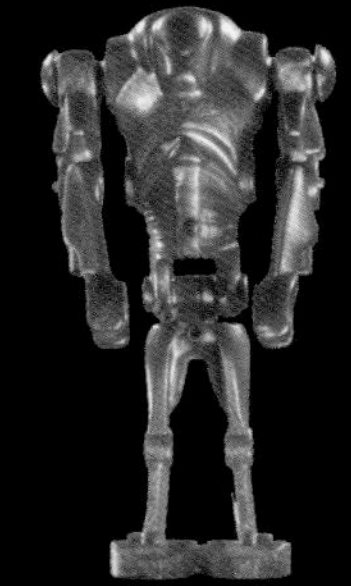

Blue beginnings
The first super battle droid minifigure is metal-blue and was released in 2002. Two come with the Republic Gunship (set 7163).

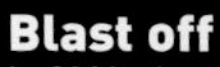

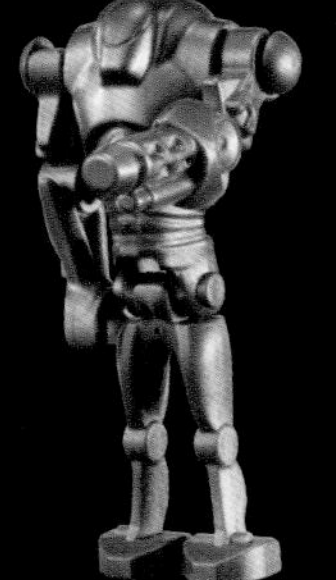

Blast off
In 2009, the super battle droid swapped one of its arms for a unique piece with a blaster molded into it. This third variant of the droid appears in two LEGO sets.

DATA FILE

SET: 8091 Republic Swamp Speeder
YEAR: 2010
PIECES: 4
EQUIPMENT: None
VARIANTS: 3

Geonosian Warrior
HIVE DRONE

2003 saw the introduction of Geonosian minifigures to the LEGO *Star Wars* theme with two variants of the warrior. The first is a basic drone; the cannon fodder of the Geonosian army. The second is a higher-caste variant with wings. One of each appears in Geonosian Fighter (set 4478).

Geonosian Fighter (set 4478)
In Geonosian Fighter, a Geonosian mans this sonic cannon on a platform that spins 360 degrees and hinges 90 degrees. The set was released in 2003 in a blue box and then in 2004 in a black box.

DATA FILE

SET: 4478 Geonosian Fighter
YEAR: 2003/4
PIECES: 4
EQUIPMENT: Blaster
VARIANTS: 2

Monochrome head-mold

The two Geonosian warrior minifigures are identical except for the addition or omission of the orange wings

Plastic wings in two parts are unique to LEGO *Star Wars*

Sonic blaster fires concussive energy

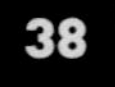

Geonosian Pilot

INSECTOID FLYER

The rocky outcrops of Geonosis house the hive colonies of an insectoid, hive-minded race, which is loyal to the Separatist cause. This 2011 Geonosian minifigure pilots a starfighter at the Battle of Geonosis. It has unique torso and leg printings and an all-new head shape that develops the original LEGO Geonosian head-mold.

Geonosian Starfighter (set 7959)
This set, which exclusively features the 2011 Geonosian pilot minifigure, revisits the Geonosian starfighter model from 2003. The ships are flown by Geonosian pilots in the Battle of Geonosis.

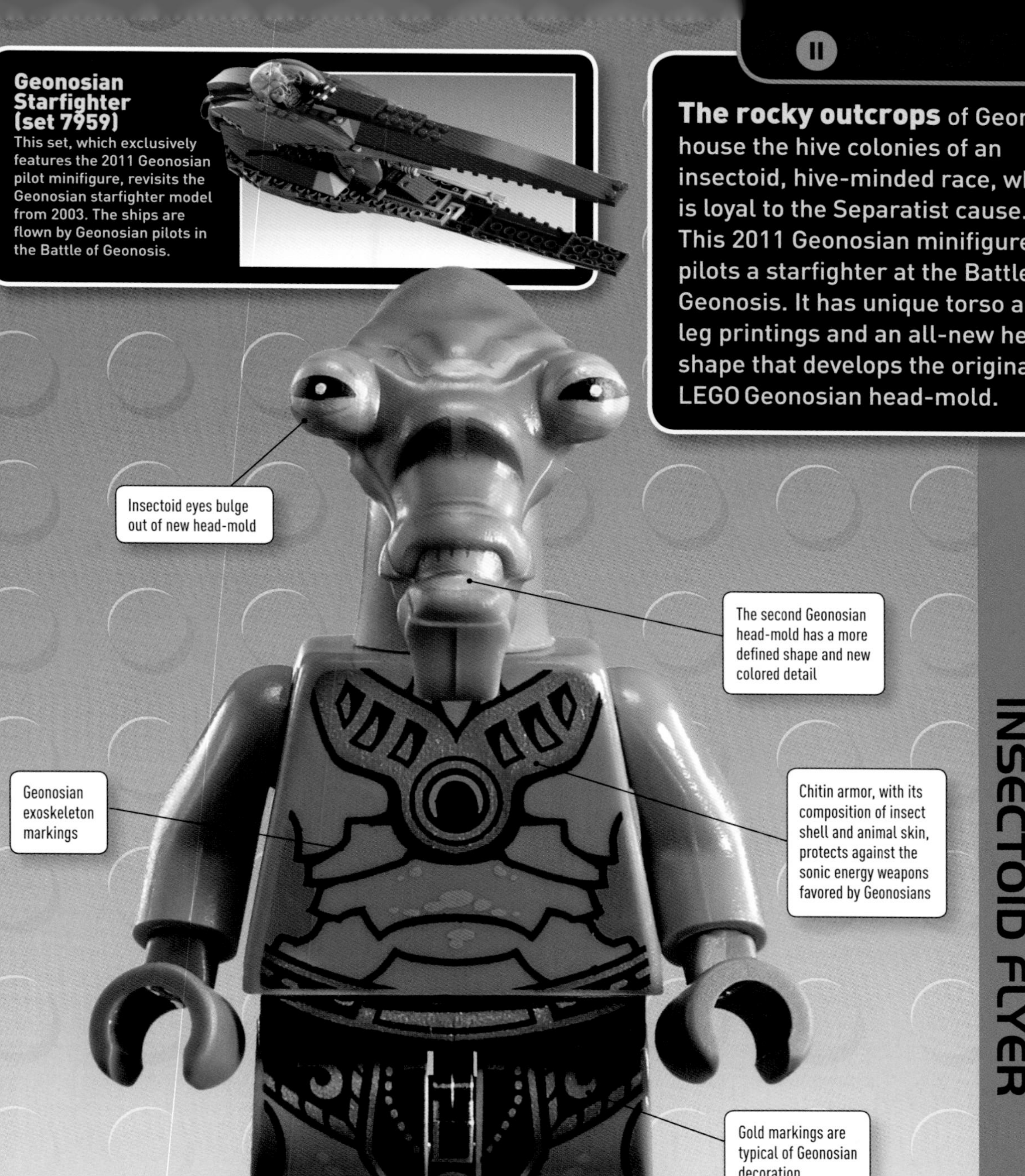
Insectoid eyes bulge out of new head-mold
The second Geonosian head-mold has a more defined shape and new colored detail
Geonosian exoskeleton markings
Chitin armor, with its composition of insect shell and animal skin, protects against the sonic energy weapons favored by Geonosians
Gold markings are typical of Geonosian decoration
Red iketa stones are symbols of war in Geonosian culture

DATA FILE

SET: 7959 Geonosian Starfighter
YEAR: 2011
PIECES: 3
EQUIPMENT: None
VARIANTS: 1

General Grievous
CYBORG COMMANDER

This vicious cyborg might look like a LEGO droid, but don't tell him that! He will react savagely, as his many victims will attest. General Grievous is Supreme Commander of the Droid Armies. His minifigure has four lightsabers—two blue and two green—to fill his four arms, making him more than a match for any Jedi!

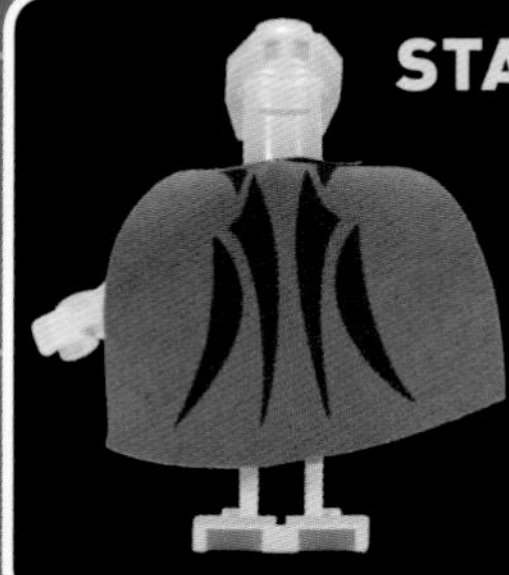

STAR VARIANT

Caped cyborg
Grievous wears an intimidating cape in General Grievous Chase (set 7255)! One side of the unique cape is gray with a slash pattern, and the underside of the cape is dark red.

DATA FILE

SET: 7656 General Grievous Starfighter
YEAR: 2007
PIECES: 7
EQUIPMENT: Blaster, four lightsabers
VARIANTS: 2

General Grievous's head-mold was specially created for his minifigure

Skull-like mask contains the cyborg's eyes and brain

General Grievous hates to be called a droid, so he won't be pleased that his LEGO arm pieces are also used on 20 LEGO *Star Wars* droids!

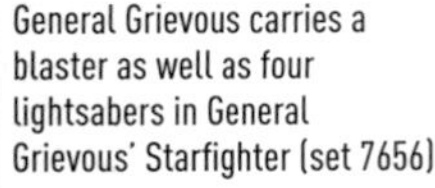

General Grievous carries a blaster as well as four lightsabers in General Grievous' Starfighter (set 7656)

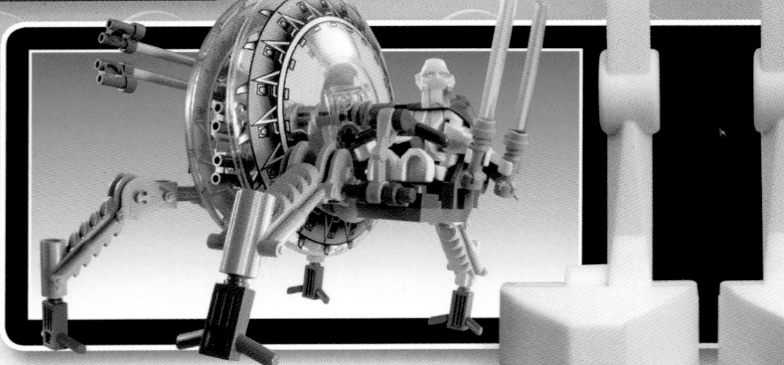

General Grievous Chase (set 7255)
General Grievous entered LEGO *Star Wars* sets astride his imposing wheel-bike. He is being chased by General Obi-Wan Kenobi, who is on a giant varactyl lizard in this 2005 set—the first to feature Grievous. The bike has two pairs of legs to help him hot-foot it out of trouble!

Obi-Wan Kenobi
JEDI MASTER

Jedi Starfighter with Hyperdrive Booster Ring (set 7661)
Obi-Wan Kenobi and his Jedi starfighter zip into hyperspace with the help of a hyperdrive booster ring in this 2007 set. It is the only set to features the latest variant of the minifigure.

Obi-Wan Kenobi is now a Jedi Master and he has achieved much military success as a General during the Clone Wars. His minifigure has appeared in four LEGO *Star Wars* sets, as a slightly different variant in each one. In Ultimate Lightsaber Duel (7257), Obi-Wan wields a light-up lightsaber when forced to fight his former apprentice, Anakin Skywalker.

Obi-Wan Kenobi wears a gold headset when piloting his Jedi Starfighter

STAR VARIANT

Light-up Jedi
A Light-up Lightsaber variant of Jedi Master Obi-Wan Kenobi appears in Ultimate Lightsaber Duel (set 7257). The variant is not wearing a pilot headset.

Cloaked Kenobi
Jedi Master Obi-Wan wears a Jedi cloak in two LEGO sets: General Grievous Chase (set 7255) and Ultimate Lightsaber Duel (set 7257). The Light-up Lightsaber variant in Ultimate Lightsaber Duel also wears a Jedi hood.

Obi-Wan is now a Jedi Master, but he still wears simple and practical Jedi robes

This Obi-Wan variant has tan legs, but all three earlier variants of the minifigure have dark orange leg pieces

DATA FILE

SET: 7661 Jedi Starfighter with Hyperdrive Booster Ring
YEAR: 2007
PIECES: 4
EQUIPMENT: Lightsaber
VARIANTS: 4

Anakin Skywalker

JEDI KNIGHT

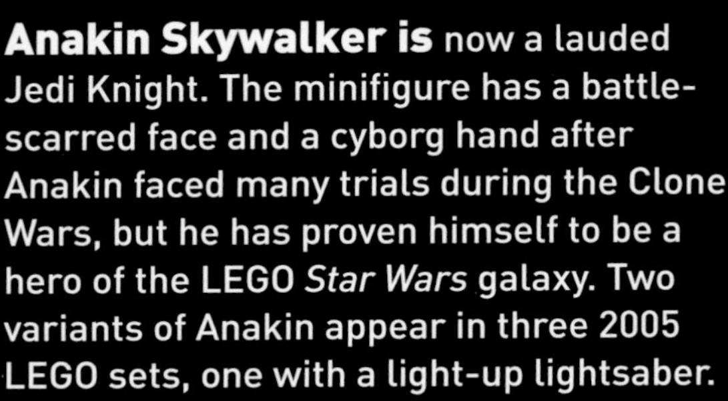

Anakin Skywalker is now a lauded Jedi Knight. The minifigure has a battle-scarred face and a cyborg hand after Anakin faced many trials during the Clone Wars, but he has proven himself to be a hero of the LEGO *Star Wars* galaxy. Two variants of Anakin appear in three 2005 LEGO sets, one with a light-up lightsaber.

Anakin is the only LEGO minifigure to wear this hair piece in a dark flesh color

Cyborg hand concealed by a black glove. Count Dooku cut off Anakin's hand

Anakin's unique LEGO head has a button to control his light-up lightsaber

Facial scars are from a duel with Asajj Ventress during the Clone Wars

Dark Jedi tunic with black surcoat—this torso piece is exclusive to Anakin's Jedi Knight minifigure

Hip piece is integrated into the torso piece on Light-up Lightsaber minifigures

The hilt of Anakin's blue light-up lightsaber is joined to his arm piece so electric current can flow through it from a battery in his torso

STAR VARIANT

Light-less
This non-Light-up Lightsaber Anakin was released in two LEGO sets: Jedi Starfighter and Vulture Droid (set 7256) and Ultimate Space Battle (set 7283). The variant wears a headset and no cape.

DATA FILE

SET: 7257 Ultimate Lightsaber Duel
YEAR: 2005
PIECES: 2
EQUIPMENT: Cape, lightsaber
VARIANTS: 2

Emperor Palpatine

DARK DICTATOR

Sith Lord Emperor Palpatine is the self-appointed ruler of the LEGO *Star Wars* galaxy. His minifigure dresses in simple black robes, and three variants carry a cane to make him look weak, but don't be fooled! This is a man of terrible power who has made his presence felt in seven LEGO sets.

STAR VARIANT

The first Emperor
The original Emperor Palpatine minifigure has different printing on his torso, yellow hands, and a yellow face with smaller (but no less terrifying!) eyes. He also walks with a cane. The variant is in three 2000–2002 sets.

Black hood hides Palpatine's face, which has been distorted by dark side energies

Lightning strike
Emperor Palpatine's red-bladed lightsaber is not his only powerful weapon. The minifigure lashes out at Luke Skywalker with deadly Force lightning on the LEGO Death Star (set 10188)!

Red-bladed Sith lightsaber

Palpatine acquired this unique gray, wrinkled LEGO head with large, staring Sith eyes in the 2008 redesign

Palpatine's black robe printing was first seen on the 2008 redesign. Only this minifigure has this torso piece

Black hands—a variant in the Imperial Inspection (set 7264) has gray hands

Hologram

The Imperial Star Destroyer (set 6211) features Emperor Palpatine's minifigure as a hologram. His printed image appears on a sticker attached to a transparent-blue LEGO brick.

DATA FILE

SET: 8096 Emperor Palpatine's Shuttle
YEAR: 2010
PIECES: 5
EQUIPMENT: Cape, lightsaber
VARIANTS: 4

Clone Pilot
FEARLESS FLIER

The clone pilot is trained to fly the super-fast Republic and Jedi starships. His minifigure's uniform includes a blue jumpsuit, an armored torso with specialist equipment, and a high-tech helmet with communications system. There are three variants of the clone pilot, each with a different helmet and head piece.

Helmet is marked with red and yellow Republic symbols

Helmet contains an air filtration system

Torso and legs are the same as Captain Jag's minifigure (p.47), but Jag wears a different pilot helmet

White airtight flight gloves

Life-support pack integrated into clone pilot uniform—in case of emergency

STAR VARIANT

Face revealed
The clone pilot of the 2010 ARC-170 Starfighter (set 8088) wears his plain helmet over a flesh-colored face printed with orange visor and chin strap.

Faceless
This original variant flies starships in two sets from 2005–2006. His white, fin-topped helmet covers a plain black head piece, and his torso features blue tubes.

DATA FILE

SET: 8096 Emperor Palpatine's Shuttle
YEAR: 2010
PIECES: 4
EQUIPMENT: None
VARIANTS: 3

Masked pilot
Beneath his helmet, the clone pilot's face is covered by a flight mask. It is printed with breathing holes and a visor.

Contingency plan
The clone pilot needs to be prepared for anything! The back of his torso is printed with a parachute.

Kit Fisto
JEDI GENERAL

Kit Fisto is a green-skinned Jedi Master. His minifigure dresses in brown and gray Jedi robes and carries a green lightsaber. The long tentacles that grow from his head can sense emotions in the people around him. As a respected Jedi General, Kit fights alongside other Jedi Knights and leads troops into battle in two LEGO sets.

Jedi Starfighter with Hyperdrive Booster Ring (set 7661)
Jedi Master Kit Fisto first appears in this set. He provides backup for Obi-Wan Kenobi, although there is no place for him aboard the starfighter—unless he pilots it instead of Obi-Wan!

Head of rubber
Kit Fisto is one of three LEGO *Star Wars* minifigures to feature a head made from rubber instead of ABS plastic. The others are Yoda (p.17) and Plo Koon (p.164). Rubber is easier to cast and can capture more detail, but it is prone to disintegrate.

Kit is a Nautolan. He has green skin, big, black eyes, and head tentacles

Unique torso with brown-and-gray Jedi robes and silver belt

Silver lightsaber hilt. The 2007 variant has a matte gray lightsaber hilt

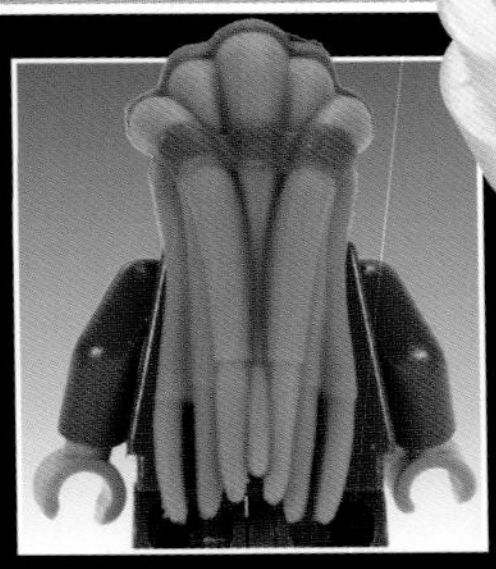

Tentacles
The back of Kit Fisto's specially designed head sculpt displays more of his sensory head tentacles.

Kit uses his ability to sense emotions to gain an advantage in battle: He can tell who is scared!

DATA FILE
SET: 8088 ARC-170 Starfighter
YEAR: 2010
PIECES: 3
EQUIPMENT: Lightsaber
VARIANTS: 1

R4-P44
RELIABLE ASTROMECH

Green astromech droid

R4-P44 helps with the navigation and repairs on Kit Fisto's ARC-170 Starfighter (set 8088). His minifigure uses the same four LEGO pieces as the other astromech droids in the LEGO *Star Wars* galaxy, but with unique coloring and printed detail. R4-P44 appears in just one LEGO set, where he plays a small but vital part in the Clone Wars.

ARC-170 Starfighter (set 8088)
R4-P44 plugs in to a droid socket between the two rear cockpits of this ARC-170 starfighter. The starfighter has twin engines, two flick-fire missiles, a double-barreled rear cannon, and wings that open out for maximum balance.

DATA FILE
SET: 8088 ARC-170 Starfighter
YEAR: 2010
PIECES: 4
EQUIPMENT: None
VARIANTS: 1

Only one other LEGO astromech droid has a blue status display, R2-Q2 (p.201)

Computer interface arm is behind this panel

Panel opens up to reveal the compartment containing R4-P44's manipulator arms

Astromech legs have built-in rocket thrusters

Captain Jag
CLONE PILOT

Clone Captain Jag is a soldier and pilot during the Clone Wars. His minifigure appears in only one 2010 set, ARC-170 Starfighter (set 8088). He wears a blue jumpsuit and a life-support pack, common to pilot minifigures. His helmet has a unique design which differentiates him from the clone pilot minifigure (p.44).

Pilot head
Captain Jag's head piece is also used for the clone pilot minifigure (p.44) and Zev Senesca (p.104).

The blue pattern design on Jag's open-fronted helmet piece is exclusive to his minifigure

Orange visor helps with visibility when flying in bright light

Helmet contains a life-support system because most starfighters do not have one on board

Front and back
The torso printing continues onto the back of Jag's torso piece. This LEGO piece was new for 2010 and is also seen on the clone pilot (p.44).

Air supply hose

Jag sometimes carries a blaster

Jag's sand-blue legs appear on 46 other LEGO minifigures, including Princess Leia in her Endor guise (p.139)

DATA FILE
SET: 8088 ARC-170 Starfighter
YEAR: 2010
PIECES: 4
EQUIPMENT: Blaster
VARIANTS: 1

Luminara Unduli
MIRIALAN MASTER

Luminara Unduli is a fierce fighter and strict Jedi Master. She wears the traditional robes of her home planet, Mirial, which allow more freedom of movement than Jedi robes. Luminara's minifigure carries a light-up lightsaber, which she puts to good use aboard the Wookiee Catamaran (set 7260).

Wookiee Catamaran (set 7260)
Luminara charges into battle on the planet Kashyyyk. She fights alongside Chewbacca, a Wookiee warrior, Yoda, and a clone trooper on the Wookiee Catamaran—the only set to include this Luminara minifigure.

Mirialan skin has a slight greenish hue

Mirialan headdress is unique to Luminara. Her Clone Wars minifigure also wears it (p.169)

Facial tattoos signify her physical accomplishments

DATA FILE
SET: 7260 Wookiee Catamaran
YEAR: 2005
PIECES: 3
EQUIPMENT: Lightsaber, cape
VARIANTS: 1

Ancient Mirialan symbol

Black cape cannot be removed as Luminara's head is not detachable

The lightsaber hilt is built into the minifigure's arm. It is part of the light-up lightsaber circuit

Push the button
Pressing down on the top of Luminara's unique head activates her green light-up lightsaber.

Barriss Offee

LOYAL PADAWAN

Republic Swamp Speeder (set 8091)
Barriss is ready to take on the Separatists in her armored swamp speeder, which "hovers" above the ground thanks to hidden LEGO wheels. Barriss's minifigure is exclusive to this set.

Young Barriss Offee learns all she can from her experienced Jedi mentor, Luminara Unduli. Barriss wears her own Mirialan robes instead of regular Jedi attire, and she has a unique face, with blue lips and tattoos. Barriss appears in just one LEGO set, in which she wields a blue lightsaber.

DATA FILE
SET: 8091 Republic Swamp Speeder
YEAR: 2010
PIECES: 4
EQUIPMENT: Lightsaber, cape
VARIANTS: 1

Black version of brown Jedi hood

Mirialan tattoos are a sign of high achievement

Barriss is skilled in lightsaber combat

Unique torso with black and blue stripes and belt pattern

Mirialan skin tone
Barriss Offee and her Jedi Master, Luminara Unduli, are from the planet Mirial. To reflect their alien origins, their minifigures' heads and hands are differentiated by a distinctive skin color, which has a greenish hue.

Chewbacca
WOOKIEE HERO

Wookiee Chewbacca is a brave fighter and long-time companion of Han Solo. Although Chewie towers over his friend in the *Star Wars* movies, his LEGO minifigure is average height. Chewbacca appears in 11 LEGO sets, never hesitating to protect his home planet of Kashyyyk from Separatist invasion or fight alongside the Rebels.

DATA FILE

SET: 7879 Hoth Echo Base
YEAR: 2011
PIECES: 3
EQUIPMENT: Bowcaster
VARIANTS: 2

The head and textured body are made from a single sandwich-board piece that fits over a standard reddish-brown minifigure torso

Molded to give hairy texture

Bandolier contains energy bolts for the Wookiee bowcaster

STAR VARIANT

Original Wookiee
The first Chewbacca minifigure is made from the same pieces as the later variant, but they are all colored brown instead of reddish brown. The minifigure appears in three 2000–2001 sets.

Comic-Con exclusive
In 2009, a handcuffed brown Chewbacca minifigure appeared in a collectible display set made exclusively for San Diego's Comic-Con, with Luke Skywalker and Han Solo minifigures in stormtrooper disguise (pp82–83).

Reddish-brown pieces replace the original brown ones

LEGO crossbow piece adapted to the distinctive Wookiee bowcaster

Wookiee Warrior

DEFENDER OF KASHYYYK

You don't want to anger a Wookiee! Although often peaceful and placid, these creatures can become ferocious when attacked. This proud Wookiee warrior minifigure springs to the defense of his homeworld when the Separatists invade Kashyyyk in two 2005 LEGO sets.

Wookiee Attack (set 7258)
Two Wookiee warriors are needed to operate this ornithopter; one pilot and one gunner. A classic example of Wookiee technology, the ornithopter flies into action against an invading dwarf spider driod and amphibious tank during the Battle of Kashyyyk in this set.

Gold-decorated helmet molded as part of head

This minifigure could be based on Tarfful as he also wears a crossed bandolier

DATA FILE
SET: 7260 Wookiee Catamaran
YEAR: 2005
PIECES: 3
EQUIPMENT: Spear
VARIANTS: 1

The Wookiee warrior minifigure comes with this LEGO spear in the Wookiee Catamaran (set 7260)

Emblem indicates clan identity of warrior

Round the back
The reverse side of the warrior's torso repeats the silver and gold bandolier molding, but it is cut short by the back of the helmet.

Kashyyyk Trooper
CAMOUFLAGED CLONE TROOPER

The Kashyyyk trooper or "Swamp Trooper" is well-equipped for operations on jungle worlds. He wears custom-made camouflage armor and carries essentials for survival in harsh environments. The minifigure has been called up for action in only one LEGO *Star Wars* set to date.

Clone Turbo Tank (set 7261)
The Kashyyyk Trooper flanks the Clone Turbo Tank on his turbine-engine BARC speeder. The speeder has controls for the minifigure to pilot the vehicle with and two blasters on either side of the seat.

Scout trooper
The Kashyyyk trooper is part of a scouting unit based in the jungle world of Kashyyyk, so his LEGO helmet is of the same design as the scout trooper minifigure (p.141). The scout trooper wears the helmet in white.

Wide visor provides greater visibility in jungle worlds

This minifigure has a unique torso piece. He wears camouflage armor to blend in with forest and swamp surroundings

Extra utility pockets for jungle survival equipment

Unique printed legs feature ammo pouches

DATA FILE
SET: 7261 Clone Turbo Tank
YEAR: 2005/6
PIECES: 4
EQUIPMENT: Blaster
VARIANTS: 1

Clone Trooper
GENETICALLY MODIFIED SOLDIER

This clone trooper minifigure is wearing advanced Phase II armor. The Phase I design (p.35) has been improved because of feedback received during the Clone Wars, and the minifigure's helmet and torso design now have a different look. This minifigure appears in three Episode III sets.

STAR VARIANT
Close clone
This clone trooper variant appears in two 2005–2007 LEGO sets. He has no dotted mouth grille pattern on his helmet, and a slightly less detailed torso piece than his 2010 counterpart.

Phase II clone troopers have blank black heads that can be seen through the open T-visor of their helmets

Heat dispersal vents aid breathing

Detailed torso design is new for the 2010 variant and is only seen on this LEGO minifigure

Phase II clone troopers have carried this blaster gun since 2007

DATA FILE
SET: 8091 Republic Swamp Speeder
YEAR: 2010
PIECES: 4
EQUIPMENT: Blaster, electrobinoculars
VARIANTS: 2

Improvements
The Phase II clone trooper minifigure has been issued with a revised version of the Phase I clone trooper's LEGO helmet. It is a different shape as it contains superior communications and breathing apparatus.

These clone trooper minifigures are highly trained combat specialists. They are the elite forces that carry out vital and dangerous missions for the Grand Army of the Republic, and are seen in only a select few LEGO sets. Each clone trooper specialist wears Phase II LEGO armor with distinguishing colors or equipment.

Shock troopers wear red-emblazoned armor to distinguish them as the elite force on Coruscant

DATA FILE

NAME: Shock trooper
SPECIALTY: Elite Coruscant guard
SET: 7671 AT-AP Walker
YEAR: 2008
PIECES: 4
EQUIPMENT: Blaster, blaster rifle
VARIANTS: 2

Short blaster gun. Shock troopers also carry blaster rifles for long-range targets

The original variant of this minifigure has black hips. It appears in the Clone Troopers Battle Pack (set 7655)

Phase II clone trooper helmet with dark-red markings

Blaster is a LEGO loudhailer with a translucent light-blue round plate

Recon trooper emblem identifies unit

DATA FILE

NAME: Recon trooper
SPECIALTY: Reconnaissance missions
SET: 7250 Clone Scout Walker
YEAR: 2005
PIECES: 4
EQUIPMENT: Blaster
VARIANTS: 1

Clone Troopers

CLONE SPECIALISTS

Audio pick-up for specialist communications

Black body glove under white armor

Green markings distinguish this minifigure as part of the 42nd Siege Battalion

DATA FILE

NAME: Siege Battalion trooper
SPECIALTY: Besieging enemy strongholds
SET: 7260 Wookiee Catamaran
YEAR: 2005
PIECES: 4
EQUIPMENT: Blaster
VARIANTS: 1

Jetpack warhead missiles

Dark visor
Like ordinary clone troopers (p.53), each of these specialized clone troopers has a plain black head, which can be seen through the open visor of his helmet so that the visor appears black.

The aerial trooper is the only minifigure to utilize this black flag LEGO piece

Super-size sniper rifle

DATA FILE

NAME: Aerial trooper
SPECIALTY: Airborne assaults
SET: 7261 Clone Turbo Tank
YEAR: 2005/6
PIECES: 16
EQUIPMENT: Jetpack, sniper rifle
VARIANTS: 1

Star Corps Trooper
ELITE CLONE TROOPER

The Star Corps trooper is one of the most skilled soldiers in the LEGO *Star Wars* galaxy. As part of the elite 327th Star Corps, his minifigure wears unique armor with yellow markings. He brings his combat expertise to two LEGO sets: Clone Turbo Tank (set 7261) and Clone Troopers Battle Pack (set 7655).

STAR VARIANT

Top trooper
An orange-and-black LEGO pauldron shows that this Star Corps trooper is a squadron leader. This variant appears in Clone Turbo Tank (set 7261).

Back armor
The back of the Star Corps trooper's torso shows his armor plates, power pack, and black body glove.

A yellow stripe extends from the Star Corps trooper's helmet through his chest armor

This torso piece is only seen on the Star Corps trooper. It features yellow markings and a blaster magazine strap over the right shoulder

A black body glove covers the Star Corps trooper's entire body

The Star Corps trooper carries two of these DC-15S blasters in the Clone Turbo Tank (set 7261)

DATA FILE

SET: 7655 Clone Troopers Battle Pack
YEAR: 2007
PIECES: 4
EQUIPMENT: Blaster
VARIANTS: 2

Droid Tri-Fighter (set 7252)

The buzz droid makes its first appearance in this 2005 set. The minifigure is housed within the central sphere of this deadly LEGO Droid Tri-Fighter, ready to be unleashed during a space dog fight!

Look out for this deadly LEGO buzz droid! Unleashed by the Separatists, this droid attaches itself to enemy starships with its legs and then destroys them with a powerful circular saw. The minifigure has wreaked havoc in three LEGO sets.

Buzz Droid

DEADLY DROID

Shock-absorbing outer hull. This piece is also used for astromech droid heads in LEGO *Star Wars*, though with different printing

Buzz droids have primary and secondary photoreceptors for homing in on targets

Inbuilt circular saw destroys starships

Circular saw
The buzz droid is the only LEGO minifigure to incorporate the circular blade saw piece. The piece is mostly used by minifigures as a tool in LEGO *Star Wars* and other LEGO themes.

DATA FILE

SET: 7751 Ahsoka's Starfighter and Vulture Droid
YEAR: 2009
PIECES: 13
EQUIPMENT: Built-in circular saw
VARIANTS: 1

These mechanical legs are seen on battle droids (p.22) and other droid minifigures in LEGO *Star Wars*

Anakin Skywalker
FALLEN JEDI

Emotionally, Anakin Skywalker has succumbed to the dark side. Now his physical transformation is almost complete, too. A charred and scarred Anakin minifigure comes aboard Emperor Palpatine's Shuttle (set 8096) for his journey to Coruscant for surgery.

STAR VARIANT

Before surgery
Anakin's first injured minifigure, from Darth Vader Transformation (set 7251), shows him before his operation. The set also contains the "after" minifigure; Vader in his trademark armor.

Anakin's red Sith lightsaber has already committed atrocities against the Jedi

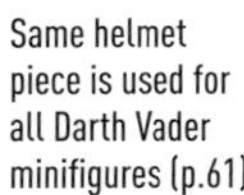

Same helmet piece is used for all Darth Vader minifigures (p.61)

Bared teeth
Under his protective helmet, Vader's harrowed, hairless face reveals the pain and rage of the dark side.

Anakin's remaining flesh-colored arm is a vestige of his past humanity; his black arm hints at Anakin's future as a Sith Lord

DATA FILE

SET: 8096 Emperor Palpatine's Shuttle
YEAR: 2010
PIECES: 4
EQUIPMENT: Lightsaber
VARIANTS: 2

Burnt remnants of Anakin's Jedi robes

Scarred Sith
Anakin has injuries on the front and back of his torso. The LEGO piece was made specifically for his battle-scarred minifigure.

2-1B
SURGICAL DROID

Endowed with the knowledge of a doctor and the skill of a surgeon, medical droids like 2-1B are literal life-savers on the battlefield. 2-1B features in two LEGO *Star Wars* sets, each containing a different variant of the minifigure. Both variants have a unique combined head-and-torso piece.

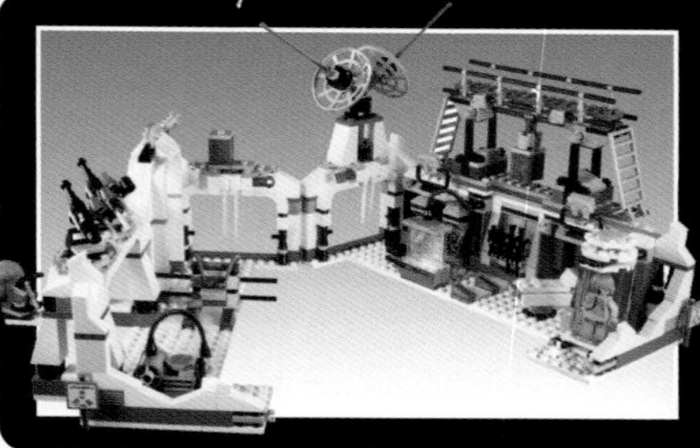

Hoth Echo Base (set 7879)
Many years after assisting at Anakin's medical transformation into Darth Vader, 2-1B treats Vader's son, Luke, at the Rebel headquarters on Hoth. Hoth Echo Base contains the second 2-1B minifigure; the blue variant from 2011.

STAR VARIANT

Vader's aide
In Emperor Palpatine's Shuttle (set 8096), the first variant of the 2-1B minifigure assists an injured Anakin. It is pearlized dark gray with a bionicle arm attachment.

Printed visual sensors

Vocoder unit for speaking

Auxiliary data input

This combined head-and-torso piece is gray on the earlier 2010 minifigure

Hydraulic systems give the robotic medic delicately controlled movements for precise and gentle surgery

The grip of the droid's two arms are at right-angles to each other. This arm is positioned to handle medical equipment

30376 3-02

Arm pieces are shared with battle droids (p.22) and classic LEGO skeletons

Solid feet for stability aboard starships

DATA FILE
SET: 7879 Hoth Echo Base
YEAR: 2011
PIECES: 4
EQUIPMENT: None
VARIANTS: 2

FX-6
MEDICAL ASSISTANT DROID

Medical droids are programmed to help anyone in need, and this multi-armed medic is responsible for bringing Darth Vader back from the brink of death. FX-6 saves the Sith's damaged body and encases it in the life-support uniform for which Vader becomes famous. This minifigure is exclusive to one LEGO set and is the only minifigure to incorporate the cone piece.

Darth Vader Transformation (set 7251)
On Coruscant, FX-6 toils away in secret. On one side of the rotatable operating table is Anakin's injured minifigure. On the other is Vader, resplendent in his new shiny suit.

DATA FILE
SET: 7251 Darth Vader Transformation
YEAR: 2005
PIECES: 21
EQUIPMENT: Closed-wrench, hammer, power drill, screwdriver, wrench
VARIANTS: 1

Data bank provides robot with medical knowledge

Toy Fair toy
FX-6 also appears in an exclusive VIP Gala edition of Darth Vader Transformation (set 7251), which was given out to guests at the 2005 LEGO International Toy Fair in New York.

Rotatable five-armed droid is an expert at multitasking

Classic tools from various other LEGO themes are used to repair Vader's body and forge his metal suit

Broad cone base gives droid stability during delicate surgical procedures

Darth Vader

SITH LORD

Darth Vader's iconic look is instantly recognizable in his LEGO minifigure form. There are nine variants, all made up of combinations of two torso designs, a cape, and four heads (with variations in the eyebrows, eye color, and scar patterns), but just one trademark helmet piece.

STAR VARIANTS

Lighting the way

2005 saw the addition of light-up lightsabers to the LEGO *Star Wars* theme. Vader's appears in TIE Fighter (set 7263) with a minifigure that uses the original Vader torso design.

Chrome Vader

Vader's black suit took on a chrome sheen for a special figure for the 10th Anniversary of LEGO *Star Wars* in 2009.

Intimidating red Sith lightsaber

Removable helmet piece is common to all Vader minifigures and was first molded in 1999

Whites of his eyes

In 2009, Vader's previously black eyes received white pupils for the first time.

The second Vader torso design, first seen in 2008, has a detailed control chestplate and a utility belt

Welcome to Toy Fair

The anniversary-edition chrome-black Darth Vader minifigure was given out to lucky guests at the 2009 Toy Fair in New York in a special LEGO Collectors Event presentation box.

DATA FILE

SET: 10212 Imperial Shuttle
YEAR: 2010
PIECES: 5
EQUIPMENT: Cape, lightsaber
VARIANTS: 9

Stormtrooper
IMPERIAL SOLDIER

Loyal to the Empire and highly disciplined, a stormtrooper is built to succeed in combat. Shielded in white space armor, these nameless soldiers have blank heads beneath their helmets to ensure anonymity. Seven stormtrooper variants have appeared in 15 sets since 2001.

Reinforced helmet with internal comlink

Dotted mouth grilles have been seen on stormtroopers from the 2007 sets onwards

Utility belt with blaster power cell reserves

E-11 blaster pistol with rangefinder

Heads up

All seven variants of the stormtrooper minifigure have blank heads but the colors vary. The two earliest variants have yellow heads, two others have light flesh heads, and the three latest variants have black heads.

STAR VARIANTS

Leg armor
This stormtrooper variant has an extension of his utility belt and armor shin plates on his hips and legs. The 2005 minifigure is exclusive to Imperial Inspection (set 7264).

Silver-trooper
This shiny chrome silver stormtrooper was released in a promotional polybag in 2010. It was sold exclusively at Toys 'R' Us stores throughout March of that year.

DATA FILE

SET: 10212 Imperial Shuttle
YEAR: 2010
PIECES: 4
EQUIPMENT: Blaster
VARIANTS: 7

Back armor
A stormtrooper has emergency breathing apparatus and a thermal detonator on the back of his armor.

C-3PO
PROTOCOL DROID

STAR VARIANTS

Chrome gold
This limited edition chrome gold C-3PO was randomly placed in 10,000 LEGO *Star Wars* sets to celebrate the 30th anniversary of *Star Wars* in 2007. The LEGO Group also made five 14-carat gold variants.

Light C-3PO
The original variant of C-3PO is light pearl-gold in color. It appeared in sets between 2001 and 2005. From 2008, the color of C-3PO changed to a richer pearl-gold.

Worrisome protocol droid
C-3PO has found himself in ten LEGO *Star Wars* sets since he was first released in 2001. C-3PO was the first LEGO *Star Wars* protocol droid and seven variants of him have since been released. All have kept his original protocol head-mold and printing but his gold tone has been refined from light pearl-gold to a brighter pearl-gold color.

Audiosensor—C-3PO has one on each side of his head

C-3PO's connection wires are exposed in his mid-body section

Behind C-3PO
C-3PO's shiny gold armor continues on the back of his torso piece. You can also see his back plate and mid-body section.

Protocol droids
C-3PO was the first LEGO protocol droid and his head-mold was specially cast for him. The LEGO Group has since produced other protocol droids using the same head-mold: R-3PO, K-3PO (pp.94–95), and the Death Star Droid (p.81).

DATA FILE
SET: 8092 Luke's Landspeeder
YEAR: 2010
PIECES: 3
EQUIPMENT: None
VARIANTS: 7

Plain pearl gold hips and legs are unique to C-3PO

Captain Antilles
ILL-FATED CAPTAIN

This cool-headed captain of the consular cruiser *Tantive IV* is on a covert mission for the Rebel Alliance—he must transport secret Death Star plans across the galaxy. When his ship is invaded by Darth Vader, brave Antilles refuses to betray the location of the plans. However, swiveling the minifigure's double-sided head reveals the fate of his own personal mission!

***Tantive IV* (set 10198)**
Captain Raymus Antilles is exclusive to this 2009 set. He commands the *Tantive IV* from a central control room, which has two monitors for the minifigure to track the ship's progress on.

LEGO Death
Captain Antilles meets a grizzly end when Darth Vader strangles him! This face shows his pained expression.

Captain Antilles happily goes about his work for the Rebel Alliance

Rank badge with five blue dots shows this minifigure is a captain

Helmet strap with white chin guard is printed on Captain Antilles's face

Torso with open utility jacket and gray undershirt is unique to this minifigure. The dark-tan shoulder panels of Captain Antilles's jacket continue on the back of his torso

DATA FILE

SET: 10198 *Tantive IV*
YEAR: 2009
PIECES: 5
EQUIPMENT: None
VARIANTS: 1

Rebel Trooper
SOLDIER OF THE REBEL ARMY

This Rebel trooper is ready to fight for the Alliance! His minifigure comes well equipped for battle in his custom-made blast helmet, wielding plenty of fire power. The Rebel trooper has starred in just two sets—he arrived with several comrades in the first, and provides vital backup for Captain Antilles in the second.

Rebel Scout Speeder (7668)
This 2008 set was the first to contain the Rebel trooper minifigure—with enough to start a Rebel Army! Four Rebel troopers fit into the repulsorlift speeder: a pilot, two soldiers, and a gunner atop the turret.

Removeable blast visor clips into holes at the sides of the helmet

Only the Rebel trooper and Captain Antilles (opposite) wear this blast helmet

Rebel helmet
This white blast helmet with an extended neck guard was specially designed for this minifigure.

Rebel troopers carry blaster guns like this as well as long blaster rifles

Although the Rebel trooper wears the standard-issue Rebel Army uniform of a sand-blue shirt and black combat vest, the torso is seen only on this minifigure

DATA FILE
SET: 10198 *Tantive IV*
YEAR: 2009
PIECES: 5
EQUIPMENT: Blaster, blaster rifle
VARIANTS: 1

Princess Leia
SENATOR OF ALDERAAN

As a member of the Galactic Senate and secret sympathizer of the Rebel Alliance, Princess Leia Organa is a symbol of hope across the LEGO *Star Wars* galaxy. She dresses in the traditional white robes of the Alderaan royal family. Her redesigned minifigure, with a double-sided head, escapes the clutches of Darth Vader in the 2011 *Millennium Falcon* (set 7965).

Princess Leia wears her hair in two braided buns when on senatorial duty. The LEGO hair piece was specially created for Leia's minifigure

Unique LEGO head is first seen on the 2011 design. It has feminine fluttering eyelashes and red lips

Leia wears this white torso piece with black and light bluish-gray printing in LEGO sets from 2007 onwards

Leia probably stole this blaster from Imperial forces!

Symbolic silver belt of Alderaan royalty

STAR VARIANT

Original Leia
The first variant of Princess Leia appears in the original *Millennium Falcon* (set 7190), released in 2000. The minifigure has a yellow head and hands, and a unique torso with light gray printing.

Serious side
While one side of Princess Leia's face has a relaxed smile, the other has a determined expression.

DATA FILE

SET: 7965 *Millennium Falcon*
YEAR: 2011
PIECES: 4
EQUIPMENT: Blaster
VARIANTS: 4

Luke Skywalker

FARMBOY OF TATOOINE

Luke Skywalker is a poor farmboy who dreams of becoming a space pilot. The sullen expression on one side of his minifigure's dual-face head shows just how much he longs to escape the daily drudgery of life on his uncle's moisture farm! But when Luke meets exiled Jedi Obi-Wan Kenobi, his life changes forever.

Luke wore standard long female LEGO hair from 2007 until this unique hair was created for his 2011 redesign
Unique head with a down-turned mouth and distinctive chin dimple is new for the 2011 redesign
Obi-Wan Kenobi gave Luke this blue lightsaber
Luke keeps farm tools in his brown utility belt pouch
Leg bindings keep out desert sand

STAR VARIANT

First Luke
The original variant of young Luke Skywalker has short tan hair, a yellow face and hands, and different printing on his torso and leg pieces. He appears in three 2000–2003 LEGO sets.

Helmet head
Luke wears a helmet with a visor as a blindfold when he practices using the Force with his lightsaber.

DATA FILE

SET: 7965 *Millennium Falcon*
YEAR: 2011
PIECES: 4
EQUIPMENT: Blaster, lightsaber
VARIANTS: 4

Skyhopper Pilot
MYSTERIOUS MINIFIGURE

This T-16 skyhopper pilot cuts a mysterious minifigure in the LEGO *Star Wars* galaxy. He is found in only one LEGO set, and his visor permanently obscures his face so he is not recognized. What we do know is that this pilot is an ace at racing around the narrow ravines of Tatooine in his T-16 skyhopper!

This pilot helmet was created for the T-16 pilot, but in 2006 Ten Numb (p.137) adopted it in reddish brown

T-16 Skyhopper (set 4477)

This 2003 LEGO set is the only one that contains the T-16 skyhopper pilot minifigure. The model bears Luke Skywalker's flying decal—perhaps a hint that the minifigure might be him!

Luke Skyhopper?
Luke Skywalker flies a T-16 skyhopper as a teenager, even though his Uncle Owen disapproves of it. Could this pilot be Luke? The pilot's visor hides much of his face, but that distinctive chin dimple might give him away!

This yellow head with a visor pattern was first used on the scout trooper minifigure (p.141) in 1999

The T-16 pilot's torso was specially made for him. It shows the utility pockets and folds of his bright red jumpsuit

Black flight gloves

This minifigure carries electrobinoculars for zooming in on distant targets and a blaster gun for shooting womp rats

DATA FILE

SET: 4477 T-16 Skyhopper
YEAR: 2003
PIECES: 4
EQUIPMENT: Blaster, electrobinoculars
VARIANTS: 1

Owen Lars
MOISTURE FARMER

Sandcrawler (set 10144)
Owen Lars is looking to buy some cheap droids for his moisture farm from passing Jawas in the Sandcrawler (set 10144), which the minifigure is exclusive to. Will Uncle Owen purchase the R2-D2 and C-3PO minifigures that also come with this set?

Poor moisture farmer Owen Lars is the uncle and guardian of Luke Skywalker. His minifigure is featured in only one LEGO set, while his loyal wife, Beru, is yet to be seen in LEGO form. When Jawas pass by his remote farm in their Sandcrawler (set 10144), Uncle Owen takes a look at the beat-up droids they are selling cheap—he could do with some help around the farm!

DATA FILE
SET: 10144 Sandcrawler
YEAR: 2005
PIECES: 4
EQUIPMENT: None
VARIANTS: 1

Uncle Owen's unique head has gray eyebrows and a stubble beard

This LEGO torso was specially made for Owen Lars. He wears a rough desert robe over a gray tunic and brown undershirt

Brown utility belt for farming tools

Farm fashion
Uncle Owen shares his short bluish-gray LEGO hair with Grand Moff Tarkin (p.79) and old Obi-Wan "Ben" Kenobi (p.75) in the LEGO *Star Wars* galaxy, but it is also used on two farmer minifigures in the LEGO City theme.

Indigenous to the desert planet Tatooine, this Jawa minifigure is a small, industrious creature, always on the look out for items it can scavenge and sell on. Its humanoid shape is reflected in a standard minifigure form, though it has short, unposeable legs and a mysterious face. Fortunately, the LEGO plastic doesn't recreate the Jawa's distinctive body odor.

Jawa
DESERT SCAVENGER

Sandcrawler (set 10144)
In this set, unwary droids need to watch out for Jawas on the prowl for anything they can sell. Here, R2-D2 is loaded by crane into the large Sandcrawler by three Jawas, eager to take him to market and make a profit.

Only the Jawa has this unique LEGO head
A heavy hood protects the Jawa from the desert sun. It is a reddish-brown LEGO Jedi hood piece
Bandolier for ionization charges
Ion blaster
Standard Jedi cape is specially adapted to accommodate shorter minifigure

Beneath the hood
Jawas rarely venture out from under their heavy cloaks so their faces are largely unknown. The minifigure has a simple head pattern: plain black with striking glowing eyes.

DATA FILE
SET: 10144 Sandcrawler
YEAR: 2005
PIECES: 6
EQUIPMENT: Cape, ion blaster
VARIANTS: 1

R5-D4
RED ASTROMECH DROID

R5-series astromech droids were originally conceived as a lower-cost, lower-functionality version of the R2-series. However, there is nothing lacking about this minifigure, which comes in three variants. The droid fulfills its piloting function in eight LEGO sets and, in Sandcrawler (set 10144), R5-D4 is sold by Jawas on Tatooine.

STAR VARIANT

Red droid
This minifigure, called "astromech droid" on LEGO packaging, appears in seven sets. It shares the same body as R5-D4's 2005 variant, but has a red-and-silver domed head. A different dome pattern appears on a 2007 variant in Y-Wing Fighter (set 7658).

LEGO adaptation
Reproducing the world of *Star Wars* in LEGO bricks can require some adaptation. R5-D4 shares the same circular dome-shaped head piece as R2-series minifigures, although the original droid has a more funnel-shaped head.

DATA FILE

SET: 10144 Sandcrawler
YEAR: 2005
PIECES: 5
EQUIPMENT: None
VARIANTS: 3

Specially printed central torso piece is used for all three variants of the red droid

Tan-colored disc is unique to the 2005 variant of R5-D4

Spacecraft linkage arms

Robotic leg pieces are unique to astromech droid minifigures

Polarity sink

System ventilation

Heat exhaust

Recharge power coupling

Droids
MECHANICAL HELPERS

These droids are programmed to perform specific tasks in the LEGO *Star Wars* galaxy, providing the LEGO minifigures with various forms of help. Some are used for maintenance work, some provide energy, and some—like the Imperial IT-O interrogator droid—are used for far more sinister ends!

Probing arm is a LEGO screwdriver piece

The IT-O records all information obtained during interrogations

DATA FILE
NAME: IT-O
ROLE: Imperial interrogator
SET: 10188 Death Star
YEAR: 2008
PIECES: 9
VARIANTS: 1

The IT-O has a light bluish-gray LEGO stand so it appears to hover in the air

Antenna is a LEGO lever piece

DATA FILE
NAME: R1-G4
ROLE: Starship technician
SET: 10144 Sandcrawler
YEAR: 2005
PIECES: 12
VARIANTS: 1

The gray plate piece with a ring clip on R1-G4's unipod body is also seen on the mouse droid (opposite)

Sandcrawler
R1-G4, the GNK droid, and the treadwell droid are all scrap droids that have been salvaged by Jawa minifigures (p.70) on the LEGO Sandcrawler (set 10144). The droids are offered for sale at the Lars's Tatooine homestead in the Sandcrawler set.

This LEGO GNK droid is light bluish gray, but the variant that appears in Jabba's Palace (set 4480) is dark gray

A GNK droid walks on two legs

DATA FILE
NAME: GNK droid
ROLE: Power generator
SET: 10144 Sandcrawler
YEAR: 2005
PIECES: 7
VARIANTS: 2

Communications antenna

The sentry droid hovers off the ground on a translucent LEGO stand

The mouse droid is used on the Death Star (set 10188) and the Imperial Star Destroyer (set 6211)

DATA FILE
NAME: Mouse droid
ROLE: Imperial messenger
SET: 10188 Death Star
YEAR: 2008
PIECES: 9
VARIANTS: 1

Gray plate piece has a ring clip to attach the wheels

DATA FILE
NAME: Sentry droid
ROLE: Imperial surveillance
SET: 8092 Luke's Landspeeder
YEAR: 2010
PIECES: 8
VARIANTS: 1

Imperial droids
The IT-O, mouse droid, and sentry droid are all used by Imperial forces in LEGO sets. On the LEGO Death Star (set 10188) the droid operating room wall has a special mouse hole for the mouse droid to pass secret Imperial messages through undetected.

A multitude of manipulator arms perform maintenance tasks. The same white arm pieces are seen on the pilot droid (p.162), General Grievous (p.40), and assassin droid (p.110) minifigures

Antenna LEGO piece is used as stand on the IT-O droid (opposite)

DATA FILE
NAME: Treadwell droid
ROLE: Repairs
SET: 10144 Sandcrawler
YEAR: 2005
PIECES: 18
VARIANTS: 1

The treadwell droid gets its name from its low, treaded base

ASP Droid
LABOR DROID

This beaten-up ASP droid belongs to a clan of Jawa minifigures, though it could be yours for the right price! The minifigure is one of the many droids for sale on the LEGO Sandcrawler (set 10144). It is a general purpose droid designed to perform menial labor tasks, with a limited vocabulary and low brain power.

Sandcrawler (set 10144)
The ASP droid has been salvaged by Jawas and patched up in their workshop aboard the Sandcrawler. It is now ready to be sold on to any willing moisture farmers on Tatooine. The ASP droid is unique to this 2005 LEGO set.

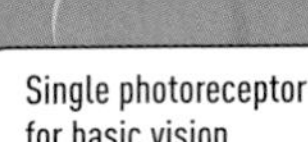

Single photoreceptor for basic vision

Tan battle droid torso. This piece was first seen on battle droid minifigures (p.22) in 1999

Fellow LEGO droids A4-D (p.174) and the rocket droid commander (p.156) have this dark bluish-gray mechanical arm piece

Wide feet for stability

Hardwearing
LEGO ASP droids closely resemble LEGO battle droids (pp.22–23). The droids' torsos, arms, and legs are identical. Both types of droid are built to last—one endures hard physical labor, while the other withstands blows on the battlefield.

DATA FILE
SET: 10144 Sandcrawler
YEAR: 2005
PIECES: 6
EQUIPMENT: None
VARIANTS: 1

Obi-Wan "Ben" Kenobi

EXILED JEDI

Luke's Landspeeder (set 8092)
Obi-Wan Kenobi accompanies Luke Skywalker in his landspeeder in this 2010 set. It has a secret compartment to hold the minifigures' lightsabers.

Now an old man, Obi-Wan Kenobi is a Jedi in exile. He lives a hermit's existence on Tatooine and goes by the name of Ben Kenobi. But his minifigure shows signs of the life he once led: He wears Jedi robes and a brown cloak, and keeps his blue lightsaber close at hand. Obi-Wan "Ben" Kenobi appears in six LEGO *Star Wars* sets.

Obi-Wan Kenobi is a Jedi in exile, but he still has his blue lightsaber

Old Obi-Wan has a gray beard and wrinkles. The minifigure has had this LEGO head since 2010

Only old Obi-Wan Kenobi wears these tan robes and simple brown belt. In sets released before 2007, he has a torso with fewer robe details and no belt

DATA FILE

SET: 7965 *Millennium Falcon*
YEAR: 2011
PIECES: 5
EQUIPMENT: Cape, lightsaber
VARIANTS: 6

STAR VARIANT

Original Obi
This variant of old Obi-Wan Kenobi appears in the Landspeeder (set 7110). He has a yellow head and hands, simple torso printing, brown hips, and no hood or cape.

Sandtrooper
DESERT SOLDIER

The sandtrooper minifigure might look a lot like a stormtrooper, but his armor has been specifically adapted to withstand extreme desert climates found on planets like Tatooine. Commander and regular officer sandtrooper minifigures have appeared in LEGO *Star Wars* sets since 2003.

STAR VARIANT

Orange pauldron
Sandtrooper squad leaders and commanders wear orange shoulder pauldrons over their armor. This sandtrooper variant appears in Mos Eisley Cantina (set 4501).

DATA FILE

SET: 8092 Luke's Landspeeder
YEAR: 2010
PIECES: 11
EQUIPMENT: Blaster, pauldron
VARIANTS: 4

Helmet is the same as that of a regular LEGO stormtrooper (p.62)

Helmet has inbuilt breathing filters to withstand the fierce desert sun

Blaster gun. Mounted sandtroopers carry long electropikes in Mos Eisley Cantina (set 4501)

Pauldron cloths denote rank. Regular sandtroopers wear black pauldrons

Sandtrooper armor has an inbuilt cooling system

Rebreather
Sandtroopers wear rebreather packs to regulate their oxygen supply in sweltering desert climes.

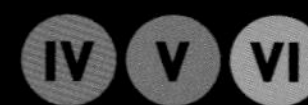

Han Solo

BRAVE BRAGGART

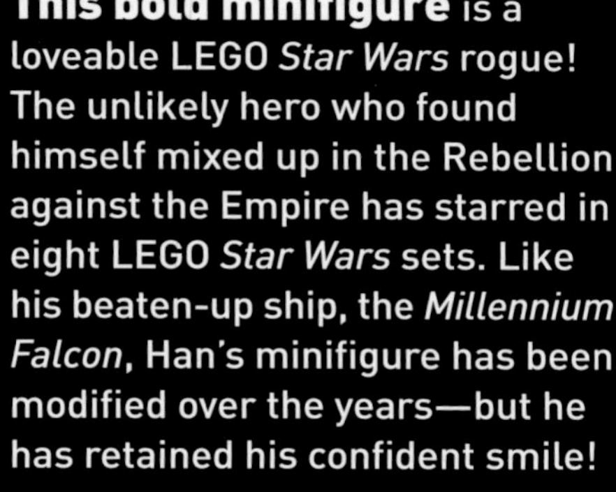

This bold minifigure is a loveable LEGO *Star Wars* rogue! The unlikely hero who found himself mixed up in the Rebellion against the Empire has starred in eight LEGO *Star Wars* sets. Like his beaten-up ship, the *Millennium Falcon*, Han's minifigure has been modified over the years—but he has retained his confident smile!

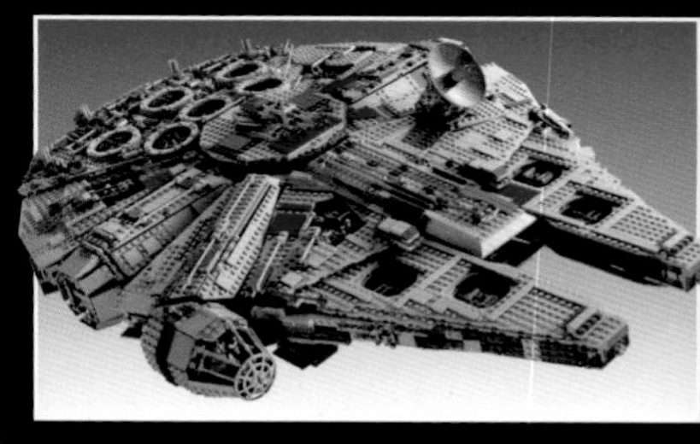

***Millennium Falcon* (set 10179)**
This 2007 version of Han's battered YT-1300 light freighter, the *Millennium Falcon*, is an Ultimate Collector's Edition set. The cockpit seats four minifigures, with Han and his right-hand Wookiee Chewbacca at the helm!

STAR VARIANT

Solo Solo
This is a rare original variant of Han Solo's minifigure. He appears in only one LEGO set: the first-ever LEGO *Millennium Falcon* (set 7190), released in 2000.

This light flesh head with white pupils is first seen in the 2011 design

Han wears a black vest and light shirt

Harrison Ford
Han Solo is the first LEGO minifigure to be based on the likeness of actor Harrison Ford, who plays Han Solo in the *Star Wars* movies—but he is not the only one to be based on Ford! There is also a LEGO Indiana Jones.

Unique painted hips feature pockets for Han's essentials, including a droid caller and blaster power cell reserves

Previous variants of this minifigure have featured brown and blue legs, but Han is hardly ever without his gun belt and quick-draw holster

DATA FILE

SET: 7965 *Millennium Falcon*
YEAR: 2011
PIECES: 4
EQUIPMENT: Blaster
VARIANTS: 5

Rodian bounty hunter Greedo is looking for Han Solo to recover money owed to his boss, Jabba the Hutt. He has caught up with Han in the Mos Espa Cantina (set 4501). But only one of them can walk out alive. A clue as to who that might be: Greedo appears in only this one LEGO *Star Wars* set!

Mos Eisley Cantina (set 4501)
This saloon on the desert planet Tatooine has shady alcoves where secret conversations can take place unseen. Here, Han Solo and Greedo discuss the unpaid debts Han owes Jabba the Hutt. Luckily, the table they have chosen has a secret compartment for Han to hide his blaster inside!

Greedo
BOUNTY HUNTER

Large disc-shaped eyes with light reflectors

Painted elongated snout

Greedo's unique arms have painted tan stripes

First Rodian
Greedo was the first Rodian minifigure and his pimpled head-mold was designed specially for him. Greedo's fellow Rodians, Onaconda Farr (p.171) and W. Wald (p.14), have since used the same head-mold but in different colors.

Tan vest over sky-blue jumpsuit

Reddish-brown hips with sky-blue legs are unique to the Greedo minifigure

DATA FILE
SET: 4501 Mos Eisley Cantina
YEAR: 2003
PIECES: 3
EQUIPMENT: None
VARIANTS: 1

Grand Moff Tarkin

IMPERIAL GOVERNER

Governer of the Imperial Outland Regions, Grand Moff Tarkin has appeared in two LEGO *Star Wars* sets since 2006. Both sets—Imperial Star Destroyer (6211) and Death Star (10188)—are jewels in the Empire's fleet, while Tarkin's intimidating countenance and obvious rank make him one of the Empire's most feared men.

Death Star (set 10188)
Grand Moff Tarkin is one of 24 minifigures included in the LEGO Death Star. Inside the superlaser control room, Tarkin just needs to say the word and the Death Star's powerful superweapon can fire a laser beam powerful enough to destroy an entire planet.

Standard short LEGO hair in light bluish-gray. The same piece is used on Owen Lars (p.69) and old Obi Wan "Ben" Kenobi (p.75) in the LEGO *Star Wars* theme

Light flesh head with drawn cheekbones and a scowl is unique to Grand Moff Tarkin

Imperial code cylinders. High-ranking Tarkin keeps one of these important security devices on each side of his tunic

Unique rank badge indicates military status. As Grand Moff, Tarkin has two rows of colored squares

Black belt with silver Imperial officer's disc

DATA FILE
SETS: 10188 Death Star
YEAR: 2008
PIECES: 4
EQUIPMENT: None
VARIANTS: 1

Imperial Officer
THE EMPEROR'S HENCHMAN

Wearing a starched gray uniform, the Imperial officer minifigure is part of the Emperor's vast army. These high-ranking soldiers work far from the battlefield, aboard starships like the Imperial Shuttle (set 10212). First appearing in 2002 with an unusually cheery smile, the Imperial officer became more stern in 2010.

Dark bluish-gray Imperial officer kepi

STAR VARIANT

First officer
This original variant is only in the 2002 set Final Duel II (set 7201). He has a sunnier disposition than his 2010 counterpart! Before the 2010 redesign, all Imperial officer minifigures had smiling faces.

Kepi
Many members of the LEGO *Star Wars* security forces wear a flat, circular cap with a peak called a kepi. The same kepi is worn in gray by Admiral Piett (p.98), in black by the Imperial pilot (p.126) and Juno Eclipse (p.204), and in blue by the Bespin guard (p.115).

The Imperial officer has a stern expression because he takes his work for the Empire very seriously. The Hoth Rebel trooper (p.103) and Hoth Imperial officer (p.99) have the same head

Imperial code cylinder—only important military officers carry these sophisticated keycards

Red and blue rank insignia plaque

Imperial officer minifigures carry no weapons because they work away from the battlefield

Dark bluish-gray tunic. All Imperial officer variants wear this uniform print, but the original, from Final Duel II (set 7201), has it in darker gray

DATA FILE

SET: 10212 Imperial Shuttle
YEAR: 2010
PIECES: 4
EQUIPMENT: None
VARIANTS: 4

Death Star Droid
RA-7 PROTOCOL DROID

This RA-7 protocol droid is informally known as a Death Star droid because its kind is generally found on the Imperial battle station. The droids look like C-3PO, but they are very different: They have low intelligence and are programmed to be stern rather than helpful. The RA-7 is exclusive to the Death Star (set 10188), where its main role is to spy on officials like Grand Moff Tarkin.

Death Star (set 10188)
The Death Star droid is exclusive to this set. If in need of repairs, the Death Star droid can take the turbolift to the Death Star's droid maintenance room (top right in picture). The facility has a work bench and tool rack.

Photoreceptors are a droid's visual organs. The RA-7 uses his to spy on officials

Vocabulator allows the RA-7 to speak—and pass on secrets

Head start
The protocol droid head piece on the Death Star droid minifigure was first created for C-3PO in 2000 (p.63). The head piece can also be found on fellow protocol droids R-3PO, and K-3PO (pp.94–95).

Primary power outlet

Printed chest plate. The same print is used on C-3PO, R-3PO, and K-3PO and continues on the back

DATA FILE
SET: 10188 Death Star
YEAR: 2008
PIECES: 3
EQUIPMENT: None
VARIANTS: 1

Luke Skywalker
STORMTROOPER DISGUISE

This Luke Skywalker minifigure is exclusive to the Death Star (set 10188). Luke is there to rescue Leia, but he must get past the Death Star's stringent security forces first. So, if you can't beat 'em, join 'em! Luke is disguised in stormtrooper armor. He can wear either a helmet or his (more recognizable) tan hair.

Death Star (set 10188)
In the depths of the Death Star, Luke, Leia, Chewbacca, and Han find themselves in the stinking trash compactor! The walls are closing in—can they escape in time? A mechanism above the room closes the walls.

DATA FILE
SET: 10188 Death Star
YEAR: 2008
PIECES: 4
EQUIPMENT: Helmet, blaster
VARIANTS: 1

This light flesh head with a distinctive chin dimple was used on six Luke Skywalker minifigures between 2006 and 2009

This blaster gun is typically used by stormtroopers (p.62)

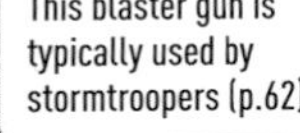

White space armor is not only a good disguise—it can protect Luke from blaster bolts

Long locks
Luke's long hair is mostly used on female characters in other LEGO themes, but several LEGO *Star Wars* males favor the long-haired look, including the Anakin Skywalker (p.42), Obi-Wan Kenobi (p.28), and Boba Fett minifigures (p.31).

Han Solo
STORMTROOPER DISGUISE

Death Star (set 10188) Both Luke Skywalker and Han Solo appear in several different guises aboard the Death Star: in stormtrooper disguise to rescue Leia from her detention cell (pictured), in their regular outfits, and Luke also appears in his Jedi Knight robes.

Quickwitted scoundrel Han Solo wears stolen stormtrooper armor to disguise himself on the Death Star. Like Luke, Han comes with both his standard reddish-brown hair and a stormtrooper helmet. He certainly needs the helmet if he is to get past the Death Star's real stormtroopers and rescue Leia—there is no hiding that trademark smirk!

DATA FILE

SET: 10188 Death Star
YEAR: 2008
PIECES: 4
EQUIPMENT: Helmet, blaster
VARIANTS: 1

Light flesh head with thick brown eyebrows and a cocksure smile

Black, temperature-controlled body glove worn under space armor

Stolen blaster

Collectible set
Han and Luke Skywalker in stormtrooper disguises were also part of the exclusive LEGO Collectible Display Set 3. The set was available for one day only at the 2009 San Diego Comic-Con. Chewbacca was also included in the set.

Luke Skywalker
X-WING PILOT

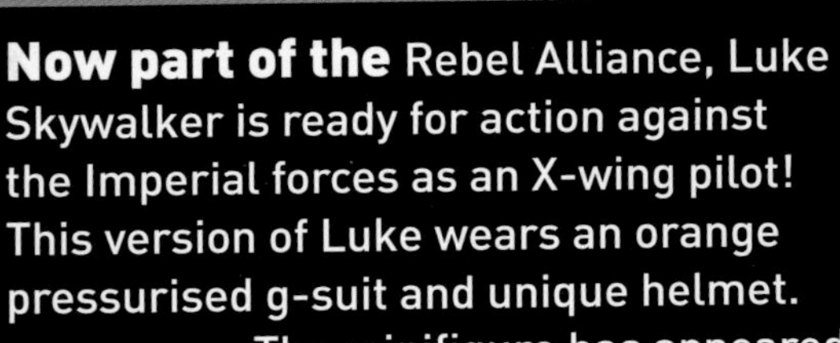

Now part of the Rebel Alliance, Luke Skywalker is ready for action against the Imperial forces as an X-wing pilot! This version of Luke wears an orange pressurised g-suit and unique helmet. The minifigure has appeared in nine LEGO *Star Wars* sets, in five different variations.

AT-AT Walker (set 8129)

The AT-AT walker has a grappling hook that X-wing pilot Luke Skywalker can hang from. Luke can climb the AT-AT's body and use his lightsaber to destroy it before it reaches the Hoth Rebel base.

Luke's blue lightsaber once belonged to his father, Anakin Skywalker

Flesh-colored head with white pupils and Luke's distinctive chin dimple is first used in the 2010 design

Luke's Insignia

Luke's insulated pilot helmet has red Rebel markings and unique patterns that continue around the back and sides.

Luke's orange g-suit is also worn by his fellow Rebel pilot Zev Senesca (p.104). The white flak vest design continues on the back of the torso

Black flight gloves

DATA FILE

SET: 8129 AT-AT Walker
YEAR: 2010
PIECES: 4
EQUIPMENT: Lightsaber
VARIANTS: 5

STAR VARIANT

Rare Rebel

This X-wing pilot Luke appears in only one 2003/4 set: Rebel Snowspeeder (set 4500). It has yellow flesh, bluish-gray hips, and a less detailed helmet and g-suit design than the 2010 variant.

Biggs Darklighter

X-WING PILOT

Brave X-wing pilot Biggs Darklighter appears with his childhood friend Luke Skywalker in the X-Wing Fighter (set 7140). He has remained exclusive to the set since its release in 1999. Known to his fellow Rebel pilots as "Red Three," Biggs's insulated flying helmet has a unique pattern on it. Biggs was killed in the Rebel's assault on the first Death Star.

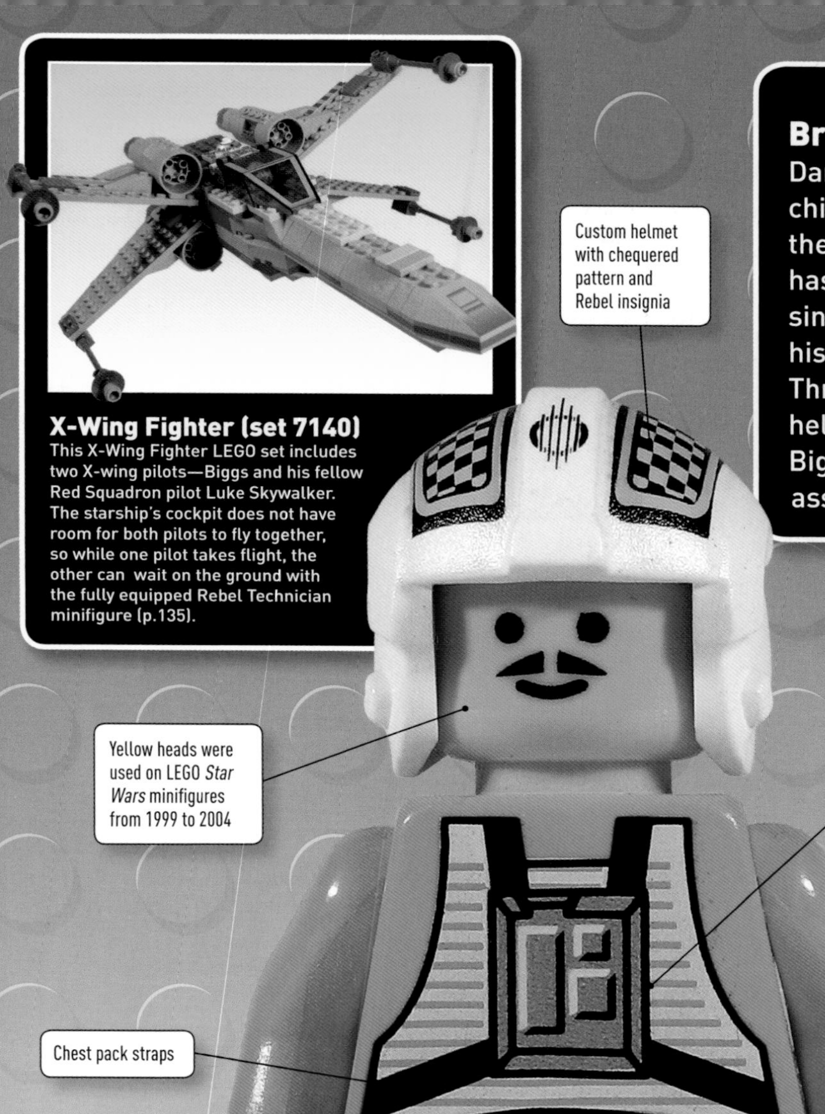

Custom helmet with chequered pattern and Rebel insignia
Yellow heads were used on LEGO *Star Wars* minifigures from 1999 to 2004
The printing on this early X-wing pilot torso piece has fewer details than that worn by Luke Skywalker (opposite)
Chest pack straps

X-Wing Fighter (set 7140)
This X-Wing Fighter LEGO set includes two X-wing pilots—Biggs and his fellow Red Squadron pilot Luke Skywalker. The starship's cockpit does not have room for both pilots to fly together, so while one pilot takes flight, the other can wait on the ground with the fully equipped Rebel Technician minifigure (p.135).

Mustache man
Biggs's mustachioed head is only used on his minifigure in the LEGO *Star Wars* theme, but it is used in lots of other LEGO themes for characters such as waiters, chefs, coast guards, and firemen.

DATA FILE

SET: 7140 X-Wing Fighter
YEAR: 1999
PIECES: 4
EQUIPMENT: None
VARIANTS: 1

Wedge Antilles
X-WING PILOT

Ace X-wing pilot Wedge Antilles is the hero of three huge battles—Yavin, Hoth, and Endor—but he has featured in only one LEGO *Star Wars* set. Humble hero Wedge blends in among the other X-wing pilot minifigures in his Rebel flight suit and standard minifigure face, but his unique helmet sets him apart from the rest.

X-Wing Fighter (set 6212)
Wedge Antilles is exclusive to the 2006 X-Wing Fighter set, which also includes X-wing pilot Luke Skywalker (p.82). The vehicle can change from Luke's Red Five to Wedge's Red Two X-wing with its unique wing details.

This simple, smiling face appears on 14 LEGO minifigures, including LEGO *Star Wars* pilots Dutch Vander (opposite) and Dak Ralter (p.105)

The same torso pattern is used—but on a red torso—for the B-wing pilot minifigure (p.136)

DATA FILE

SET: 6212 X-Wing Fighter
YEAR: 2006
PIECES: 4
EQUIPMENT: None
VARIANTS: 1

Black flight gloves

This orange pressurized g-suit is standard issue flight wear for LEGO X-wing pilots. It protects them from dangerous acceleration g-forces when flying at high speeds

Custom helmet
Wedge's custom-made X-wing pilot helmet has dark bluish-gray rectangles and a circle pattern along the sides.

Dutch Vander

Y-WING PILOT

Daring Jon "Dutch" Vander has the call-sign Gold Leader when he flies into battle as a Rebel pilot, but he is shot down in the Battle of Yavin. He is one of the only minifigures to have ever flown a LEGO Y-wing fighter. He appears in the starships in three LEGO *Star Wars* sets (and in two re-releases).

STAR VARIANT

Yellow Dutch
This Dutch Vander variant has a yellow head with red hair and eyebrows and a headset to help him communicate with his squadron. It appears in the 1999 set TIE Fighter and Y-Wing (set 7150) and its 2002 and 2004 re-releases.

DATA FILE

SET: 7658 Y-Wing Fighter
YEAR: 2007
PIECES: 4
EQUIPMENT: Blaster
VARIANTS: 3

Dutch wears a unique helmet with a yellow grid pattern and Rebel insignia

X- and Y-wing pilots wear these life support units to help them breathe during flight

Dutch is one of the only Rebel pilots to carry a blaster

This Dutch has blue-gray hips, but an early variant has dark gray hips

TIE Pilot

ELITE IMPERIAL PILOT

These elite pilots of the Imperial Navy are referred to as "bucketheads" by Rebel pilots because of their bulky helmets. Their unique headgear and flight suits are a self-contained life-support system that helps them survive in the vacuum of space. The TIE pilot minifigure has fought in five sets since 2001.

This custom TIE helmet is first seen in 2010. It is the same mold as the white helmet worn by the AT-AT driver minifigure (p.101)

TIE Defender (set 8087)
The redesigned TIE pilot has only appeared in the 2010 set TIE Defender (set 8087). The minifigure has no seat or controls in the starfighter's cramped cockpit, but it rotates as the starfighter twists and turns in battle.

STAR VARIANT

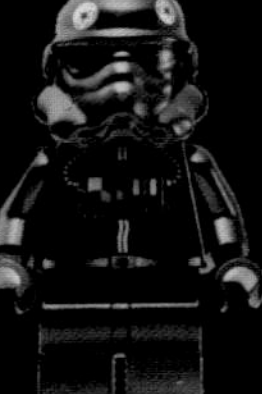

Imperial helmet
Before 2010, the TIE pilot's helmet was the same design as the stormtrooper helmet (p.62). This original variant appears in two LEGO sets: TIE Fighter (set 7146) and TIE Bomber (set 4479).

Breather tubes transfer oxygen

The TIE pilot has worn this unique torso piece since its 2001 debut. The life-support chest piece helps the pilot adapt for changing altitudes

Hidden heads
A peek under the oversized helmet of the latest TIE pilot reveals a plain black head. A 2006 variant of the minifigure also has a black head, but the two earlier variants have brown and reddish-brown heads.

DATA FILE

SET: 8087 TIE Defender
YEAR: 2010
PIECES: 4
EQUIPMENT: None
VARIANTS: 4

Book Luke
Luke with his medal of honor has not been seen in LEGO sets. It only appears in this book: DK's *LEGO* Star Wars: *The Visual Dictionary.*

This Luke Skywalker minifigure was specially created to celebrate ten years of LEGO *Star Wars*. The minifigure himself has cause for celebration—Luke has been honored with a medal for bravery after destroying the first Death Star! This minifigure is exclusive to DK's *LEGO* Star Wars: *The Visual Dictionary*.

Luke Skywalker
MEDAL WINNER

This long, tan LEGO hair is also seen on Tatooine Luke (p.67) and Luke in his stormtrooper disguise (p.82)

DATA FILE
SET: N/A
YEAR: 2009
PIECES: 4
EQUIPMENT: None
VARIANTS: 2

A variant of this Luke minifigure has white pupils on his eyes

Princess Leia Organa awards Luke with this medal of bravery for destroying the first Death Star at the Battle of Yavin

Luke might be celebrating, but he stays armed with this gun belt

Pants pair
Luke is not the only minifigure to sport pants with a gun belt pattern. They are also worn by two versions of his friend Han Solo's minifigure. Han has worn the pants on Tatooine (p.77) and Hoth (p.92).

Han Solo
DECORATED HERO

This proud Han Solo minifigure is exclusive to this book! Han has received the highest medal of honor for his role in the destruction of the first Death Star. Cocky Han doesn't feel the need to dress up for the medal ceremony—what could look better than his cool blue jeans and black vest?

DATA FILE
SET: N/A
YEAR: 2011
PIECES: 4
EQUIPMENT: None
VARIANTS: 1

Standard reddish-brown LEGO hair

Special Solo
If you are reading this book, you may now be the lucky owner of Han Solo wearing his celebratory medal! The minifigure does not star in any LEGO sets.

Princess Leia Organa has awarded Han with this medal of honor for his heroics in the Battle of Yavin

Han's unique torso features his favorite black waistcoat and light-colored shirt

Lighter blue legs with a similar gun belt pattern are also seen on the regular Han Solo minifigure (p.77)

Fifth figure
This is the fifth version of Han Solo in LEGO form. The only LEGO *Star Wars* character available in more versions is Luke Skywalker, but three characters match Han Solo's number: Anakin Skywalker, Princess Leia, and Obi-Wan Kenobi.

Hoth Wampa Cave (set 8089)
Poor Luke dangles from the roof of a cave awaiting his fate at the hands of the hungry wampa in this 2010 set! Can he escape? Luke in his Hoth uniform appears in no other LEGO sets.

Commander Luke Skywalker is stationed with his Rebel Alliance squadron on the ice planet Hoth. The minifigure finds himself in a chilling situation when he is captured by a wampa ice creature in Hoth Wampa Cave (set 8089). Luckily LEGO Luke is braced to withstand subarctic temperatures in his insulated uniform and snow goggles.

Luke Skywalker

HOTH REBEL COMMANDER

These white snow goggles are also seen on the Hoth Rebel trooper minifigure (p.103)

Snow goggles
Luke's snow goggles clip into two sets of holes in his helmet so he can wear them over his eyes or on his helmet.

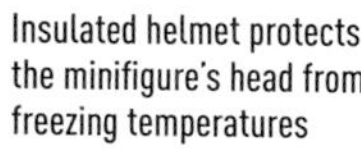

Insulated helmet protects the minifigure's head from freezing temperatures

Communications chip helps Luke give signals to his squadron

Rebel rank insignia shows that Luke is a commander

These dark bluish-gray gloves help Luke to stay warm

Luke is one of many troopers serving at the Rebel base on Hoth, but he is the only LEGO minifigure to wear this torso piece

DATA FILE
SET: 8089 Hoth Wampa Cave
YEAR: 2010
PIECES: 5
EQUIPMENT: Lightsaber
VARIANTS: 1

Han Solo
HOTH HERO

Rebel Captain Han Solo is stationed on the ice planet Hoth. Han hates the cold, so his minifigure wraps up in a heavy-weather dark-blue parka when he leaves Hoth Echo Base (set 7879) on patrol duty. Back at the base, Han's minifigure can replace his parka hood with reddish-brown hair. Han in his Hoth gear appears in six LEGO *Star Wars* sets.

Parka hood
Han has a dark blue parka hood with a tan fur trim. The piece is first seen on this 2011 Hoth Han minifigure.

STAR VARIANTS

Cool Han
Han isn't quite so wrapped up for cold weather in the 2010 set AT-AT Walker (set 8129). Han's unique torso has an open jacket and white shirt, and wears brown pants.

Yellow Han
This yellow variant of Han Solo in Hoth gear appears in a special promotional version of the 2003/4 *Millennium Falcon* (set 4504). It is a very rare find!

The fur trim of Han's parka hood continues on his unique torso piece

Stolen Imperial electrobinoculars hang from Han's torso

Blue hips with a painted gun belt and tan legs. Two earlier variants of Han have brown painted legs and hips

Han Solo carries a blaster pistol. The piece is first seen in 2011 LEGO *Star Wars* sets

DATA FILE

SET: 7879 Hoth Echo Base
YEAR: 2011
PIECES: 5
EQUIPMENT: Blaster pistol
VARIANTS: 6

Princess Leia
HOTH COMMANDER

Princess Leia has pulled back her hair, donned insulated gear, and is now ready for action on Hoth! Leia is an inspirational leader of the Rebel Alliance at Hoth Echo Base (set 7879). She is a key command figure, organizing troops and tactics from her command post, so her minifigure is unarmed. This version of Leia has two variants, which have starred in three LEGO sets.

STAR VARIANT

First Leia
This variant of Leia in her Hoth gear appears in two sets: *Millennium Falcon* (set 4504) and X-Wing Fighter (set 6212). She wears Leia's trademark two-bun hair piece. She also has a different head and torso, and flesh-colored hands.

On duty on Hoth, Leia wears her hair back in braids. This LEGO hair piece is also seen on Leia in her Endor outfit (p.139)

Head first
Before Princess Leia acquired her current head, all LEGO Leias had the same head, which they shared with three other minifigures: Mon Mothma in LEGO *Star Wars* (p.129) and two female soccer players in LEGO Soccer.

Look of concern
Leia's head has two sides: one looks happy, while the other has a concerned expression.

Leia's unique torso has an insulated vest and zipped-up white jumpsuit

Rebel rank insignia shows Leia is a Rebel leader

White-gloved hand pieces

Leia still wears the symbolic white clothing of Alderaan royalty

DATA FILE

SET: 7879 Hoth Echo Base
YEAR: 2011
PIECES: 4
EQUIPMENT: None
VARIANTS: 2

R-3PO
REBEL ESPIONAGE DROID

With his bright red coloring and a markedly moody disposition, R-3PO might not seem like the best choice for a spy droid detector at Hoth Echo Base (set 7879), but that's exactly why he is one! No one suspects a thing, and this inquisitive minifigure has foiled many Imperial infiltration attempts on Hoth. R-3PO makes his first appearance in LEGO *Star Wars* in 2011.

Hoth Echo Base (set 7879)
R-3PO serves under the Rebel Alliance at their secret base on Hoth. He is known for having a very moody disposition, and proves to be a general annoyance around the place. His minifigure first appears in this 2011 set.

R-3PO performs his espionage duties by closely observing others with his photoreceptors

R-3PO cuts a conspicuous figure in his red protocol droid armor

Although R-3PO is a droid, he has a human-like build, so his minifigure has standard arm, hand, torso, and leg pieces

Printed plate pattern continues on the back of R-3PO's torso

DATA FILE
SET: 7879 Hoth Echo Base
YEAR: 2011
PIECES: 3
EQUIPMENT: None
VARIANTS: 1

No tattoo
R-3PO is thought to sport a tattoo on his left posterior that says "Thank the Maker," but there is no sign of it on his LEGO minifigure! R-3PO has plain red minifigure hip and leg pieces.

K-3PO
Rebel Lieutenant

K-3PO is a one-of-a-kind droid in more ways than one. The white protocol droid is an invaluable tactical expert in the Rebel army—so much so that the Alliance High Command awarded him the position of lieutenant. He is also a limited-edition LEGO *Star Wars* minifigure that is exclusive to one set: Hoth Rebel Base (set 7666), released in 2007.

Hoth Rebel Base (set 7666)
K-3PO has only ever appeared in this limited edition 2007 set, making him a rare LEGO minifigure. K-3PO watches from the sliding doors of the command center as Hoth Rebel trooper minifigures face off with Imperial snowtroopers who are attacking the Rebel base.

K-3PO is branded with two red dots that identify him as a Rebel lieutenant

K-3PO has the same head-mold as fellow protocol droids C-3PO (p.63), R-3PO (opposite), and the Death Star droid (p.81), but only he has it in white

Protocol print
Although K-3PO has special rank branding on his torso piece, the rest of his printing is the same as that seen on other protocol droid minifigures. Their back armor details are also identical.

Ridged pelvic armor plate

K-3PO's entire form is covered with white armor. He would feel naked without it!

DATA FILE
SET: 7666 Hoth Rebel Base
YEAR: 2011
PIECES: 3
EQUIPMENT: None
VARIANTS: 1

Luke Skywalker
INJURED AT THE INFIRMARY

After a near-death experience in the frozen wilderness of Hoth, Luke Skywalker is injured and unconcious at the Hoth Echo Base infirmary (set 7879). It is lucky that the Rebels are equipped with a healing LEGO bacta tank to aid his recovery! Luke's unique double-sided head shows his horrible injuries on one side, and Luke in recovery on the other.

Hoth Echo Base (set 7879)
Injured Luke fits inside the large bacta tank at Hoth Echo Base, which is the only LEGO set to feature this version of Luke. A 2-1B medical droid minifigure (p.59) is on hand to oversee his recovery and nurse him back to health.

This hair piece was designed specifically for Luke in 2011. It is also seen on LEGO Luke in his Tatooine clothing (p.67)

A breath mask provides Luke with oxygen when he is submerged in a rejuvenating bacta tank

Feeling better
Swiveling Luke's head reveals a different face. Luke's injuries have healed, but he has a tired-looking smile.

Oxygen tube

Luke hangs from a harness during his bacta tank treatment. These arm straps can also be seen on the back of his torso piece

This part of the bacta tank harness secures Luke's hips

Luke wears white briefs at the Hoth infirmary

DATA FILE
SET: 7879 Hoth Echo Base
YEAR: 2011
PIECES: 4
EQUIPMENT: None
VARIANTS: 1

Imperial Probe Droid

ROVING RECONNAISSANCE

DATA FILE

SET: 7666 Hoth Rebel Base
YEAR: 2007
PIECES: 21
EQUIPMENT: None
VARIANTS: 1

This mysterious minifigure is an Imperial probe droid. If you have spotted it, it has probably already spotted you, so watch out for its blaster fire! The LEGO Imperial probe droid carries out reconnaisance missions for the Empire, seeking out its target's secrets. The minifigure has only ever been seen in one LEGO set.

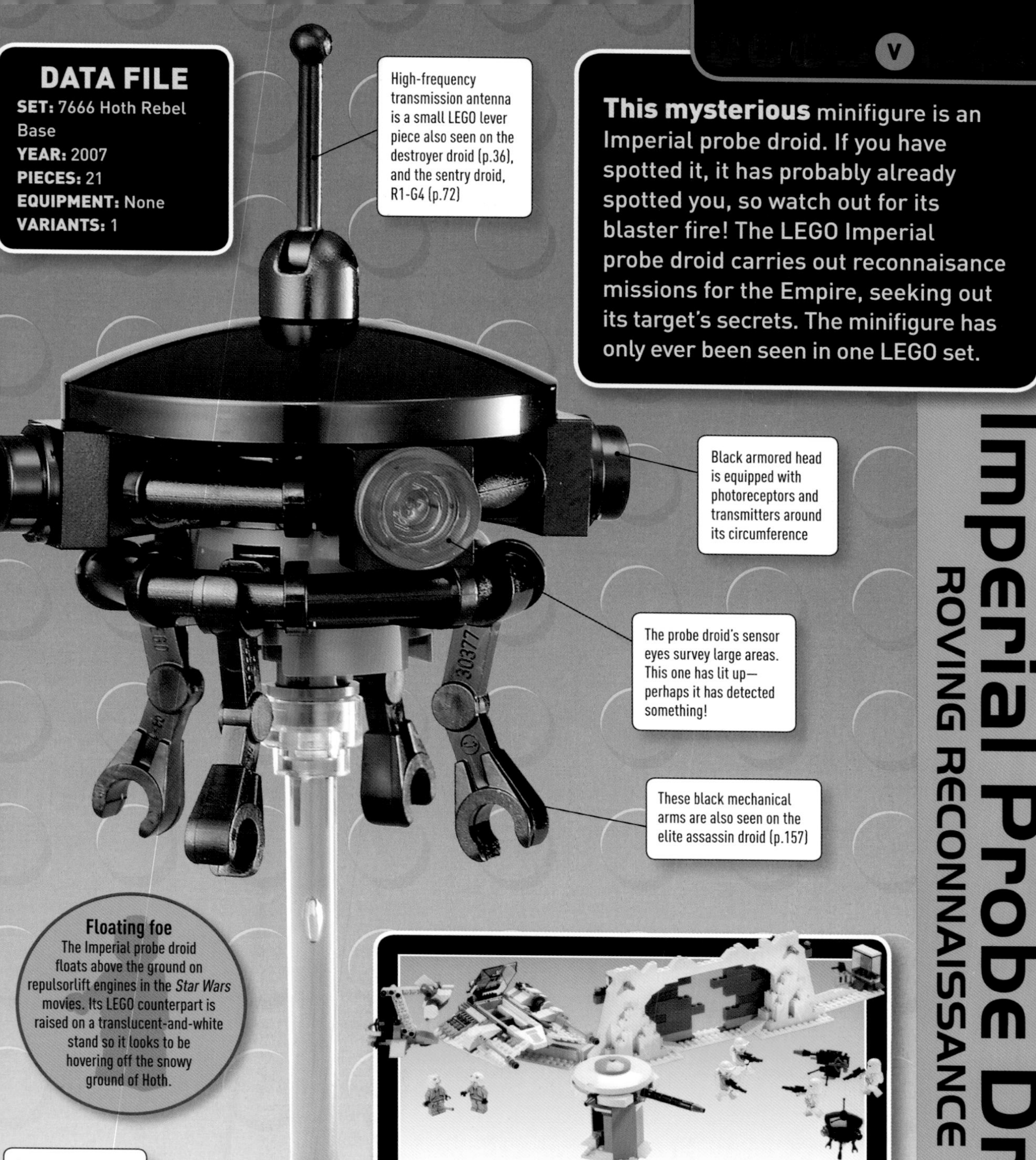

High-frequency transmission antenna is a small LEGO lever piece also seen on the destroyer droid (p.36), and the sentry droid, R1-G4 (p.72)

Black armored head is equipped with photoreceptors and transmitters around its circumference

The probe droid's sensor eyes survey large areas. This one has lit up—perhaps it has detected something!

These black mechanical arms are also seen on the elite assassin droid (p.157)

An inverted white dish piece makes a stable base for the Imperial probe droid

Floating foe
The Imperial probe droid floats above the ground on repulsorlift engines in the *Star Wars* movies. Its LEGO counterpart is raised on a translucent-and-white stand so it looks to be hovering off the snowy ground of Hoth.

Hoth Rebel Base (set 7666)
The Imperial probe droid has discovered the secret Rebel base on Hoth! It communicates its findings to Imperial forces and the Battle of Hoth begins. The Imperial probe droid is exclusive to this limited-edition set, released in 2007.

Admiral Firmus Piett

IMPERIAL ADMIRAL

Admiral Firmus Piett is the intelligent, but secretly incompetent, admiral of the Ultimate Super Star Destroyer (set 10221). He is skilled at avoiding conflict with Darth Vader by staying under the radar—much like his LEGO minifigure, which has long been absent from the LEGO *Star Wars* galaxy.

Ultimate Super Star Destroyer (set 10221)
Admiral Piett's first and only LEGO appearance is in this set from 2011. In it, he commands the imposing Star Dreadnought *Executor* warship.

Unwanted guests
Piett must sit with three bounty hunters on board the *Executor*, even though he considers them to be "scum."

Piett wears a dark gray cap called a kepi atop his stern, humorless face

Admiral Piett's insignia displays his high rank on the front of his unique torso

Piett's minimal gray tunic enhances his austere image

Piett's belt buckle has an Imperial silver officer's disk that can store top secret data

DATA FILE
SET: 10221 Ultimate Super Star Destroyer
YEAR: 2011
PIECES: 4
EQUIPMENT: None
VARIANTS: 1

Back to back
Admiral Piett is the first Imperial officer to feature printed details on the back of his torso. The Imperial officer minifigure (p.80) and even powerful Grand Moff Tarkin (p.79) do not have printing depicting the backs of their gray uniforms.

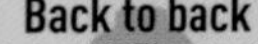

General Veers
IMPERIAL GENERAL

Ruthless and aggressive, Veers is the Major General of the Empire's Imperial Army. He leads the assault on Hoth and helps Darth Vader to capture Echo Base with his AT-AT Walker (set 8129). Parts of his minifigure are seen on other Imperial LEGO minifigures, but his disdainful facial expression remains unique to General Veers.

STAR VARIANT

In an AT-AT
The Motorized Walking AT-AT (set 10178) from 2007 includes this variant of General Veers. He wears darker gray headgear plus goggles and a chin-strap. He does not wear black gloves in this LEGO set.

Light gray, cowl-like helmet piece also appears on the Hoth Imperial officer from the Snowtrooper Battle Pack (set 8084).

The 2010 variant has no chin-strap or goggles, so you can see his chin dimple

Smiles Ahead
The Hoth Imperial officer is exactly the same minifigure, except for his more smiley face.

This variant of General Veers wears a detailed armor pack. The 2007 variant wears a plain officer tunic

Veers's torso pack can also be seen on the Hoth Imperial officer. The red and blue stripes near his left shoulder denote military rank

General Veers wears black flight gloves for piloting the AT-AT walker

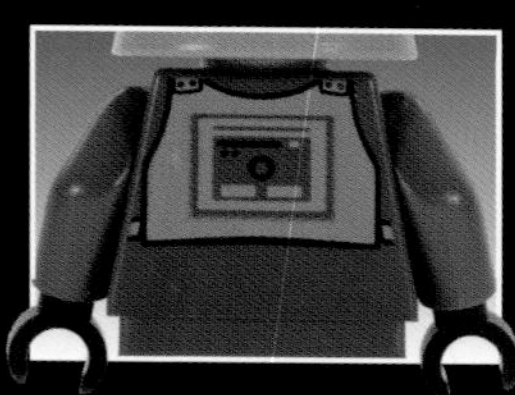

Backplate
Veers's LEGO torso piece shows straps connecting the front and back armor plates.

DATA FILE
SET: 8129 AT-AT Walker
YEAR: 2010
PIECES: 4
EQUIPMENT: None
VARIANTS: 2

AT-ST Driver
GUARD IN GRAY

Driving the two-legged AT-ST (All Terrain Scout Transport) requires lots of training and skill. Luckily, the AT-ST driver has been taught by Imperial experts. His gray-clad minifigure is exclusive to a single LEGO set, where his jumpsuit and open-faced helmet allow him to sit comfortably in the AT-ST's cramped LEGO cockpit.

DATA FILE

SET: 7657 AT-ST
YEAR: 2007
PIECES: 4
EQUIPMENT: Blaster
VARIANTS: 1

AT-ST (set 7657)
The AT-ST's driver fits completely into the walker's enclosed cockpit, where he can rest his blaster in the gun-holder. There is also a bar for the minifigure to hold on to when surveying the area for any concealed Rebel minifigures.

Anti-shock helmet is also worn by the General Veers minifigure (p.99)

Unique torso features a gray utilitarian jumpsuit with black stitching

The AT-ST driver scouts many different terrains. His polarized visor shields his eyes from bright snow or harsh sunlight

Thick, black driving gloves

Black belt with silver buckle

Imperial heads
The AT-ST driver's head piece is printed with a black visor, a downturned mouth, and a gray chin-strap. The same head piece is used for the 2007 General Veers minifigure (p.99).

AT-AT Driver
ALL TERRAIN TERROR

The AT-AT driver is a top Imperial soldier. His minifigure commands a deadly AT-AT (All Terrain Armored Transport) walker. Three variations of the AT-AT driver have appeared in four LEGO sets since 2003. His minifigure wears a gray jumpsuit under blaster-proof armor. He also has a unique, specialized helmet.

STAR VARIANT

Helmet
The AT-AT driver minifigure from Motorized Walking AT-AT (set 10178) has a smaller helmet. It is the same LEGO piece used for stormtrooper helmets, but with specially designed AT-AT markings (p.62).

Life-support back
The printed back of the AT-AT driver's torso reveals the life-support's oxygen pack, which contains emergency supplies.

Helmet is marked with Imperial symbols

Specialized AT-AT helmet has a breathing apparatus that enables the driver to breathe on any land-based terrain he explores

The unique torso's life-support system connects the air supply to the helmet through two tubes

Energy monitor

Identity chip

The AT-AT driver wears a light-gray harness

DATA FILE
SET: 8129 AT-AT Walker
YEAR: 2010
PIECES: 4
EQUIPMENT: Blaster
VARIANTS: 3

Imperial pilots
The AT-AT driver is sometimes considered to be a pilot, even though AT-ATs are not flying machines. He shares his helmet piece with another Imperial pilot: the TIE pilot (p.88), who has a black version of the helmet and a similar torso.

This highly specialized snowtrooper is built to survive in extremely cold climates. The minifigure's airtight white body glove provides insulation from the cold as well as camouflage on icy planets, while his unique masked helmet, backpack, and torso have been created specifically for his use.

STAR VARIANT

Snow clone

This variant of the snowtrooper minifigure has black hands and clone trooper armor printing on his torso. The minifigure appears in the 2003 *Millennium Falcon* (set 4504, blue box edition only).

Snowtrooper

SUBARCTIC STORMTROOPER

Backpack

The snowtrooper minifigure wears a backpack with an inbuilt heater. It is integrated into his helmet piece.

Snowtroopers have blank black heads beneath their unique helmets

The snowtrooper's unique torso has an armored breastplate that can deflect blaster fire

Suit heater and communication controls

This snowtrooper has light bluish-gray hips, but a variant in AT-AT (set 4483) has light-gray hips

DATA FILE

SET: 7879 Hoth Echo Base
YEAR: 2011
PIECES: 4
EQUIPMENT: Blaster
VARIANTS: 3

Hoth Rebel Trooper

SUBARCTIC SOLDIER

The secret Rebel headquarters are now on the hostile ice planet Hoth, so the Rebel trooper minifigure wears an insulated uniform and helmet. He appears in six sets, each containing a different variant—but all six are dressed to battle both the cold weather and the Empire!

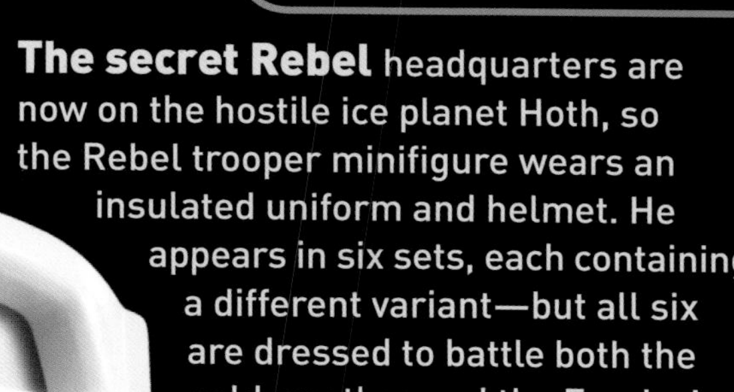

Hoth Helmets
These variants of the Hoth Rebel trooper minifigure wear different Hoth head gear. Each has a white aviator helmet, and one has a brown visor, one has rounded white snow goggles, and another has new-style snow goggles.

This tan insulated helmet is first seen on the 2010 design. Luke Skywalker in his Hoth gear also wears the helmet (p.91)

Backpack is attached around the minifigure's neck. All six variants of the Hoth Rebel trooper wear this piece

Backpack
Only the Hoth Rebel trooper minifigure wears this white backpack with a bedroll in LEGO *Star Wars*.

Unique torso design with a white scarf, tan utility belt, and thermal jacket is first seen in 2010

DL-21 blaster with targeting scope

DATA FILE

SET: 8129 AT-AT Walker
YEAR: 2010
PIECES: 6
EQUIPMENT: Blaster
VARIANTS: 6

Zev Senesca
X-WING PILOT

Zev Senesca is a brave Rebel X-wing pilot who fights on Hoth. He is the only X-wing pilot to carry a weapon, making him especially effective during combat. His minifigure appears in two sets and is a pioneer in its design. Zev's 2009 head and torso have since appeared elsewhere in the LEGO *Star Wars* galaxy.

Each X-wing pilot wears a unique helmet. Zev's has distinctive gray markings

All in a name
Zev Senesca was the first named character to feature in a LEGO *Star Wars* battle pack. Previously, the minifigures included in the LEGO battle packs were generic troopers and pilots.

Zev's head is printed with an orange visor and chin strap. It is also seen on the Clone pilot (p.44) and Captain Jag (p.47) minifigures

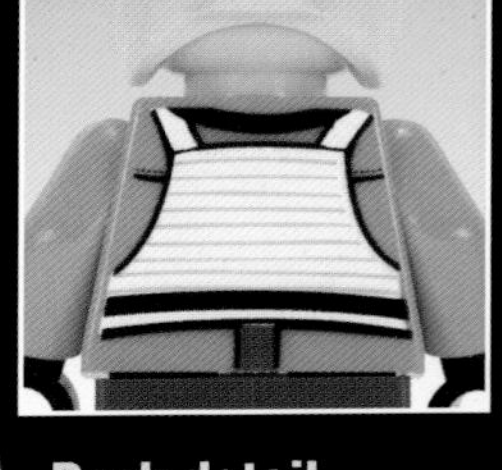

Back detail
Zev was the first LEGO X-wing pilot to feature a double-sided torso. X-wing pilot Luke Skywalker (p.84) adopted the torso piece later in 2010.

Zev does not rely on his X-wing's fire power alone—he also keeps a blaster close at hand during flight

Zev's flight suit torso features a white flak vest and detailed life-support chest pack

Standard-issue orange pressurized jumpsuit

DATA FILE

SET: 8089 Hoth Wampa Cave
YEAR: 2010
PIECES: 4
EQUIPMENT: Blaster
VARIANTS: 1

Dak Ralter
X-WING PILOT

Doomed Rebel pilot Dak Ralter is a gunner in Luke Skywalker's snowspeeder on Hoth. His happy and naive expression belies a murky fate. Dak looks a lot like other X-wing pilot minifigures but his helmet makes him unique. Dak has appeared in three LEGO sets.

STAR VARIANT

Yellow head
Dak Ralter has yellow flesh and darker gray hips in the 1999 Snowspeeder (set 7130). Another variant in the 2003 Rebel Snowspeeder (set 4500) also has yellow flesh, but he has the same light bluish-gray hips as seen on the 2007 variant.

There are two blue Rebel Alliance symbols on Dak's unique helmet

Visor visibility
X-wing pilots' helmets often have an orange visor that contains a special computer screen to help them with targeting during battle. However, Dak's minifigure does not have one—he must think he doesn't need it!

Dak's torso piece is also worn by his fellow Rebel pilots Luke Skywalker, Biggs Darklighter, Wedge Antilles, and Dutch Vander (pp.84–87)

Dak wears standard issue X-wing pilot black flight gloves

Bending Dak's poseable legs at his hip joint allows the minifigure to fit in the snowspeeder cockpit alongside his co-pilot, Luke Skywalker

DATA FILE

SET: 7666 Hoth Rebel Base
YEAR: 2007
PIECES: 4
EQUIPMENT: None
VARIANTS: 3

Luke Skywalker
JEDI IN TRAINING

On a quest to become a Jedi, this Luke Skywalker minifigure is dressed for extreme training. His green tank top and gray pants are easy to maneuver in, and they also provide camouflage on the swamp planet Dagobah. Luke's face is set in a determined expression—his mentor, Master Yoda, is a hard taskmaster and Luke must use all his strength to succeed!

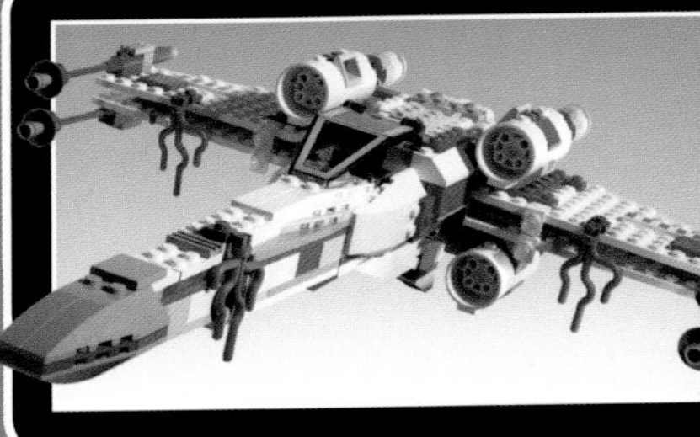

X-Wing Fighter (set 4502)
Luke's minifigure fits easily into the cockpit of his trusty X-wing starfighter. When he crashes on the swamp planet Dagobah, the X-wing can be separated into two large pieces and covered in green reeds.

In the LEGO *Star Wars* theme, this tan hair piece is only used for Luke minifigures

Jedi training
Luke's minifigure trains hard to improve his strength and willpower. He carries his mentor Yoda on his back. Yoda is small enough to stand on Luke's backpack, which is decorated with a bedding tile.

Rebel pilot
Luke's minifigure also has a helmet marked with Rebel symbols. Luke's flight suit, however, is not included in this set.

Luke's training oufit becomes tattered from all his hard work!

This torso is unique to this version of Luke

In this set, Luke comes with a green lightsaber, even though his training as a Jedi is not yet complete

DATA FILE

SET: 4502 X-Wing Fighter
YEAR: 2003
PIECES: 4
EQUIPMENT: Lightsaber, pilot helmet
VARIANTS: 1

Dengar

BANDAGED BOUNTY HUNTER

DATA FILE

SET: 10221 Ultimate Super Star Destroyer
YEAR: 2011
PIECES: 4
EQUIPMENT: Blaster rifle
VARIANTS: 2

This minifigure might wear makeshift armor, but don't underestimate him! Dengar is a dangerous bounty hunter. He is hired by Darth Vader to capture the *Millennium Falcon* and its passengers. Two variants of Dengar appear in two LEGO *Star Wars* sets, both with his huge Valken-38 blaster rifle close at hand.

Dengar once suffered a severe head injury. Imperial agents fixed most of the damage, but Dengar always wears a head bandage

Scarred face from a swoop-racer crash

STAR VARIANT

Ninja bandage
The 2006 Dengar variant comes with the LEGO set *Slave I* (set 6209). His torso and legs are different and the minifigure's standard LEGO head piece is covered with a white Ninja hood.

Dengar's armor is built from discarded Imperial materials. It includes pieces of armor from sandtroopers, snowtroopers, and stormtroopers

Dengar painted his armor gray

White gloves to protect hands

Bounty hunters
Most of the bounty hunters hired by Darth Vader to track down the Rebels can be found in LEGO *Star Wars* sets. Dengar, Boba Fett, Bossk, and IG-88 (pp.105–108) have all been made into LEGO minifigures. Only Zuckuss and 4-LOM remain elusive.

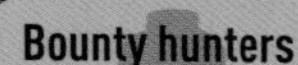

I II III IV V VI CW EU

Boba Fett
BOUNTY HUNTER

Mandalorian bounty hunter
Boba Fett appears in eight LEGO *Star Wars* sets, in six distinct variations. Boba's latest incarnation is battle-worn, but he is equipped with everything he needs to catch his prey: a probing rangefinder, a powerful jetpack, and his favorite EE-3 carbine blaster rifle.

Blue-gray detachable rangefinder fits into a hole in Boba's helmet

Gray markings are battle damage

DATA FILE
SET: 8097 *Slave I*
YEAR: 2010
PIECES: 7
EQUIPMENT: Jetpack, blaster, pauldron cloth
VARIANTS: 6

STAR VARIANTS

Bronze Boba
There are only two of these solid bronze Boba Fetts in existence. One was given away to a lucky competition winner as part of the LEGO "May the 4th" promotion in 2010.

Cloud City
This variant of Boba Fett has lots of detail, with printing on his arms and legs. It has only ever appeared in one LEGO *Star Wars* set—Cloud City (set 10123), released in 2003.

Jetpack (behind) is a sand-green version of the white jetpack used on the clone jetpack trooper (p.154)

Wookiee hair is worn as a prize

Tattered fabric pauldron cloth is unique to Boba

Gray circular barrel is a Technic piece attached to a blaster gun

The man beneath
Boba never removes his helmet in public, but a peek under his LEGO helmet reveals a battle-scarred face.

Bossk

ALIEN BOUNTY HUNTER

This terrifying Trandoshan bounty hunter made his minifigure debut alongside redesigns of Boba Fett and Han Solo in 2010's *Slave I* (set 8097), although he doesn't actually have a place to sit aboard the LEGO starship! Bossk's reptilian head, complete with smooth horns and sharp teeth, was specially cast for this dangerous LEGO minifigure.

***Slave I* (set 8097)**
Bossk helps his fellow bounty hunter Boba Fett to capture Han Solo inside a block of carbonite in this 2010 set. Bossk doesn't have a seat aboard Fett's starship, *Slave I*, but he can fit beneath the cabin during flight.

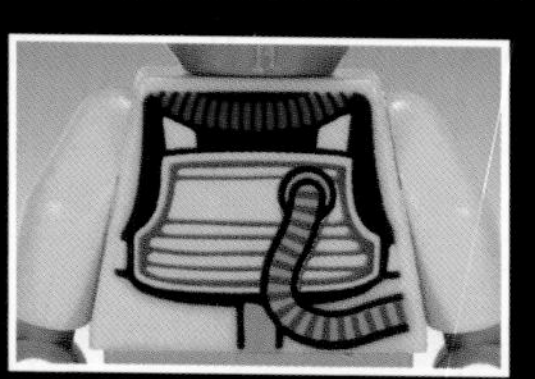

Flying in style
Bossk's flight suit has intricate details on the back as well as the front.

Painted infrared-vision eyes

Unique sand-green head is made from hard ABS plastic

Painted white teeth

Blaster rifle is the weapon of choice for many LEGO *Star Wars* minifigures, including assassin droids (p.157) and senate commandos (p.184)

White flak vest

Yellow high-altitude pressure suit

Bossk's body
The torso design on Bossk's flight suit is unique to him. It is more detailed than the flight suit sported by Rebel pilots Luke Skywalker, Biggs Darklighter, Wedge Antilles, Dutch Vander (pp.84–87), and Dak Ralter (p.105).

DATA FILE
SET: 10221 Ultimate Super Star Destroyer
YEAR: 2011
PIECES: 3
EQUIPMENT: Blaster rifle
VARIANTS: 1

IG-88
BOUNTY HUNTER

Assassin droid IG-88 stalks the LEGO *Star Wars* galaxy in three sets, and in each one he has a slightly different look—though each is as intimidating as the last. The monstrous minifigure is obsessed with hunting and killing, and he comes well equipped to pursue his passion. His round, sensor-filled head can see in all directions at once!

IG-88 has individual orange sensors on his silver head plate. Pre-2011 variants of his minifigure have a translucent orange round plate piece

Cone-shaped head has motion, sound, and heat sensors that help IG-88 catch his prey

IG-88's body is made up of identical pieces to the LEGO battle droid (p.22)

One of IG-88's hands is at a 90 degree angle to his opposite hand so he can hold his blaster vertically

STAR VARIANTS

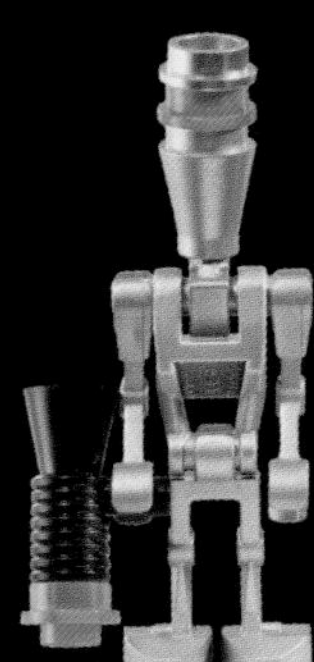

Silver assassin
This metallic silver variant of IG-88 appears in *Slave I* (set 6209), released in 2006. He carries an older version of a LEGO *Star Wars* blaster.

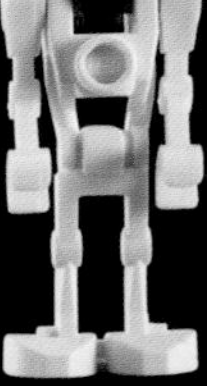

White assassin
This white droid appears on the LEGO Death Star (set 10188). He is thought to be a variant of IG-88, but he is not named as him on the set box.

DATA FILE

SET: 10221 Ultimate Super Star Destroyer
YEAR: 2011
PIECES: 8
EQUIPMENT: Blaster, blaster rifle
VARIANTS: 3

Lando Calrissian
BARON OF CLOUD CITY

DATA FILE
SET: 10123 Cloud City
YEAR: 2003
PIECES: 5
EQUIPMENT: Blaster, cape
VARIANTS: 1

Lando's head
This Lando Calrissian has a unique brown head with a suave slim mustache and winning smile! The two other versions of LEGO Lando (p.121; p.130) have the same head piece in a reddish-brown color.

This cool customer is the Baron Administrator of Cloud City. Lando Calrissian has a flamboyant personality and sense of style—something that is reflected in his LEGO minifigure, with his extravagant yellow-lined cloak and baronial outfit. Lando in all his finery only stars in the 2003 set Cloud City (set 10123), alongside his old gambling partner Han Solo.

The version of Lando dressed in his General outfit (p.130) has this same short black hair piece

Unique torso features a dark-blue collared shirt and matching Baron Administrator state belt

Lando's exclusive cape is blue on the outside and yellow on the inside. It is a status symbol that distinguishes him as Baron Administrator of Cloud City

Blaster is made from a LEGO loudhailer piece

Lobot
CYBORG COMMAND CENTER

Half-man, half-robot, Lobot is Lando Calrissian's cyborg assistant. Lobot's double-sided head is the only clue that he is not fully human: One side has a human face, while the other is printed with a computer implant. As Cloud City's computer liaison officer, Lobot is one of a kind—and so is his rare minifigure.

Twin-Pod Cloud Car (set 7119)
Lobot is the only minifigure to come with the Twin-Pod Cloud Car set. He fits snugly into one of the pods, from which he pilots the atmospheric vehicle around Cloud City to run errands.

The radio is a common piece in other LEGO themes, but it is exclusive to Lobot in LEGO *Star Wars*

Unique double-sided yellow head piece

Unique torso is printed with Lobot's plain, functional gray tunic and black belt over a tan shirt

Unusual behavior
It is only in a LEGO *Star Wars* set that Lobot would pilot a Twin-Pod Cloud Car. Usually, Lobot would leave the flying of vehicles to Cloud Car pilots, and focus on controlling the computer systems on Cloud City.

Lobot uses his radio to send messages to Lando Calrissian and other workers on Cloud City

Super computer
A computer device is implanted into Lobot's brain so he can control Cloud City's computer system with his mind.

DATA FILE
SET: 7119 Twin-Pod Cloud Car
YEAR: 2002
PIECES: 3
EQUIPMENT: Radio
VARIANTS: 1

Princess Leia
CLOUD CITY CAPTIVE

Cloud City (set 10123)
Leia's unique Cloud City minifigure is exclusive to this LEGO set. She can use the sliding cafeteria door to hide from stormtroopers, while Luke's Cloud City minifigure duels Darth Vader at the city's spiky core.

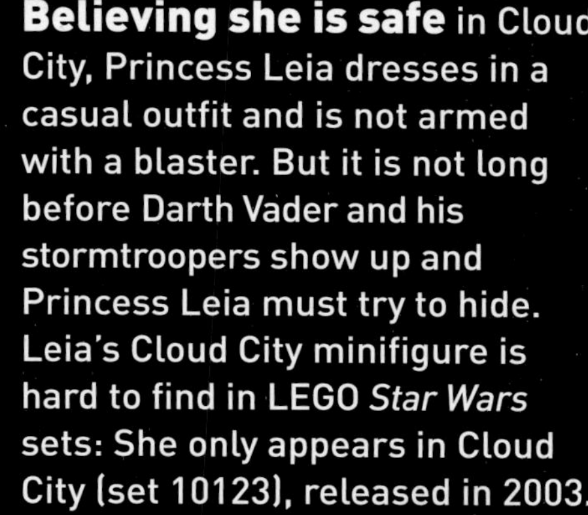

Believing she is safe in Cloud City, Princess Leia dresses in a casual outfit and is not armed with a blaster. But it is not long before Darth Vader and his stormtroopers show up and Princess Leia must try to hide. Leia's Cloud City minifigure is hard to find in LEGO *Star Wars* sets: She only appears in Cloud City (set 10123), released in 2003.

Hair tied into a single, long braid

Shared hair
The same long, top-braided hairstyle worn by Leia when she relaxes on Cloud City is also worn by Padmé, Leia's mother. The hair piece was first used for Padmé Naberrie's 1999 minifigure (p.7) and is exclusive to LEGO *Star Wars*.

A flesh-colored version of this head piece is used for Mon Mothma's minifigure (p.129)

Unique torso printed with a collared white cloak

This is the only Princess Leia minifigure without a flesh-colored variant

Leia's brown and dark orange top is decorated with a triangle-shaped belt

DATA FILE
SET: 10123 Cloud City
YEAR: 2003
PIECES: 4
EQUIPMENT: None
VARIANTS: 1

Luke Skywalker
CLOUD CITY

Luke arrives on Cloud City to rescue his friends. But it is a trap! Darth Vader is waiting for him. This exclusive minifigure is dressed in a tan jumpsuit, which is not restrictive, allowing Luke to put up a good fight against Vader. But there is nothing Luke can do to protect his minifigure's right hand, which he loses in battle.

Cloud City (set 10123)
Luke's minifigure wields his blue lightsaber against Darth Vader. But Vader uses the Force to make a LEGO wall collapse! When Luke reaches the window, a LEGO mechanism catapults him out over the city's reactor core.

This LEGO head piece is only used for Luke Skywalker minifigures

Tan torso
This tan torso is unique to Luke's Cloud City minifigure in the LEGO *Star Wars* theme. However, it has also been used for farmer and worker minifigures in the LEGO City and LEGO Town themes.

Luke's tan jumpsuit has a lot of utility pockets

Brown hip piece is printed with a silver belt buckle

LEGO hand piece can be removed to show the terrible outcome of Luke's duel with Darth Vader

Unique leg pieces are printed with pockets

DATA FILE
SET: 10123 Cloud City
YEAR: 2003
PIECES: 4
EQUIPMENT: Lightsaber
VARIANTS: 1

Bespin Security Guard

CLOUD CITY COP

The Bespin security guard only appears in one LEGO set, but he has a very important job. His minifigure helps keep the peace on Cloud City. The security guard's official blue uniform is enough to deter most minifigures from breaking the rules, but some criminals don't take the hint. He might have a smiling LEGO face, but beware of his deadly blaster!

***Slave I* (set 6209)**
The Bespin security guard makes his only LEGO *Star Wars* appearance in the 2006 set *Slave I*. He helps carry Han Solo's carbonite-frozen minifigure to Boba Fett's ship, *Slave I*, which has a special compartment that opens to store the carbonite block containing Han Solo.

The Bespin guard is the only LEGO minifigure to have this standard LEGO head piece in reddish brown

Sergeant Edian?
This security guard minifigure might be Sergeant Edian, a loyal guard who works for Lando Calrissian on Cloud City—although he is not named in the LEGO set he comes in.

Unique torso is printed with a gold trim and the insignia of the Bespin security guards

Relby-K23 blaster pistols are standard issue for Bespin security guards

Unique arm pieces are printed with red markings, which indicate the rank of sergeant

DATA FILE
SET: 6209 *Slave I*
YEAR: 2006
PIECES: 4
EQUIPMENT: Blaster
VARIANTS: 1

Han Solo
FROZEN IN CARBONITE

Han Solo has been captured by Darth Vader! Dressed in casual brown pants and a plain white shirt, Han's minifigure is frozen inside a block of carbonite and delivered to Jabba the Hutt. His minifigure is so unprepared for his imminent capture that he is even without his trusty blaster!

STAR VARIANT

Uncreased
The original variant of this minifigure has yellow skin, light eyebrows, and no creases on his shirt—even though it appears in Desert Skiff (set 7104), when Han has just escaped after a few days in a cramped carbonite prison.

This face printing was first seen in 2010 and is used only for Han Solo

Ford's hair
The reddish-brown variant of this common LEGO hair piece is used only for Han Solo in the LEGO *Star Wars* theme. The same color is also used for Indiana Jones's minifigure, which is based on a character also played by actor Harrison Ford.

Trapped!
Han is frozen in a block of carbonite! This unique piece cleverly traps Han's minifigure by securing him with clips inside the 3D mold.

Detailed printing on Han's unique torso gives his shirt some creases

Apart from his stormtrooper disguise, this is the only Han Solo minifigure without a gun holster printed on his pants. Han won't be needing a gun where he is going!

DATA FILE

SET: 8097 *Slave I*
YEAR: 2010
PIECES: 4
EQUIPMENT: None
VARIANTS: 3

Jabba The Hutt
INTERGALACTIC GANGSTER

Jabba the Hutt is a slimy, green crime lord who orchestrates shady schemes across the LEGO *Star Wars* galaxy. The vile villain's head-and-torso piece is a unique LEGO mold. It is almost impossible to miss Jabba's enormous slug-like minifigure—even though he only comes in two LEGO sets.

Jabba's Palace (set 4480)
Jabba sits on a raised throne in his royal palace, where he keeps an eye on his slave, Princess Leia. There is a sneaky trapdoor beneath the throne, which Jabba can open to dispose of anyone who is silly enough to get on his nerves!

DATA FILE
SET: 4480 Jabba's Palace
YEAR: 2003
PIECES: 3
EQUIPMENT: None
VARIANTS: 1

Facial features are defined by the unique mold, not by any printed detail

Jabba's sand-green coloring matches the skin tone of his Gamorrean guards

Although Jabba's head and torso is a single LEGO piece, the arms are poseable

Jabba's favorite snack is a slimy gorg. LEGO gorgs are actually transparent green frog pieces

Tail tales
Jabba's minifigure requires some assembly: His slimy tail comes in two pieces that clip together. The end piece is also used for the tail of Obi-Wan's varactyl, Boga, and for the tails of the dewback creatures of Tatooine.

Gamorrean Guard
JABBA'S PIG GUARD

The Gamorrean guard protects Jabba the Hutt in two LEGO sets. Brutish, strong, and dull-witted, his minifigure does whatever his boss Jabba tells him and never makes a fuss. His minifigure wears sand-green armor that is attached to his unique head piece, and is armed with a deadly vibro-ax.

Vibro-ax can inflict a lethal wound with minimal effort

Gamorreans are boar-like creatures with horns and a snout

Head and torso armor are a single, unique piece. It fits over a plain reddish-brown LEGO torso

DATA FILE

SET: 6210 Jabba's Sail Barge
YEAR: 2006
PIECES: 3
EQUIPMENT: Vibro-ax
VARIANTS: 2

STAR VARIANT

Gray-armed guard
The original variant of this minifigure comes in the 2003 set Jabba's Prize (set 4476). He has gray arms, green hands, and a brown hip piece—but is just as ugly as the 2006 variant.

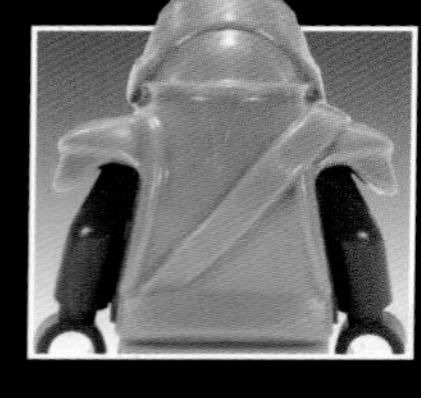

Turn around
The Gamorrean guard is well protected. His armor fits over the front and back of his torso.

Jabba's Sail Barge (set 6210)
The Gamorrean guard watches over Jabba's prisoners Han Solo and Luke Skywalker in this set. Little does he know that his fellow skiff guard is actually Lando Calrissian in disguise (p.123)!

Bib Fortuna

TWI'LEK ASSISTANT

Bib Fortuna is Jabba the Hutt's eerie assistant. The Twi'lek minifigure decides who gets to speak to Jabba—and who doesn't. His rare minifigure only comes in one LEGO set, dressed in dark blue robes with a metal chestplate and black cape. His chestplate might protect him from armed intruders, but it's no good against a Jedi mind trick!

Jabba's Message (set 4475)
Bib Fortuna guards the entrance to Jabba's palace in this set—the only one he comes in. When R2-D2 and C-3PO turn up, Bib and the eye droid in the palace door interview the droids before they enter.

Twi'leks
Just two Twi'lek minifigures have been released in LEGO *Star Wars*: Bib Fortuna and Aayla Secura (p.177). Both Twi'leks have tentacles that clip onto a standard LEGO head piece, although Bib's are longer, because he is older.

Bib is very old, and has lived in Jabba's palace for many years. His skin in pale and wrinkled from decades without sunlight

Unique hat piece depicts Bib's bulging head and fully grown Twi'lek tentacles

Unique torso is printed with a blue belt that fastens Bib's robes

Metal chestplate protects against attacks made by Jabba's enemies

DATA FILE
SET: 4475 Jabba's Message
YEAR: 2003
PIECES: 5
EQUIPMENT: Cape
VARIANTS: 1

EV-9D9

SADISTIC DROID

New droids in Jabba's palace report for work to the red and gray droid EV-9D9. With her wicked grin and deranged eyes, she is a scary-looking minifigure—and she enjoys watching other droids suffer! EV-9D9 is a distinctive droid, but fortunately for the droids in the LEGO *Star Wars* galaxy, this sadistic robot comes only in one set.

Jabba's Palace (set 4480)
EV-9D9 is exclusive to the Jabba's Palace set. The demented droid has her own workspace beneath Jabba's throne, where she assesses new droids and puts them to work. The set includes a computer monitor to keep track of the droids and a poor GNK droid who is at EV-9D9's mercy!

Unique head piece is printed with EV-9D9's cruel-looking face, complete with three yellow eyes

Dark red torso piece is also used for the security battle droid minifigure (p.23)

Outlet for power coupler

DATA FILE

SET: 4480 Jabba's Palace
YEAR: 2003
PIECES: 6
EQUIPMENT: None
VARIANTS: 1

Droid parts
Droids come in all shapes and sizes, but EV-9D9's minifigure is very similar to a battle droid (p.22). The same arm, leg, and torso pieces are used, although in different colors. Only the neck and head pieces are different.

Although EV-9D9's leg piece is not unique, she is the only LEGO minifigure to have it in dark gray

B'omarr Monk

WALKING BRAIN

DATA FILE

SET: 4480 Jabba's Palace
YEAR: 2003
PIECES: 13
EQUIPMENT: None
VARIANTS: 1

Brain jar
The transparent jar that houses the B'omarr monk's brain is an upside-down crystal ball LEGO piece! It has appeared in various sets in the LEGO Harry Potter, LEGO Atlantis, and Fantasy Era themes.

Perhaps the strangest creatures in Jabba's palace are the B'omarr monks. These ancient beings used to be fully alive, but now only their brains remain, attached to a four-legged, spider-like droid body. The monk's minifigure is made from 13 separate pieces, and is exclusive to Jabba's Palace (set 4480).

The B'omarr monk's legs are LEGO samurai sword pieces. It is the only LEGO minifigure to feature the piece

Telepath response unit allows the monks to communicate silently with each other

Locomotion unit connects the brain support unit to the legs

Disembodied brain of the original B'omarr monk is kept alive in a fluid-filled container

Transparent orange stud piece is used as the brain

Droid legs are automated to carry the brain around Jabba's palace

LEGO crystal ball piece has a thick section of plastic at the top, which looks like a collection of fluid

Princess Leia
JABBA'S SLAVE

Demure Princess Leia is now a scantily clad slave girl—property of Jabba the Hutt! Leia's minifigure is dressed in a gold and dark red slave outfit for the entertainment of the grotesque gangster, with a chain around her neck to keep her in her place. But Jabba better watch out for that chain—Leia might just manage to wrap it around his neck!

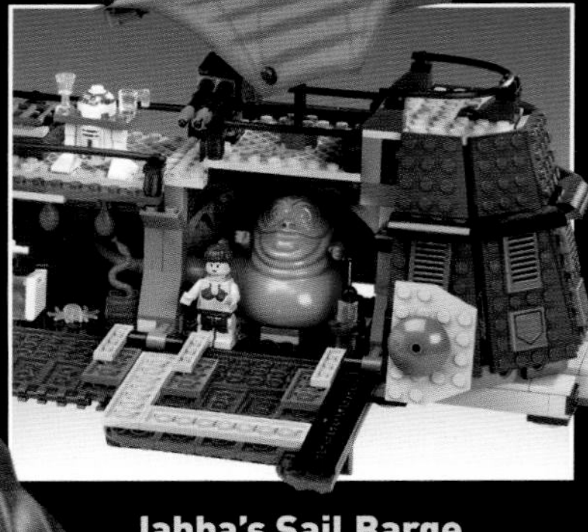

Jabba's Sail Barge (set 6210)
Princess Leia is at the mercy of Jabba the Hutt on his sail barge. The enormous crime lord attaches a neck brace and chain to Leia's minifigure to keep his slave close by at all times.

Only Leia wears this reddish-brown ponytail piece in LEGO *Star Wars*

All versions and variants of Princess Leia in LEGO sets released before 2011 have this same face, with red lips and dainty eyebrows

STAR VARIANT

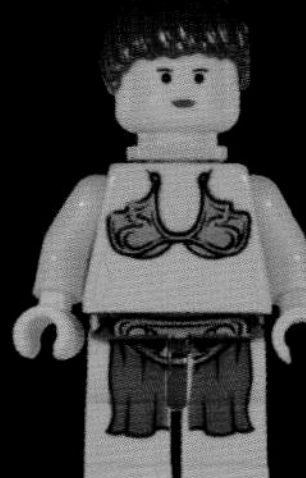

Yellow slave
A variant of Leia in her slave bikini appears in Jabba's Palace (set 4480), released in 2003. She has yellow flesh and brown hair, but the same face and slave outfit pattern.

Jabba the Hutt forces Leia to wear this revealing gold slave-girl harness

Leia's unique hips and legs are printed with a dark red silk skirt and gold harness briefs

DATA FILE
SET: 6210 Jabba's Sail Barge
YEAR: 2006
PIECES: 4
EQUIPMENT: None
VARIANTS: 2

Lando Calrissian

JABBA'S GUARD

Disguised as a skiff guard on Jabba's Sail Barge (set 6210), Lando Calrissian is now known as Tamtel Skreej. Don't blow his cover, or he won't manage to rescue his friends from Jabba's clutches. This LEGO Lando appears in only one set—he is careful not to get into such a sticky situation again!

As a skiff guard, Lando carries a LEGO vibro-ax. Its blade is seen in many other LEGO themes, including LEGO Vikings

Lando's skiff guard helmet is unique to his minifigure

Integrated face guard obscures Lando's face

Unique torso with brown tunic and gold chest armor

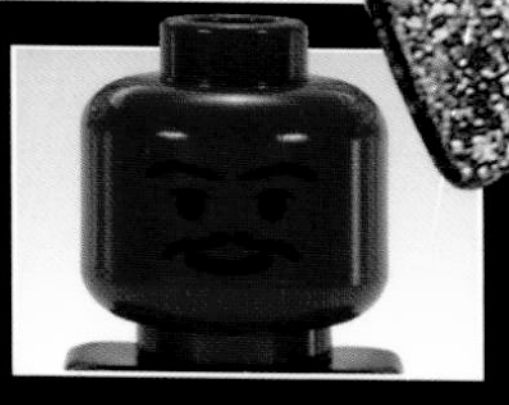

Hidden head
If anyone removes Lando's guard helmet, they will discover his unmistakable mustachioed head!

DATA FILE

SET: 6210 Jabba's Sail Barge
YEAR: 2006
PIECES: 4
EQUIPMENT: Vibro-ax
VARIANTS: 1

Jabba's Sail Barge (set 6210)
Lando delivers Han Solo and Luke Skywalker to the Great Pit of Carkoon on Jabba's sand skiff. There, the minifigures will be fed to the LEGO Sarlacc beast!

Luke Skywalker
JEDI KNIGHT

Dressed in black Jedi clothing, Luke Skywalker has become a brave Jedi Knight. This minifigure appears in seven sets, and in each he has a slightly different look, with changes to his head and hand pieces. But Luke's new green lightsaber is always close at hand!

Luke has a green LEGO lightsaber after losing his blue one during a duel with Darth Vader

This head with white-eye pupils and Luke's distinctive chin dimple was first seen on the 2010 design of Jedi Knight Luke

Mechanics
Jedi Knight Luke lost his right hand to Darth Vader during a duel, but variants of his minifigure released in sets before 2008 do not have a black cybernetic hand—they have two matching yellow or flesh-tone hands instead.

All variants of Jedi Knight Luke have worn the same torso with black Jedi robes and black legs

Luke now wields his lightsaber with a black cybernetic hand

STAR VARIANTS

Two-hand Luke
Jedi Knight Luke has two flesh-colored hands in Jabba's Sail Barge (set 6210), released in 2006. He also has a different head to the later 2010 variant.

Hooded figure
This variant of Luke has a black hood and cape to keep a low profile in the *Star Wars* #2 LEGO minifigure pack (set 3341). He doesn't come with hair.

DATA FILE

SET: 10212 Imperial Shuttle
YEAR: 2010
PIECES: 4
EQUIPMENT: Lightsaber
VARIANTS: 7

Death Star Guard

FEARSOME FIGHTER

With a stern countenance and full black attire, the Death Star guard is a deliberately intimidating minifigure. He is part of a handpicked, elite fighting force that can handle any number of combat and non-combat roles for the Imperial Navy, appearing aboard the LEGO Death Star (set 10188) and at The Battle of Endor (set 8038).

Death Star (set 10188)
Aboard the LEGO Death Star, two elite Death Star guard minifigures control the mechanism for the superlaser firing dish. The huge laser is ready to destroy anything in its path at Darth Vader's command.

With its extended neck guard, the Death Star guard's helmet bears a resemblance to that worn by Darth Vader (p.61)

The Rebel trooper (p.65) also has this LEGO head with printed black chin guard

Black attack
The Death Star guard is the only LEGO minifigure to wear his helmet in black. However this style is popular with other Imperial minifigures: General Veers (p.99) and the Imperial AT-ST driver (p.100) wear it in gray tones.

The Death Star guard wears the same torso as the Imperial pilot (p.126). It features a black imperial tunic and utility belt

Black gloves complete the all-black look

The minifigure has a LEGO blaster to use when he requires it, but for many of his duties he remains unarmed

DATA FILE

SET: 8038 The Battle of Endor
YEAR: 2009
PIECES: 4
EQUIPMENT: Blaster
VARIANTS: 1

Imperial Pilot

MAN IN BLACK

The Imperial pilot transports many high-ranking officials aboard the Imperial shuttle. He is always dressed in his freshly pressed black uniform and cap because his next passenger might be Darth Vader—or even the Emperor himself! This minifigure has piloted the Imperial shuttle in two LEGO sets since 2001.

STAR VARIANT

Happy pilot
The original variant of this minifigure has a yellow head with the basic LEGO smiling face. He also wears an all-black uniform, but with much less detail. This rare, cheerful pilot only appears in the 2001 set Imperial Shuttle (set 7166).

Imperial Shuttle (set 10212)
The Imperial pilot and three other minifigures can all fit into the spacious cockpit of the 2010 Imperial shuttle. Now the pilot can transport his Sith Masters in style!

Black cap is also worn by another Imperial pilot, Juno Eclipse (p.204)

This pilot takes his job very seriously

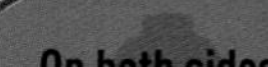

On both sides
The Imperial pilot's fierce, flesh-colored head appears on both sides of the Empire/Rebel conflict. It is used for the Hoth Imperial officer (p.99), as well as for the Hoth Rebel trooper minifigure (p.103).

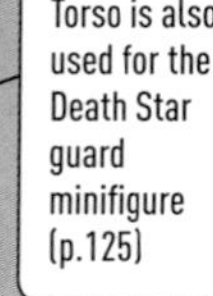

Torso is also used for the Death Star guard minifigure (p.125)

The Imperial pilot does not fly battle craft, so he does not require the life-support equipment that LEGO TIE pilots wear (p.88). His uniform is a plain black suit with a black, blaster-proof vest

Belt holds several small storage pouches

DATA FILE

SET: 10212 Imperial Shuttle
YEAR: 2010
PIECES: 4
EQUIPMENT: None
VARIANTS: 2

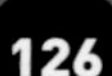

Royal Guard

CRIMSON PROTECTOR

The mysterious Royal Guard is the Emperor's deadly personal bodyguard. The minifigure is dressed in a full crimson uniform and cape. Even his hands and eyes are concealed. In his bright and otherworldly uniform, the Royal Guard stands out among other minifigures. His presence will make any minifigure think twice about attacking the Emperor!

Imperial Inspection (set 7264)
In their crimson uniforms, the Royal Guards stand out from other Imperial soldiers in Imperial Inspection. The Royal Guard minifigures in this 2005 set are identical to the 2008 variant, except that they have red hands.

Unique hood mold was designed especially for the Royal Guard

Standard black LEGO head piece makes it look like the Royal Guard minifigure is wearing a black visor

Standard LEGO spear is used as a force pike, which employs vibrating energy to stun opponents

Black combat gloves

The Royal Guard is the only LEGO *Star Wars* minifigure to wear a red LEGO cloth cape

DATA FILE

SET: 10188 Death Star
YEAR: 2008
PIECES: 5
EQUIPMENT: Force pike, cape
VARIANTS: 2

R2-Q5 is an astromech droid with a secret. His black and bronze minifigure has been fitted with Imperial spying technology, so he is not to be trusted! Two variants of R2-Q5's astromech minifigure have appeared in two sets since 2006: He works aboard the Death Star (set 10188) and the Imperial Star Destroyer (set 6211).

STAR VARIANT

Original R2-Q5
The original variant of R2-Q5 comes with Imperial Star Destroyer (set 6211). This 2006 R2-Q5 has an identical body piece to the 2008 minifigure, but features less printing on the domed head piece.

R2-Q5
DEVIOUS DROID

DATA FILE

SET: 10188 Death Star
YEAR: 2008
PIECES: 4
EQUIPMENT: None
VARIANTS: 2

Identity crisis
When R2-Q5 was first released as a LEGO minifigure in Imperial Star Destroyer (set 6211) in 2006, the astromech droid was incorrectly labeled as "R2-D5" on the box.

Radar eye can record surroundings

R2-Q5 is printed with all the familiar tools and access panels of a typical astromech droid, but he also contains hidden spy devices

Head piece is unique to the 2008 variant

R2-Q5 is the only minifigure to have black LEGO Technic leg pins

Holographic projector reveals his secret findings

Inference pulse stabilizers

Mon Mothma
REBEL COMMANDER

***Home One* Mon Calamari Star Cruiser (set 7754)**
On board Rebel ship *Home One*, Mon Mothma briefs the other Rebel leaders about plans for the attack on the second Death Star. They gather in the command center around an orange hologram of the Death Star.

Former Senator Mon Mothma is the Supreme Commander of the Rebel Alliance. In her all-white outfit and rare white LEGO cape, her minifigure commands respect from all the Rebel leaders. Mon Mothma is exclusive to the LEGO *Star Wars* set *Home One* Mon Calamari Star Cruiser (set 7754), where she discusses the latest Rebel plans to defeat the Empire once and for all.

DATA FILE
SET: 7754 *Home One* Mon Calamari Star Cruiser
YEAR: 2009
PIECES: 5
EQUIPMENT: Cape
VARIANTS: 1

Same head piece as Princess Leia, another former senator

Unique torso printed with silver Chandrilian Freedom Medal

Tousled hair
Mon Mothma's tousled reddish-brown hair is the same piece as that used for the Clone Wars version of Anakin Skywalker's minifigure (p.147).

Mon Mothma is the only minifigure to wear a white cape in LEGO *Star Wars*

Admiral Ackbar
REBEL SUPREME COMMANDER

Admirable Admiral Ackbar commands the Rebel assault on the second Death Star from his flagship *Home One* (set 7754). Ackbar appears only in this one LEGO set—but his minifigure plays a pivotal part in LEGO *Star Wars* history! Ackbar is one of three Mon Calamari minifigures, but his unique commander uniform makes him stand out.

***Home One* Mon Calamari Star Cruiser (set 7754)** Admiral Ackbar coordinates the Rebel assault on the second Death Star in this set. He has a swiveling and sliding command chair, and a tactical computer that can mount his lap. The set even contains his coffee cup!

Solid plastic Mon Calamari head with large, bulbous eyes. The Mon Calamari officer (p.133) and Nahdar Vebb (p.173) have the same head piece

Metallic command insignia denotes Ackbar's high rank

Unique LEGO torso features a cream Mon Calamari naval jerkin over a white space suit

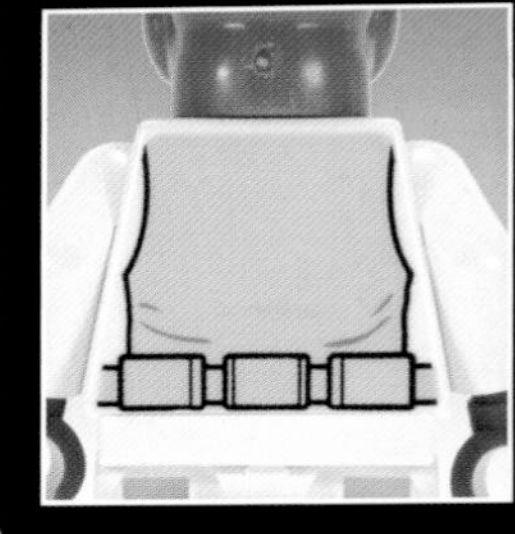

Admiral attire The details of Ackbar's jerkin and utility belt continue on the back of his torso piece. Ackbar keeps vital command equipment in the six pockets of his belt.

Reddish-brown webbed hands

Special set
Admiral Ackbar also appears in the exclusive LEGO *Star Wars* Collectible Display Set 2, which was available for one day only at the 2009 San Diego Comic-Con. Crix Madine (p.131) and Jedi Knight Luke Skywalker (p.124) were also included in the set.

DATA FILE
SET: 7754 *Home One* Mon Calamari Star Cruiser
YEAR: 2009
PIECES: 3
EQUIPMENT: None
VARIANTS: 1

General Crix Madine

REBEL LEADER

General Crix Madine has not always been loyal to the Rebel cause—he was once an Imperial Army officer—but he is now an important leader of the Rebel Alliance with invaluable insider knowledge. His minifigure is exclusive to just one limited edition LEGO set, but he is there when it counts—the most crucial battle in the LEGO *Star Wars* galaxy!

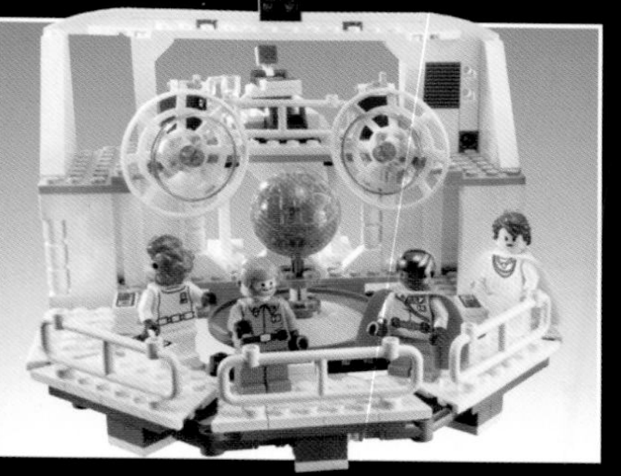

***Home One* Mon Calamari Star Cruiser (set 7754)**
Together with other Rebel leaders Mon Mothma, Admiral Ackbar, and Lando Calrissian, General Crix Madine plans the destruction of the second Death Star during the Battle of Endor.

Hair first
General Crix Madine was the first LEGO minifigure to sport the standard short hair piece in a dark tan color. It has since been seen on only one other minifigure: a faceless mannequin in a shop in the LEGO City theme.

General Crix Madine's happy, brown-bearded face is unique to his minifigure

Collar pips denote rank

Communications badge allows Madine to contact Rebel command and other leaders

Black-gloved hands

This tan torso piece was created specifically for Madine's minifigure

DATA FILE

SET: 7754 *Home One* Mon Calamari Star Cruiser
YEAR: 2009
PIECES: 4
EQUIPMENT: None
VARIANTS: 1

Lando Calrissian
REBEL GENERAL

General Lando Calrissian is one of the Rebel generals on board the *Home One* Mon Calamari Star Cruiser (set 7754), which is in battle against the second Death Star. His minifigure has a unique LEGO cape which makes him even more boldly confident than usual! It appears to help him direct a particularly assertive attack on the colossal Imperial battle station.

Home One Mon Calamari Star Cruiser (set 7754)

It is the Rebels' final assault on the second Death Star and Lando is a general in this 2009 set. He spends a lot of time in the briefing area of the command center.

General Lando's reddish-brown head is also seen on his skiff guard minifigure (p.123). When he is a Baron of Cloud City (p.111), he has a darker brown head

The brown sash across Lando's chest is a gun holster. He wears a matching brown utility belt for storing ammunition

This badge displays Lando's rank, as do the pips on his collar

Lando carries a blaster during battle

Classic cape

This minifigure's cape design appears on many other LEGO minifigures. However the sand-blue color is unique to Lando. His cape denotes his authority and rank as a Rebel general. It fastens with a blue cord.

DATA FILE

SET: 7754 *Home One* Mon Calamari Star Cruiser
YEAR: 2009
PIECES: 5
EQUIPMENT: Blaster, cape
VARIANTS: 1

Mon Calamari Officer

AMPHIBIOUS HUMANOID

***Home One* Mon Calamari Star Cruiser (set 7754)**
The officer mans the repair station in the hangar bay, but also has a seat in the briefing chamber.

Part-man, part-amphibious humanoid, this officer—exclusive to 2009's *Home One* Mon Calamari Star Cruiser (set 7754)—is one of three Mon Calamari LEGO minifigures. His main job is to maintain and repair the A-wing starship when it is not on a mission.

The Mon Calamari officer's distinctive head-mold is exactly the same as that used for his fellow Mon Calamari, Admiral Ackbar (p.130) and Nahdar Vebb (p.173)

Vote winner
The Mon Calamari Officer minifigure helped this limited-edition set to win the 2009 LEGO *Star Wars* Fan's Choice Competition, which fans voted for online.

This officer has a unique torso. The dark bib protects his tan uniform from oil and dirt in the repair station

Utility belt with pockets for storing repair equipment

He uses a wrench when in the repair station

The Mon Calamari wear tan overalls in battle, which makes them blend in better with the human Alliance members

DATA FILE
SET: 7754 *Home One* Mon Calamari Star Cruiser
YEAR: 2009
PIECES: 3
EQUIPMENT: Wrench
VARIANTS: 1

A-Wing Pilot
REBEL PILOT

The A-wing pilot is part of a force known as Green Squadron because of his distinctive green flight jumpsuit. His minifigure plays a crucial role in the Battle of Endor, flying his A-wing fighter in three LEGO *Star Wars* sets—most recently the *Home One* Mon Calamari Star Cruiser (set 7754) in 2009. There are three variants of his minifigure, each with subtle differences.

Translucent yellow visor clips into holes at the sides of the pilot's helmet. A variant in the 2006 A-Wing Fighter (set 6207) has a translucent black visor

Rebel pilots
Only the A-wing pilot minifigure wears a green flight suit in the LEGO *Star Wars* galaxy. X-wing and Y-wing pilots wear orange flight suits, while B-wing pilots wear red ones.

Standard flesh-colored LEGO head with a happy smile

Classic LEGO helmet with a red and white stripe pattern. The B-wing pilot (p.136) wears the same helmet piece with different printing

DATA FILE
SET: 7754 *Home One* Mon Calamari Star Cruiser
YEAR: 2009
PIECES: 5
EQUIPMENT: None
VARIANTS: 3

The A-wing pilot's green torso features a flight vest and life-support unit. The printing is unique to his minifigure

STAR VARIANT

Yellow pilot
The original A-wing pilot has a yellow face with a printed headset and a slightly different helmet design. His body is the same as the 2009 variant. He is only in the A-Wing Fighter (set 7134), released in 2000.

Dark green legs with black hips do not appear on any other LEGO *Star Wars* minifigure

Rebel Technician

REBEL MECHANIC

The Rebel Technician debuted in 2000 in B-Wing at Rebel Control Center (set 7180) with a yellow LEGO head and tan uniform. In 2006, he switched to a flesh-colored head and a gray uniform with a sturdier helmet for added protection. He wears a simple uniform, reflecting his practical role in LEGO *Star Wars*.

A-Wing Fighter (set 6207)

The Rebel technician rides around on a yellow transport cart, or military cargo speeder, with joystick controls. His cart has a ladder integrated into it. The technician uses the ladder to board the A-wing fighter in this set.

This helmet design can be seen in varying colors on many LEGO minifigures in other themes, including skateboarders in LEGO Gravity Games

This standard LEGO smiling expression has appeared on hundreds of LEGO minifigures

Unique torso with plain gray tunic that has pockets for storing repair equipment

Practical plain brown belt

DATA FILE

SET: 6207 A-Wing Fighter
YEAR: 2006
PIECES: 4
EQUIPMENT: None
VARIANTS: 2

Engineer

The A-Wing Fighter (set 7134) from 2000 contains a Rebel engineer minifigure, which is very similar to the original Rebel technician. He has the same body and cap, but his face has a straighter mustache and no stubble.

STAR VARIANT

Rebel control
In the 2000 set B-Wing at Rebel Control Center (set 7180), the Rebel technician wears a tan uniform and a tan cap. He has a yellow LEGO head with a large mustache and stubble.

B-Wing Pilot
SPACE ACE

The B-wing pilot is ready to fly the largest single-seat starship in the Rebel fleet! His minifigure has appeared in two LEGO sets since 2000, both times with his B-wing starfighter. Like other Rebel pilots, he wears a jumpsuit and life-support pack, but he is distinguished by his bright red coloring and unique helmet.

STAR VARIANT

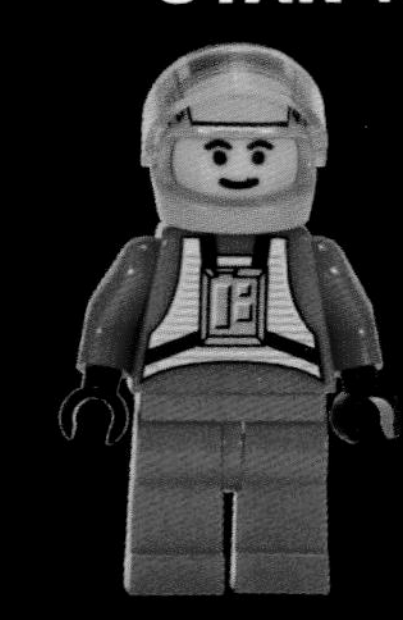

Yellow face
This yellow-faced variant appears in the 2000 LEGO set B-Wing at Rebel Control Center (set 7180). Apart from skin color, variations include a face with eyebrows and a transparent yellow visor instead of a black one.

Pilot torso
The B-wing pilot's red torso is unique to his minifigure, but the same design is used on an orange torso for X-wing pilots Luke Skywalker, Biggs Darklighter, Wedge Antilles, Dutch Vander (pp.84–87), and Dak Ralter (p.105).

Unique yellow and black printing decorates helmet

Standard LEGO head piece printing gives the B-wing pilot a cheerful disposition

Life-support pack is standard issue for Rebel pilots

The pilot wears a red jumpsuit and white flak vest

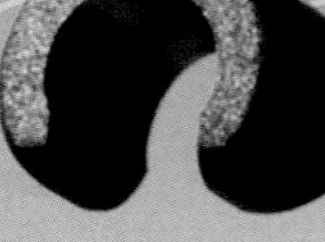

Only two other LEGO *Star Wars* minifigures have red leg pieces: the Royal Guard (p.127) and Chancellor Palpatine (p.186)

Black flight gloves

DATA FILE

SET: 6208 B-Wing Fighter
YEAR: 2006
PIECES: 5
EQUIPMENT: None
VARIANTS: 2

Ten Numb
BLUE FIVE

Sullustan pilot Ten Numb flies a B-wing during the Battle of Endor. His Rebel call sign is Blue Five. Ten is the only Sullustan minifigure to date, and his face is printed with creases that are a common Sullustan feature. His minifigure wears a brown helmet and white jumpsuit with a unique torso pattern. Ten is exclusive to B-Wing Starfighter (set 6208).

B-Wing Fighter (set 6208)
Ten Numb fits comfortably into the B-wing's cockpit, where he mans the controls. From the cockpit, Ten can activate any of the starfighter's weapons, including the laser cannon, ion cannons, twin blaster, and torpedo launchers.

The same helmet is worn in red by the T-16 skyhopper pilot (p.68)

Ten's Sullustan face is printed wearing his breathing mask, which is attached to the life-support pack on his chest

Ten's life-support pack is different from human packs because Sullustans breathe differently

Gear harness

Torso is printed with data readers and power gauges, which monitor Ten's air supply and life-support pack

Color confusion
In Episode VI, Sullustan pilots wear red jumpsuits, like the B-wing pilot (opposite). Ten's minifigure was created from a pre-production image that showed Ten dressed in a white jumpsuit.

DATA FILE
SET: 6208 B-Wing Fighter
YEAR: 2006
PIECES: 4
EQUIPMENT: None
VARIANTS: 1

Luke Skywalker
CAMOUFLAGED ON ENDOR

Luke Skywalker dons a camouflage-patterned tunic over his black Jedi robes on Endor, making his minifigure difficult to spot in the dense foliage of the forest moon. This Luke minifigure seems to be doing a good job of staying out of sight—he appears in only one 1999 LEGO *Star Wars* set!

Speeder Bikes (set 7128)
Luke is pursued by two scout troopers on speeder bikes through the forests of Endor in this 1999 set. Luke's minifigure can stand on a LEGO tree to hide from the scout trooper minifigures.

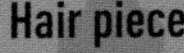

Hair piece
Luke's short hair is a classic LEGO piece, but only Luke Skywalker minifigures wear it in tan in LEGO *Star Wars*. However, it is seen in other themes, including LEGO Harry Potter and LEGO Soccer.

Luke is the only LEGO minifigure to have this head piece with small eyebrows and a chin dimple. It is seen on four other versions of his minifigure, including Luke in his Dagobah gear (p.106) and Cloud City Luke (p.114)

Luke's torso is unique to his minifigure. The camouflage pattern does not continue on the back—it is plain khaki instead

Black cybernetic hand

This minifigure comes with a green lightsaber. Like Luke's green torso, it can blend in with the scenery

DATA FILE
SET: 7128 Speeder Bikes
YEAR: 1999
PIECES: 4
EQUIPMENT: Lightsaber
VARIANTS: 1

Princess Leia
EQUIPPED FOR ENDOR

Rebel leader Princess Leia Organa is ready to fight Imperial forces in dense forests in The Battle of Endor (set 8038). This Leia minifigure, dressed in a unique camouflaged torso, is exclusive to the 2009 set. Leia's natural diplomacy skills help her befriend three Ewok minifigures who also feature in the set.

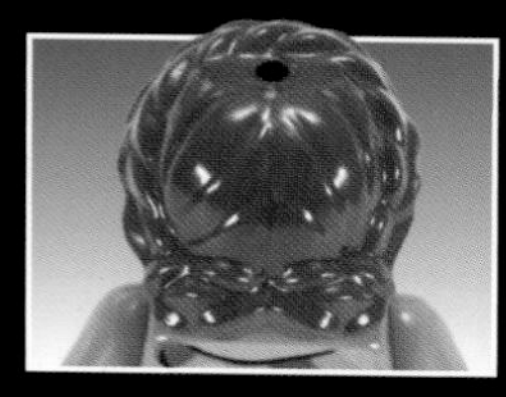

Royal locks
Leia's hair was first seen on a queen in the LEGO Fantasy Era theme. It has a hole for the queen's crown to fit into.

Leia's minifigure dressed in Hoth gear also has this reddish-brown braided hair piece (p.93)

Mon Mothma (p.129) also has this head piece

Leia's camouflage Rebel tunic helps her hide from Imperial scout troopers in the dense forests of Endor

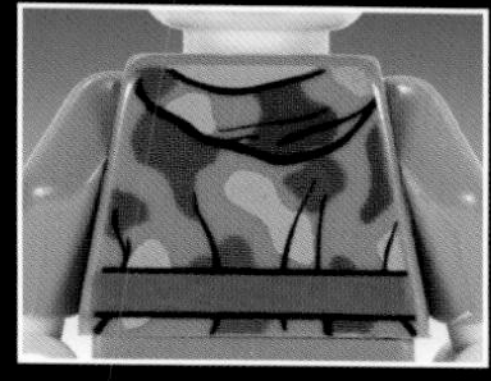

Tunic torso
The camouflage pattern on Leia's loose-fitting tunic continues on the back of her torso piece.

Utility belt for essential survival equipment

Leia protects herself from Imperial forces with this blaster

DATA FILE

SET: 8038 The Battle of Endor
YEAR: 2009
PIECES: 4
EQUIPMENT: Blaster
VARIANTS: 1

Rebel Commando
CAMOUFLAGED WARRIOR

The Rebel commandos are on a mission to destroy the shield generator bunker! There are two versions of the camouflaged commando minifigure, and both appear only in The Battle of Endor (set 8038). The minifigures are dressed in identical green fatigues with lots of printed detail, but each has an individual head.

Toothy
The Rebel commando's backpack is actually a LEGO plate with a "tooth" piece attached. The same piece, in white, is used for icicles in Hoth Wampa Cave (set 8089).

Backpack
A gray bracket fits around the commando's neck. To this, he can clip his dark green LEGO backpack.

No beard
The second Rebel commando in this set has a clean-shaven, frowning head piece. The same head is used for Galen Marek's minifigure (p.203).

Unique LEGO helmet is perfect for camouflage in the forest

Bearded head piece is unique to the Rebel commando

Green backpack contains the commando's supplies and extra battle gear

Unique torso printed with camouflage jacket and ammunition belt

Only two other LEGO *Star Wars* minifigures have sand-green legs: Onaconda Farr (p.171) and the Gamorrean guard (p.118)

DATA FILE

SET: 8038 The Battle of Endor
YEAR: 2009
PIECES: 6
EQUIPMENT: Blaster rifle
VARIANTS: 1

Scout Trooper

SOLO SENTRY

The Imperial scout trooper is often sent on dangerous missions on his own. His minifigure wears a specialized scout helmet and white armor that is more lightweight than regular stormtrooper armor. He also carries a powerful blaster. Two variants of the scout trooper minifigure have appeared in five LEGO sets since 1999.

The Battle of Endor (set 8038)

The scout trooper chases Ewok and Rebel minifigures through the forest of Endor in this LEGO set. He flies a repulsorlift speeder bike, which has a lightweight blaster cannon and is easy to maneuver through thick trees.

Black LEGO head piece is visible beneath the helmet, creating a visor effect

Electronic visor enhances the minifigure's vision

Built-in comlink system can support long-distance communication

Kashyyyk trooper

This helmet piece is used in sand-green for the Kashyyyk trooper minifigure (p.52). Kashyyyk troopers are a scouting unit based in the jungles of Kashyyyk, where they require camouflaged armor.

The scout trooper often undertakes long, solo missions. He carries survival rations with him at all times

Unique torso has dark bluish-gray printing

DATA FILE

SET: 7956 Endor Battle Set
YEAR: 2011
PIECES: 4
EQUIPMENT: Blaster
VARIANTS: 2

Visor head

The original scout trooper variant has a yellow head printed with a black visor. The minifigure has appeared in three sets from 1999 to 2002.

Wicket W. Warrick

EWOK WARRIOR

Wicket Wystri Warrick is a wide-eyed Ewok native to the emerald moon of Endor. He is a minifigure of firsts in two ways: he is the first Ewok to befriend Princess Leia in The Battle of Endor (set 8038), and one of the first Ewoks to appear in LEGO form. Wicket wears a distinctive orange hood that sets him apart from other LEGO Ewoks.

STAR VARIANT

Original Ewok
The original Wicket W. Warrick is all brown, with no printing on his head-and-torso piece. The variant appears exclusively in the 2002 set Ewok Attack (set 7139).

DATA FILE

SET: 8038 Battle of Endor
YEAR: 2009
PIECES: 3
EQUIPMENT: Spear
VARIANTS: 2

Detailed face printing is first seen on the 2009 design

Wicket's dark orange hood has stitching where he once tore it

The 2009 variant is made up of reddish-brown LEGO pieces

Unique head-and-torso sandwich-board piece has textured fur

LEGO Ewoks
Along with his fellow Ewok warrior Paploo (p.144), Wicket was one of the earliest LEGO Ewoks. Chief Chirpa (opposite) followed in 2009, while Logray and a black Ewok appeared in 2011 (pp.145–146).

Ewoks are small in stature, so Wicket has short, unposeable LEGO legs

Chief Chirpa
EWOK LEADER

Leader of the Ewoks, Chief Chirpa is a wizened old minifigure who commits his tribe to the fight against the Empire in The Battle of Endor (set 8038). Chief Chirpa's tribe of Ewok minifigures may be diminutive but they are fierce warriors when called into battle. Chirpa has a unique ruling staff that is topped with the horns of animals he has hunted.

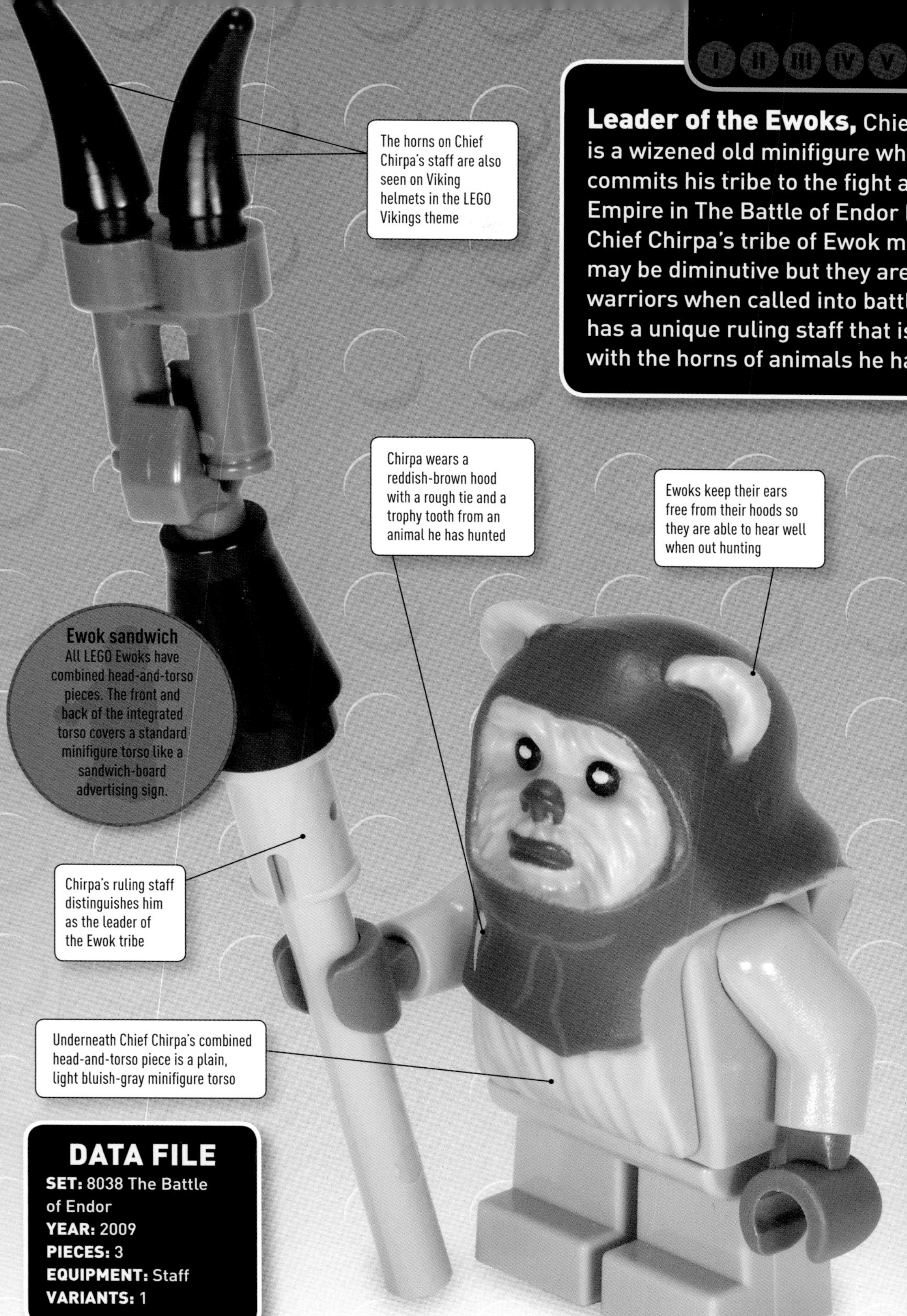

The horns on Chief Chirpa's staff are also seen on Viking helmets in the LEGO Vikings theme
Chirpa wears a reddish-brown hood with a rough tie and a trophy tooth from an animal he has hunted
Ewoks keep their ears free from their hoods so they are able to hear well when out hunting
Chirpa's ruling staff distinguishes him as the leader of the Ewok tribe
Underneath Chief Chirpa's combined head-and-torso piece is a plain, light bluish-gray minifigure torso

Ewok sandwich
All LEGO Ewoks have combined head-and-torso pieces. The front and back of the integrated torso covers a standard minifigure torso like a sandwich-board advertising sign.

DATA FILE
SET: 8038 The Battle of Endor
YEAR: 2009
PIECES: 3
EQUIPMENT: Staff
VARIANTS: 1

Paploo
BRAVE EWOK

Like his good friend Wicket, Paploo is one of the first LEGO Ewoks. His minifigure has appeared in two sets, and in each he has a different look. His redesigned 2009 minifigure has printing on his face that makes him look more realistic than his 2002 counterpart. Paploo bravely fights alongside the Rebels in The Battle of Endor (set 8038).

The Battle of Endor (set 8038)
The 2009 variant of Paploo appears exclusively in this set. He appears alongside his friend Wicket W. Warrick and his uncle Chief Chirpa. The scout trooper minifigures in the set should hold on to their speeder bikes—Paploo might just steal one!

STAR VARIANT

First Paploo
The original Paploo minifigure has a combined head-and-torso piece that is entirely tan. The rest of his body is brown-colored. The variant exclusively appears in Ewok Attack (set 7139), released in 2002.

Paploo has a distinctive orange feather pattern on his tan hood

Paploo has stitched up a tear in his hood

Paploo's furry head piece extends down to cover a plain reddish-brown torso piece

LEGO Ewoks' legs are unposeable

DATA FILE

SET: 8038 The Battle of Endor
YEAR: 2009
PIECES: 3
EQUIPMENT: Bow and arrow, spear
VARIANTS: 2

Logray
EWOK SHAMAN

This Ewok shaman and medicine man is suspicious of outsiders, so watch out or his minifigure might just put a curse on you! Logray is exclusive to the 2011 set Ewok Attack (set 7956). His striped fur, tribal headdress, medicine bag, and mysterious powers make him an unusual LEGO *Star Wars* minifigure.

Shaman spear
Logray carries a brown spear in LEGO *Star Wars*, but in Episode VI he carries a staff of power adorned with the bones and feathers of defeated enemies.

Brown LEGO spear

Shaman headdress adorned with a churi bird skull and brown feathers

Striped, fur-textured head-and-torso piece was specially created for Logray's minifigure

Shaman medicine bag

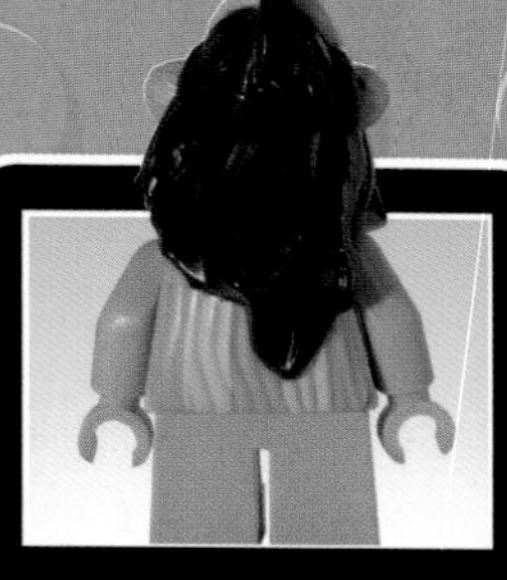

Flowing feathers
Logray's brown-feathered headdress runs down the back of his torso and his striped fur pattern also continues.

DATA FILE
SET: 7956 Ewok Attack
YEAR: 2011
PIECES: 3
EQUIPMENT: Spear
VARIANTS: 1

Black Ewok
EWOK SCOUT

This minifigure may not be very tall because of his short LEGO legs, but he is a good shot with his bow and arrow—especially when hidden high in the trees of Endor in Ewok Attack (set 7956). His green hood helps him hide in dense foliage. The black Ewok battles in only one LEGO set alongside his tribe's shaman, Logray.

DATA FILE

SET: 7956 Ewok Attack
YEAR: 2011
PIECES: 3
EQUIPMENT: Bow and arrow
VARIANTS: 1

Combined head-and-torso piece is the same as that seen on fellow Ewoks Wicket, Chief Chirpa, and Paploo (pp.142–144) but with different colors and printing

Ewoks carry primitive tools like this bow and arrow

The black Ewok has a feather in his hood

This minifigure is the only black Ewok in LEGO *Star Wars*

Tokkat?
The black Ewok minifigure is based on the Ewok scout called Tokkat, although he is not officially named as this on the set packaging for Ewok Attack (set 7956).

Anakin Skywalker

CLONE WARS JEDI

Dathomir Speeder (set 7957)
This 2011 LEGO set is the latest to feature the Clone Wars version of Anakin Skywalker. Asajj Ventress and her new Sith apprentice Savage Oppress attempt to take flight in their Dathomir speeder, but Anakin has other ideas!

During the Clone Wars, Anakin Skywalker becomes known throughout the LEGO *Star Wars* galaxy as the "Hero With No Fear." His minifigure battles for the Republic in eight LEGO sets, but could the exhausted, drawn expression on Anakin's unique face hint at the growing darkness within the brave Jedi Knight?

Tousled reddish-brown hair is also seen on Mon Mothma's minifigure (p.129)

Anakin's face has become battle-scarred during the Clone Wars

Anakin's Jedi robes have a more cartoon-like pattern than those seen on his classic Jedi Knight minifigure (p.42)

Clone Wars Anakin carries a blue lightsaber

Clone Wars
LEGO *Star Wars: The Clone Wars* minifigures have a more cartoon-like appearance than their classic *Star Wars* counterparts. They reflect how the characters look in the animated *Clone Wars* movie and TV series.

DATA FILE
SET: 7957 Dathomir Speeder
YEAR: 2011
PIECES: 4
EQUIPMENT: Lightsaber
VARIANTS: 1

R2-D2
CLONE WARS ASTROMECH

Faithful astromech droid R2-D2 serves under Anakin Skywalker during the Clone Wars. Although R2-D2 has many adventures in classic LEGO *Star Wars* sets, this Clone Wars version of R2-D2 has only appeared in one set. From his droid socket in Anakin's Y-Wing Starfighter (set 8037), R2 helps Anakin and his apprentice Ahsoka Tano fight for the Republic.

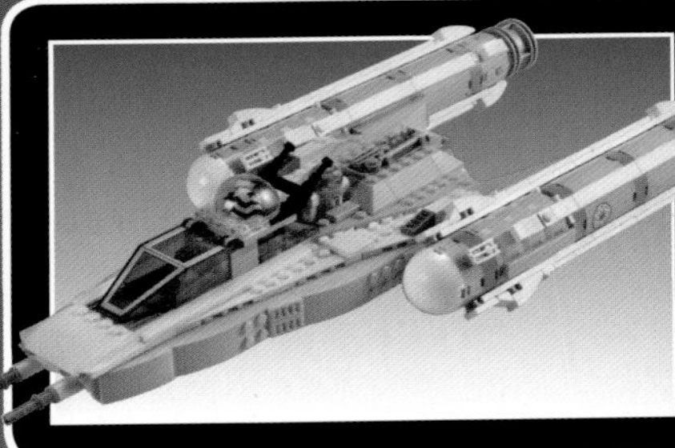

Anakin's Y-Wing Starfighter (set 8037)
Clone Wars R2-D2 only appears in this 2009 set. The droid not only navigates the starfighter, he attaches to a spring mechanism that pokes out from beneath the ship—pulling him back like a lever fires a missile!

DATA FILE

SET: 8037 Anakin's Y-Wing Starfighter
YEAR: 2009
PIECES: 4
EQUIPMENT: None
VARIANTS: 1

Cartoon Artoo
Although the Clone Wars version of R2-D2 is made up of the same pieces as the classic *Star Wars* R2-D2 (p.9), the printing on his head and torso pieces is less detailed, with thicker blue lines. This makes R2-D2 look more cartoon-like.

Clone Wars R2-D2 has a pearlescent sheen to his light bluish-gray head piece

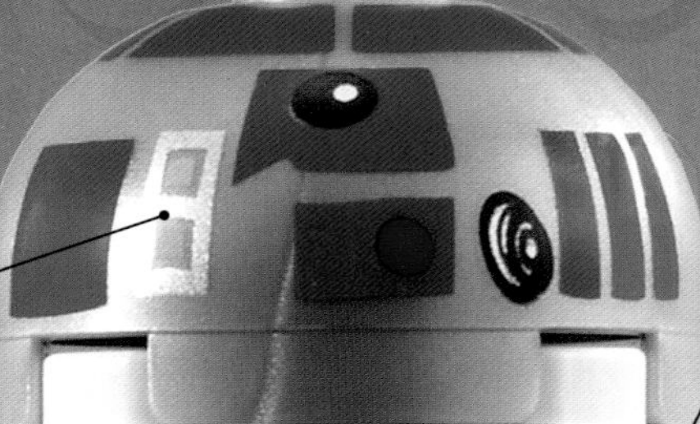

Logic function displays aid communication between R2 and his owner, Anakin Skywalker

R2-D2 has an arm inside this compartment to help him with maintenance jobs

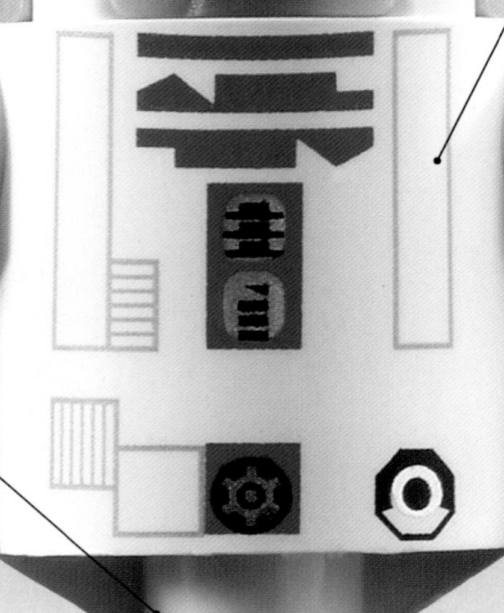

R2-D2 connects with Anakin's Y-Wing starfighter through a hole in his base

R2-D2's wide leg bases can tackle almost any terrain

Obi-Wan Kenobi

CLONE WARS NEGOTIATOR

Obi-Wan Kenobi is a public symbol of hope during the Clone Wars. Although his minifigure carries a lightsaber, Obi-Wan is known throughout the galaxy as "The Negotiator" because of his diplomacy skills and reluctance to use the powerful weapon in combat. Clone Wars Obi-Wan's calm demeanor has been tested in two sets since 2008.

Republic Attack Gunship (set 7676)

Obi-Wan Kenobi tackles his bitter enemy Asajj Ventress in this 2008 set, which was the first to feature the Clone Wars version of Obi-Wan's minifigure. Jedi Plo Koon provides back-up.

This dark orange combed-over hair piece is only seen on Obi-Wan's Clone Wars minifigure

Obi-Wan's unique head piece has big, cartoon-like eyes and a dark orange beard

Traditional Jedi utility belt with a metallic clasp

Obi-Wan prefers to use his lightsaber to defend, not attack

Loose-fitting Jedi pants

Different strokes

Obi-Wan has a different lightsaber in Pirate Tank (set 7753): Its hilt is light bluish-gray instead of metallic silver.

DATA FILE

SET: 7753 Pirate Tank
YEAR: 2009
PIECES: 4
EQUIPMENT: Lightsaber
VARIANTS: 1

Ahsoka Tano
EAGER PADAWAN

Ahsoka Tano is Anakin Skywalker's enthusiastic Padawan. She has fought for the Republic in six Clone Wars sets since her 2008 release. As a Togruta, Ahsoka's minifigure has brightly colored skin and striped head-tails. She wears an unusual Jedi costume, including a brown top and matching gloves.

LEGO Togrutas
For a while, Ahsoka was the only Togruta character available in minifigure form. In 2011, however, Jedi Master Shaak Ti's red-skinned minifigure was released, with fully grown, adult-length head-tails (see p.194).

Unique head piece features Ahsoka's orange skin and white face markings

Ahsoka's head-tails aren't yet full-length because she is still young

Head-tails
Ahsoka's hair piece is not hair at all! It is a unique mold of the blue and white head-tails that grow from the heads of all Togrutas.

Unique torso is printed with Ahsoka's orange skin and distinctive Jedi costume. There is no printing on the back

Utility belt with storage pouch and food capsules

Until 2009, Ahsoka's lightsaber hilt was a matte gray color

Boba Fett (p.108) is the only other minifigure to have the same brown hip piece and light-gray legs combination

DATA FILE

SET: 8098 Clone Turbo Tank
YEAR: 2010
PIECES: 4
EQUIPMENT: Lightsaber
VARIANTS: 1

R7-A7
AHSOKA'S ASTROMECH

Ahsoka's Starfighter and Vulture Droid (set 7751)
R7-A7 proves his worth in the one LEGO set he appears in. The plucky droid helps Ahsoka fight off a buzz droid that has latched onto her Delta-7 starfighter.

R7-A7 is a brave astromech droid who helps navigate and repair Ahsoka Tano's starfighter. His minifigure has a dark red body unit and a white head, with lime green and silver access panels. The helpful droid only appears in one LEGO set. R7-A7's brightly colored printing matches Ahsoka's red and green starship, which has a droid socket for him to plug into.

DATA FILE
SET: 7751 Ahsoka's Starfighter and Vulture Droid
YEAR: 2009
PIECES: 4
EQUIPMENT: None
VARIANTS: 1

Head piece is the same mold as other LEGO astromech droids, but the coloring is unique to R7-A7

Dark red pins
R7-A7 should be proud of his bright, unique coloring. He is the only astromech droid to have LEGO Technic leg pieces in dark red. In fact, these dark red pin pieces are not found in any other LEGO sets.

Logic function display indicates what R7-A7 is thinking

R7-A7 has many of the same functions as R2-D2, but he is not quite as intelligent

Acoustic signaler allows R7-A7 to communicate

Astromech droids have two fixed legs and a third retractable leg that is stored inside the unit

Recharge power coupling can be attached to the power source on Ahsoka's starship

The Clone Wars clone trooper has fought for the Republic in eight Clone Wars sets since 2008. His Phase I armor has been updated with a more stylized graphic pattern and, unlike the classic clone trooper minifigures (p.35; p.53), this soldier has an identity! Instead of a plain black head piece, this trooper has a new clone face under his sleeker, simpler helmet.

STAR VARIANT

Signs of rank
High-ranking clone troopers often wear extra LEGO pieces over their basic white armor. Modifications include a visor shield that clips to the helmet, a shoulder pauldron to denote rank, and a kama blaster-shield around the waist.

DATA FILE

SET: 8098 Clone Turbo Tank
YEAR: 2010
PIECES: 4
EQUIPMENT: Blaster rifle
VARIANTS: 1

Clone Trooper
CLONE WARS SOLDIER

Clone Wars clone troopers wear full helmets that are printed with a black visor

White plastoid armor is lightweight and blaster-resistant

Utility belt holds survival gear, ammunition, and assault equipment

DC-15 blaster rifle

Face of a clone
This flesh-colored head piece was first released in 2008. It is used for most Clone Wars clone trooper minifigures.

Clone Commander
LEADER OF HORN COMPANY

The clone commander leads a regiment of troopers into battle against the Separatists. He wears battle armor that has been customized with green markings and highlights to reflect his rank and unit. The minifigure appears alongside two bomb squad troopers and an ARF trooper in the Clone Trooper Battle Pack (set 7913).

Clone Trooper Battle Pack (set 7913)
The clone commander is exclusive to this LEGO set. He flies a green and white BARC speeder, which is the perfect vehicle for chasing down fast-moving enemy targets.

Unique helmet is printed with green markings and a smaller visor than the clone trooper (opposite)

Clone torsos
The Clone Wars clone trooper torso design (opposite) is used on almost every Clone Wars trooper minifigure. To differentiate minifigures by rank and unit, different colors and insignia are printed over the basic armor pattern.

Green insignia identifies unit. This commander is part of Horn Company

Black body glove is worn beneath white armor

Small blaster pistols were released in 2011 and are exclusive to LEGO *Star Wars*

Unique leg printing shows the edges of the clone commander's blast-resistant armor

DATA FILE
SET: 7913 Clone Trooper Battle Pack
YEAR: 2011
PIECES: 4
EQUIPMENT: Twin blaster pistols
VARIANTS: 1

Clone Troopers
CLONE SPECIALISTS

These clone troopers carry out specialist missions for the Republic in several LEGO Clone Wars sets. Their minifigures all wear Phase I LEGO armor, and have identical flesh-colored clone trooper head pieces beneath their helmets. Some of these specialist troopers have unique armor markings and possess equipment that is crucial for their specific jobs or missions.

Helmet fin makes jetpack troopers aerodynamic

LEGO jetpack piece is also used for the Mandalorian (p.199) and Boba Fett (p.108) minifigures

DATA FILE
NAME: Clone Jetpack Trooper
SPECIALTY: Aerial assaults
SET: 7748 Corporate Alliance Tank Droid
YEAR: 2009
PIECES: 5
EQUIPMENT: Blaster, jetpack
VARIANTS: 1

Rangefinder clips to helmet so the minifigure can measure the distance to his target

Unique helmet is insulated from battle noise and printed with black Republic symbols

Clone Wars
Minifigures released in LEGO Clone Wars sets have been designed with a "cartoon" feel. These Clone Wars troopers have stylized torso patterns and brighter, bolder coloring than the classic LEGO *Star Wars* troopers (pp.54–55).

Unique torso is printed with an extra chestplate to absorb kickback from firing large weapons

DATA FILE
NAME: Clone Gunner
SPECIALTY: Heavy artillery
SET: 8014 Clone Walker Battle Pack
YEAR: 2009
PIECES: 5
EQUIPMENT: Blaster
VARIANTS: 1

Unique helmet is printed with red Republic symbols and yellow markings that signify pilot status
Utility belt with extra ammunition
Clone pilot wears a life-support pack over the standard clone trooper armor
Unique orange helmet is extra sturdy to protect against bomb blasts
Blaster rifle keeps the bomb squad trooper safe during a mission
Orange markings denote bomb squad affiliation
Leg piece is printed with unique orange armor markings

DATA FILE

NAME: Clone Pilot
SPECIALTY: Flying Republic starships
SET: 8019 Republic Attack Shuttle
YEAR: 2009
PIECES: 4
EQUIPMENT: Blaster
VARIANTS: 1

Pilot in blue
This Clone Wars pilot minifigure is unique. However, a classic clone pilot minifigure also takes to the skies in LEGO *Star Wars*. It first appeared in 2005 wearing a blue jumpsuit and white helmet (p.44).

DATA FILE

NAME: Bomb Squad Trooper
SPECIALTY: Disarming bombs and explosive devices
SET: 7913 Clone Trooper Battle Pack
YEAR: 2011
PIECES: 4
EQUIPMENT: Blaster rifle
VARIANTS: 1

Rocket Droid Commander
AIRBORNE DROID

The rocket droid commander is a specialist Separatist droid who leads a battalion of rocket battle droids. His minifigure has a rocketpack on his back and wears lightweight armor for space combat. This droid only appears in one LEGO set, where he uses his superior programming to attack the Republic.

DATA FILE
SET: 8086 Droid Tri-Fighter
YEAR: 2010
PIECES: 7
EQUIPMENT: Blaster, jetpack
VARIANTS: 1

Unique head piece is the same mold as the battle droid minifigure (p.22), but with different coloring

Receiver for central droid command signal

One of the arm pieces has a hand that is turned 90 degrees so it can hold a blaster

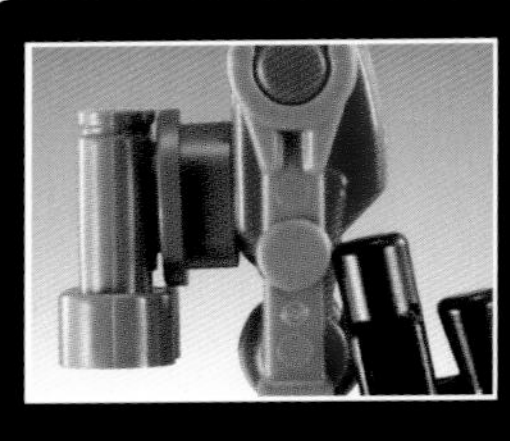

Unusual jetpack
The rocket droid commander's jetpack is actually a LEGO binoculars piece! It is also used for the destroyer droid's blasters (p.36).

Yellow markings indicate rank of commander

He uses the same E-5 blaster as regular battle droids

Rocketpack clips onto his back

Droid Tri-Fighter (set 8086)
The rocket droid commander is exclusive to this LEGO set. The set also comes with two rocket battle droid minifigures, which are the same as the commander, but without the yellow armor markings.

Same leg piece as the battle droid minifigure

Elite Assassin Droid

VILLAIN-FOR-HIRE

The elite assassin droid is the best of the best. Encased in black armor, this skilled assassin can blend into the shadows during a top-secret mission. His tall, thin minifigure has appeared in three LEGO sets since 2009—always in the unsavory company of bounty hunters or other assassin droids.

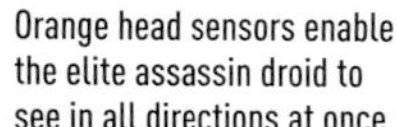

Orange head sensors enable the elite assassin droid to see in all directions at once

Cone head piece is unique to assassin droids in LEGO *Star Wars*

Assassin droid has the same torso piece as the battle droid minifigure (p.22) and rocket droid commander (opposite)

His body is covered with blaster-proof armor

Long-range blaster rifle is perfect for carrying out assassinations without being detected

Bounty Hunter Assault Gunship (set 7930)

The elite assassin droid joins bounty hunters Embo, Aurra Sing, and Sugi on board the assault gunship. This villainous group are on the hunt for Jedi, who they can capture and lock up in the ship's prison cell.

DATA FILE

SET: 7930 Bounty Hunter Assault Gunship
YEAR: 2011
PIECES: 8
EQUIPMENT: Blaster rifle
VARIANTS: 1

Assassin droid

The regular assassin droid minifigure is exactly the same as the elite assassin droid, apart from his color. The assassin droid is silver, and comes in just one LEGO set, Assassin Droids Battle Pack (set 8015). One of the more famous assassin droids is IG-88 (p.110).

Yoda
CLONE WARS JEDI LEADER

Yoda's Clone Wars minifigure is just as wise and powerful as his classic minifigure, but he has a different look. The Clone Wars version of the ancient Jedi Grand Master has a bigger green head-mold—now with printed eyes—and a new, unique torso. But Yoda still wields his green lightsaber as he leads the clone army into battle against Separatist forces.

Armored Assault Tank (set 8018)
Clone Wars Yoda only appears in this one set, where he and a single clone trooper take on two battle droids, three super battle droids, and an armored assault tank! Although the AAT has missile launchers and a laser cannon, Yoda uses the Force to triumph.

Two Yodas
This Clone Wars Yoda has been designed to look more cartoon-like than the classic Yoda minifigure (p. 17) to reflect the animated *Clone Wars* series. He has a bigger head, different ears, and large, painted eyes.

Yoda's head is made from rubber, like the Plo Koon (p.164), Kit Fisto, (p.45) and classic Yoda (p.17) minifigures

Yoda's head-mold has larger ears than the classic Yoda minifigure

Unique torso is printed with Yoda's simple tan robes and brown undershirt

Yoda might be small, but he is a lightsaber expert!

Yoda has short, unposeable leg pieces

DATA FILE
SET: 7964 Republic Frigate
YEAR: 2011
PIECES: 3
EQUIPMENT: Lightsaber
VARIANTS: 1

Rotta The Hutt
JABBA'S SON

Often referred to as "the Huttlet," Rotta is the slimy, green son of Jabba the Hutt. Poor Rotta has been captured by the Separatists. Can Anakin Skywalker and Ahsoka Tano rescue him and return him to his worried father? The Jedi will have to search hard for Rotta's small minifigure, as he only comes in two LEGO sets.

AT-TE Walker (set 7675)
Rotta makes his first LEGO appearance in the 2008 set AT-TE Walker. Jabba's young son is in good LEGO hands when he is rescued by the Jedi. Anakin and Ahsoka are joined by two clone troopers and an enormous AT-TE walker—together they have no trouble defeating the battle droid on his flying STAP.

DATA FILE
SET: 7675 AT-TE Walker
YEAR: 2008
PIECES: 3
EQUIPMENT: None
VARIANTS: 1

Rotta's mold
Rotta's minifigure is built from three unique, sand-green LEGO pieces. The two arm pieces clip into the head and body piece, which is a unique mold, made especially for this minifigure.

Rotta may not be much use on the battlefield, but Ahsoka thinks he is cute!

Like most Clone Wars minifigures, Rotta has painted eyes

Although he is small now, one day Rotta might grow up to be as large as his father Jabba (p. 117)

Rotta has a hollow circle in the base of his minifigure so he can be clipped onto a regular minifigure's hand

Asajj Ventress
SITH ASSASSIN

Asajj Ventress is a deadly assassin who works for the Sith Lord Count Dooku. Her fearsome minifigure has a unique head, torso, and legs, and wields twin red-bladed lightsabers. Asajj has dark side powers and a fiery temper—and she is on a mission to cause trouble for the Jedi in two LEGO Clone Wars sets.

Extra printing
As well as her tattoo markings, Asajj Ventress's sleeveless body suit armor printing also continues on to the back of her torso piece. The 2008 variant doesn't have printing on the back.

Asajj's Sith training gives her expert lightsaber skills

Purple tattoo markings are continued on the back of the head

Unique head piece is printed with tattoos, which are in memory of Asajj's former master, Ky Narec

Unique torso is printed with Asajj's gray and black body suit and the top of her blue, flowing skirt

Asajj wields a red lightsaber. The curved hilt is unique to her minifigure in LEGO *Star Wars*

DATA FILE
SET: 7957 Dathomir Speeder
YEAR: 2011
PIECES: 3
EQUIPMENT: Twin lightsabers
VARIANTS: 2

Change of clothes
Asajj also appears in the 2008 LEGO set Republic Attack Gunship (set 7676). Her minifigure still carries deadly twin lightsabers, but she is dressed in a different outfit with a unique torso and black cloth skirt.

Count Dooku

CLONE WARS SITH

Count Dooku's Solar Sailer (set 7752)
Count Dooku's Clone Wars minifigure is exclusive to this set, which also features his solar sailer ship and small, one-seater speeder bike (pictured). The solar sailer has a secret cargo bay in which the speeder can be hidden when Count Dooku isn't using it.

Count Dooku is the powerful leader of the Separatists—but he is also a Sith Lord! His Clone Wars minifigure is dressed in dark colors, with a cape and hood, so he can carry out secret missions in shadowy corners of the LEGO *Star Wars* galaxy. Dooku's mysterious minifigure only appears in one set.

Red lightsaber blades are only used by the Sith

Unique face is printed with hooded eyes and wrinkles that are a result of Dooku's dark side training

Hair-raising
Count Dooku's gray, swept-back hair with a widow's peak is also used for the Chancellor Palpatine minifigure, but in a tan color (p.186). (The exact same gray piece is only used for one other minifigure: Madam Hooch in LEGO *Harry Potter*.)

Dooku's unique torso is printed with a brown belt and an ornate cape chain clasp

Dooku's special curved lightsaber hilt also comes with the classic Count Dooku minifigure (p.27)

DATA FILE
SET: 7752 Count Dooku's Solar Sailer
YEAR: 2009
PIECES: 5
EQUIPMENT: Lightsaber, cape, hood
VARIANTS: 1

Hooded villain
As well as his gray hair piece, Count Dooku comes with a brown hood so he can travel and cause trouble in disguise.

Pilot Droid

COUNT DOOKU'S CHAUFFEUR

Count Dooku's personal pilot droid is the only one of his kind in LEGO *Star Wars*, but he is entirely made up of LEGO pieces seen on other minifigures. His body is made from battle droid parts, and his head is seen on skeletons in other LEGO themes, including Fantasy Era. The FA-4 model droid exclusively pilots Count Dooku's Solar Sailer (set 7752).

Count Dooku's Solar Sailer (set 7752)
The pilot droid sits on a sliding seat inside the working cockpit of Count Dooku's *Punworcca 116*-class interstellar sloop. He navigates through a rounded cockpit window.

Rounded head piece has ridges on the other side

Leg head
The pilot droid's head can be found on many other minifigures, but it has never before been used as a head piece—it mostly functions as a leg piece on LEGO skeletons.

This white mechanical torso piece is commonly used on battle droids (pp.22–23)

General Grievous (p.40) has these same white mechanical arms, but his minifigure has four of them!

Some FA-4 pilot droids move around on wheels, but the LEGO FA-4 has white mechanical legs

DATA FILE
SET: 7752 Count Dooku's Solar Sailer
YEAR: 2009
PIECES: 5
EQUIPMENT: None
VARIANTS: 1

MagnaGuard
MECHANICAL MONSTER

The MagnaGuard minifigure is an advanced battle droid designed by General Grievous to pose a threat to any clone troopers or Jedi Knights that cross his path. Dressed to intimidate in a unique Kaleesh warrior headwrap and cape, the MagnaGuard carries an impenetrable electrostaff that is resistant to lightsaber blades.

MagnaGuard Starfighter (set 7673)
Two MagnaGuards appear in this 2008 set. Their specialized starfighter has deadly flick-fire missiles. The MagnaGuards store their electrostaffs at the back of the ship's wings during flight.

Glowing red photoreceptors

Only the MagnaGuard minifigure carries a powerful LEGO electrostaff

Headwrap is integrated in the MagnaGuard's unique head piece

Torso piece was first seen on the MagnaGuard. Fellow Separatist droid A4-D (p.174) adopted it in 2010

Mechanical arm is in two parts

This large red round plate piece is a second photoreceptor

The super battle droid (p.37) and TX-20 (p.196) have the same mechanical legs

DATA FILE

SET: 7752 Count Dooku's Solar Sailer
YEAR: 2009
PIECES: 9
EQUIPMENT: Cape, electrostaff
VARIANTS: 1

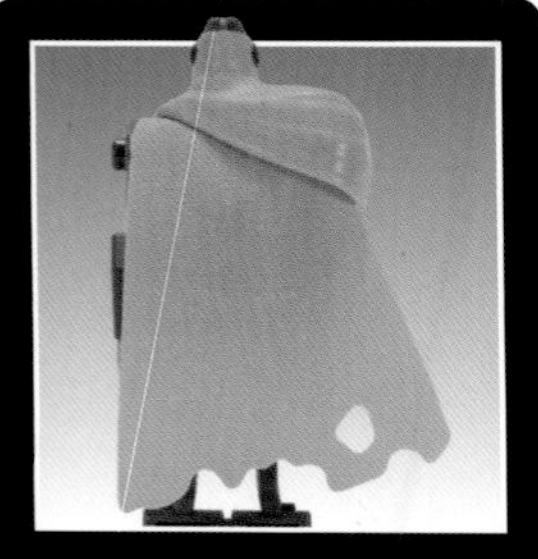

Cruel cape
The MagnaDroid is the only LEGO minifigure to feature this tan cloth cape with a tattered edge.

Plo Koon is a Kel Dor from the planet Dorin. He is a Jedi Master during the Clone Wars and a highly skilled pilot. His minifigure has a unique torso showing his Jedi robes and a unique head piece that displays both his Kel Dor origins and the antiox mask he wears so he can breathe when not on Dorin.

Republic Attack Gunship (set 7676)

In this 2008 set, the Republic's clone army has boarded a huge gunship to take on the Separatists in the harshest battlefields. Plo Koon rides a small speeder bike that can be deployed from the back of the heavily armored gunship.

Plo Koon
JEDI PILOT

Blade change

Plo Koon made his debut in 2008 in the Republic Gunship (set 7676). The set's box artwork originally showed Plo Koon with a green lightsaber, but this was changed to blue before its final release.

Dark orange and dark bluish-gray rubber head-mold

Plo Koon wears a fanged antiox breathing mask and he is rarely seen without his protective goggles

Blue-bladed lightsaber with silver hilt

Dark brown Jedi robe with white undershirt. The robe printing continues on the back of the torso

DATA FILE

SET: 8093 Plo Koon's Jedi Starfighter

YEAR: 2010

PIECES: 3

EQUIPMENT: Lightsaber

VARIANTS: 1

R7-F5

BROWN ASTROMECH DROID

Astromech droid R7-F5 co-pilots Plo Koon's Jedi Starfighter (set 8093) during the Clone Wars. The leg design of this exclusive LEGO minifigure means he can rotate to provide extra navigation assistance to Plo Koon during battle. He is the only brown astromech droid minifigure.

Plo Koon's Jedi Starfighter (set 8093)
R7-F5 sits in front of Plo Koon on his starfighter. They are part of a task force on a mission to find a Separatist superweapon. He keeps an eye on Plo's lightsaber in its holder on the side of the ship.

DATA FILE
SET: 8093 Plo Koon's Jedi Starfighter
YEAR: 2010
PIECES: 4
EQUIPMENT: None
VARIANTS: 1

One of a kind
R7-F5 is known as R7-D4 in the *Clone Wars* series, but when he appeared in the LEGO *Star Wars* galaxy in 2010, he had been re-named. There are several conflicting sources regarding this character's name.

Photoreceptor searches for Grievous's ship

Function indicators monitor the starfighter's in-flight performance

Reddish-brown cylindrical body piece. The design on it shows his arm compartments and system ventilation

White legs are fixed to R7-F5's body with LEGO Technic pins

Recharge power coupling

General Grievous
CLONE WARS CYBORG

General Grievous's cyborg minifigure has been updated for a 2010 LEGO Clone Wars appearance. His four-armed minifigure is now built entirely from exclusive pieces! Grievous is still a vicious villain with an untempered hatred of the Jedi and a ghastly lightsaber collection, but his menacing minifigure is now one-of-a-kind.

General Grievous's Starfighter (set 8095)
The Clone Wars General Grievous minifigure is exclusive to this set. His luxurious starfighter includes a medical room, lightsaber rack, an opening cockpit with controls, and hidden missiles.

Grievous's rotting red and yellow eyes are printed on his head piece. The classic Grievous minifigure has no face printing (p.40)

Grievous's four arms have hinged joints so they can be positioned in many ways

Grievous collects the lightsabers of his Jedi victims

Not a droid
Grievous hates being called a droid. He is a cyborg: part flesh, part metal. Grievous's classic minifigure (p.40) is built from some droid parts, but his Clone Wars minifigure is completely unique—something Grievous would probably approve of.

DATA FILE
SET: 8095 General Grievous' Starfighter
YEAR: 2010
PIECES: 8
EQUIPMENT: Four lightsabers, blaster
VARIANTS: 1

Dark bluish-gray and tan colors are new to this Grievous minifigure

Commander Cody

OBI-WAN'S CLONE COMMANDER

Clone Commander Cody leads a battalion of clone troopers and reports to Jedi General Obi-Wan Kenobi. His minifigure wears clone trooper armor that has been modified to reflect Cody's unit and his rank as commander. He has appeared in two LEGO sets since 2008, in which he fights bravely during the Clone Wars.

Geonosian Starfighter (set 7959)
Commander Cody fights alongside Ki-Adi-Mundi in this 2011 LEGO set. They face a Geonosian starfighter, flown by a Geonosian pilot, which is fitted with a rotating cannon and opening cockpit.

DATA FILE

SET: 7959 Geonosian Starfighter
YEAR: 2011
PIECES: 7
EQUIPMENT: Twin blaster pistols, visor shield, pauldron, kama
VARIANTS: 1

Visor shield only worn by LEGO *Star Wars* clone commanders

Unique helmet with orange commander markings

Orange markings denote Cody's affiliation with the 212th Attack Battalion

Cody wears the same basic armor as his fellow clone troopers, but his torso has orange arms and extra orange markings

Cody has been trained as an ARC trooper, so he is familiar with a variety of weapons

Armor additions
Cody's minifigure comes with a gray pauldron that fits round his neck and a kama leg armor that clips under his torso. These extra pieces of armor designate Cody's rank as commander.

Commander Fox makes only one appearance in the LEGO *Star Wars* galaxy in Separatist Spider Droid (set 7681) in 2008. He is well armed and armored for this battle against the huge, spindly Separatist spider droid. His minifigure has a unique red-patterned torso and helmet.

Commander Fox
CLONE TROOPER COMMANDER

Rangefinder feeds into a computer screen in Fox's visor

Separatist Spider Droid (set 7681)
The spider droid looks intimidating, but with such long legs, it isn't always stable, so Fox has a chance of winning this mighty battle.

Distinctive helmet with dark red markings instantly identifies Fox

Blaster pistol

Extra protection
Commander Fox also comes with full shoulder protective armor. His torso has detailed printing on the back.

The red ranking stripes and decoration on Fox's unique torso and helmet represent his deployment on Coruscant

Dark bluish-gray anti-blast kama leg armor

DATA FILE
SET: 7681 Separatist Spider Droid
PIECES: 7
EQUIPMENT: Two blaster pistols, pauldron, kama
VARIANTS: 1

Luminara Unduli
CLONE WARS JEDI MASTER

Luminara Unduli is a skilled and disciplined Jedi Master. This Clone Wars version of her minifigure has a double-sided head and wears more detailed Jedi robes than her classic minifigure (p.48). Clone Wars Luminara comes in just one set wearing all unique pieces apart from her headdress.

Battle for Geonosis (set 7869)
In this set, Luminara arrives on her BARC speeder to face a Separatist proton canon. There is nowhere for Luminara to store her lightsaber in the speeder, but she is very resourceful.

Non light-up lightsaber

Luminara's head piece is unique to this minifigure. It is more detailed than her 2005 classic version

No cape
This Clone Wars version of Luminara's minifigure appears without her cape. The headdress piece on this minifigure is the same as on the classic version of this dedicated Jedi Master.

Highly detailed torso with unique printing of Luminara's Jedi robes with colorful Mirialan symbol

Ornate Mirialan sash

Goggles on
The other side of Luminara's head piece shows her wearing goggles to keep out sand during sandstorms.

DATA FILE
SET: 7869 Battle for Geonosis
YEAR: 2011
PIECES: 4
EQUIPMENT: Lightsaber
VARIANTS: 1

Captain Rex
CLONE TROOPER CAPTAIN

Captain Rex is a clone captain who serves under General Anakin Skywalker in the Battle for Geonosis (set 7869). He is featured in two LEGO sets, also appearing in 2008's AT-TE Walker (set 7675). He is not a typical clone underneath his helmet, as he has a unique LEGO head piece. Rex is heavily armored and carries two blasters making him particularly bold in battle.

Rangefinder assists navigation

Unique clone
Although he is a clone, Rex has his own unique head piece. His face has a 5 o'clock shadow pattern printed on it.

As well as this helmet with blue battle honors, Rex also has a clone trooper visor

Dark bluish-gray pauldron armor to protect the clone trooper's shoulders during intense combat

Rangefinder
Captain Rex's minifigure is almost exactly the same in the two sets he comes in. The only difference is that he wears a dark bluish-gray rangefinder on his helmet in the 2011 set Battle for Geonosis (set 7869).

Bluish-gray blaster pistols

Rex wears an anti-blast kama around his waist that protects most of his legs from close-range blasts

DATA FILE
SET: 7869 Battle for Geonosis
YEAR: 2011
PIECES: 7
EQUIPMENT: Two blaster pistols, pauldron, kama
VARIANTS: 1

Onaconda Farr
RODIAN SENATOR

Separatist Shuttle (set 8036)
Onaconda Farr is exclusive to this LEGO set. He greets a Separatist shuttle that has landed on Rodia. Nute Gunray, two battle droids, and a pilot battle droid are on board. They want Onaconda to pledge his support to the Separatists and betray Padmé.

Onaconda Farr is a Senator from the planet Rodia. He is loyal to the Republic and a dear and trusted friend of Senator Padmé Amidala. His minifigure has green Rodian skin, unique blue face markings, and is dressed in his official senatorial robes. Onaconda appears in just one Clone Wars set, where he must choose whether to oppose the Separatists or betray an old friend.

Sensory organs give Rodians exceptional powers of hearing and smell

Rodians have large, glassy eyes that sometimes sparkle

Rodians
Onaconda's head-mold was created initially for bounty hunter Greedo's 2003 minifigure (p.78). The same mold was used again for the slave W. Wald in 2011 (p.14). All three Rodian head pieces have different colors and printing.

Onaconda's unique torso is printed with his senatorial outfit

Onaconda is the only minifigure in LEGO *Star Wars* to have dark purple arm pieces

Onaconda's sand-green senatorial pants are made from expensive fabric available only on Rodia

DATA FILE
SET: 8036 Separatist Shuttle
YEAR: 2009
PIECES: 3
EQUIPMENT: None
VARIANTS: 1

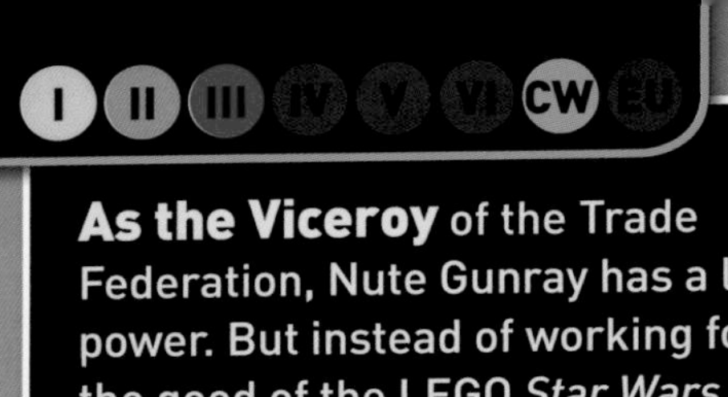

Nute Gunray

TRADE FEDERATION VICEROY

As the Viceroy of the Trade Federation, Nute Gunray has a lot of power. But instead of working for the good of the LEGO *Star Wars* galaxy, this Neimoidian minifigure is motivated by greed. Nute's well-dressed but miserable minifigure is the only Neimoidian to have been created in LEGO bricks. He appears in just one set.

Elaborate Neimoidian headdress

Nute's head piece is printed with his mottled, gray Neimoidian skin—and his perpetual frown

Iron deposits build up in Neimoidians, turning their eyes orange

Nute's elaborate official robes are printed on his unique torso

Metal badge in the shape of the official Trade Federation insignia

Gray, scaly Neimoidian hands

Nute's Viceroy robes are bright in color so he gets more attention than lesser officials

Separatist Shuttle (set 8036)
Nute is a cowardly minifigure. On a mission to meet Senator Onaconda Farr in this set, Nute travels with two battle droid guards, and hides in a secret chamber on board the shuttle.

DATA FILE

SET: 8036 Separatist Shuttle
YEAR: 2009
PIECES: 4
EQUIPMENT: None
VARIANTS: 1

Nahdar Vebb

MON CALAMARI JEDI

Nahdar Vebb is a Mon Calamari Jedi Knight who trained under Jedi Master Kit Fisto. His minifigure only appears in one LEGO set, where he attacks General Grievous on his starfighter. Nahdar is sometimes impatient, but he is always passionate about protecting the LEGO *Star Wars* galaxy.

Jedi robes
The Jedi robes and belt that are printed on Nahdar's unique torso continue on the reverse, too.

Bulging yellow eyes on either side of head have a wide field of vision

Mon Calamari can breathe underwater for up to 30 hours

Mon Calamari
Nahdar's squid-like head is not unique: The solid plastic Mon Calamari head-mold is also used for the Admiral Ackbar (p.130) and Mon Calamari officer (p.133) minifigures.

Nahdar wears Jedi robes in the traditional style, which include a tan tunic, white undershirt, and brown belt

Although young, Nahdar is skilled with a lightsaber. He can defeat four MagnaGuards on his own!

DATA FILE
SET: 8095 General Grievous' Starfighter
YEAR: 2010
PIECES: 3
EQUIPMENT: Lightsaber
VARIANTS: 1

A4-D
SADISTIC ROBOT DOCTOR

A4-D is a sadistic medical droid and General Grievous's personal doctor in just one LEGO set. His minifigure is built out of standard droid parts, but with many medical modifications! Extra arms on A4-D's torso hold all manner of equipment, which he is more than happy to use—no matter how much pain he causes!

General Grievous' Starfighter (set 8095)
A4-D ensures that General Grievous's cyborg body is well maintained in this LEGO set. The medical room has a swiveling chair and a rack for Grievous's large lightsaber collection.

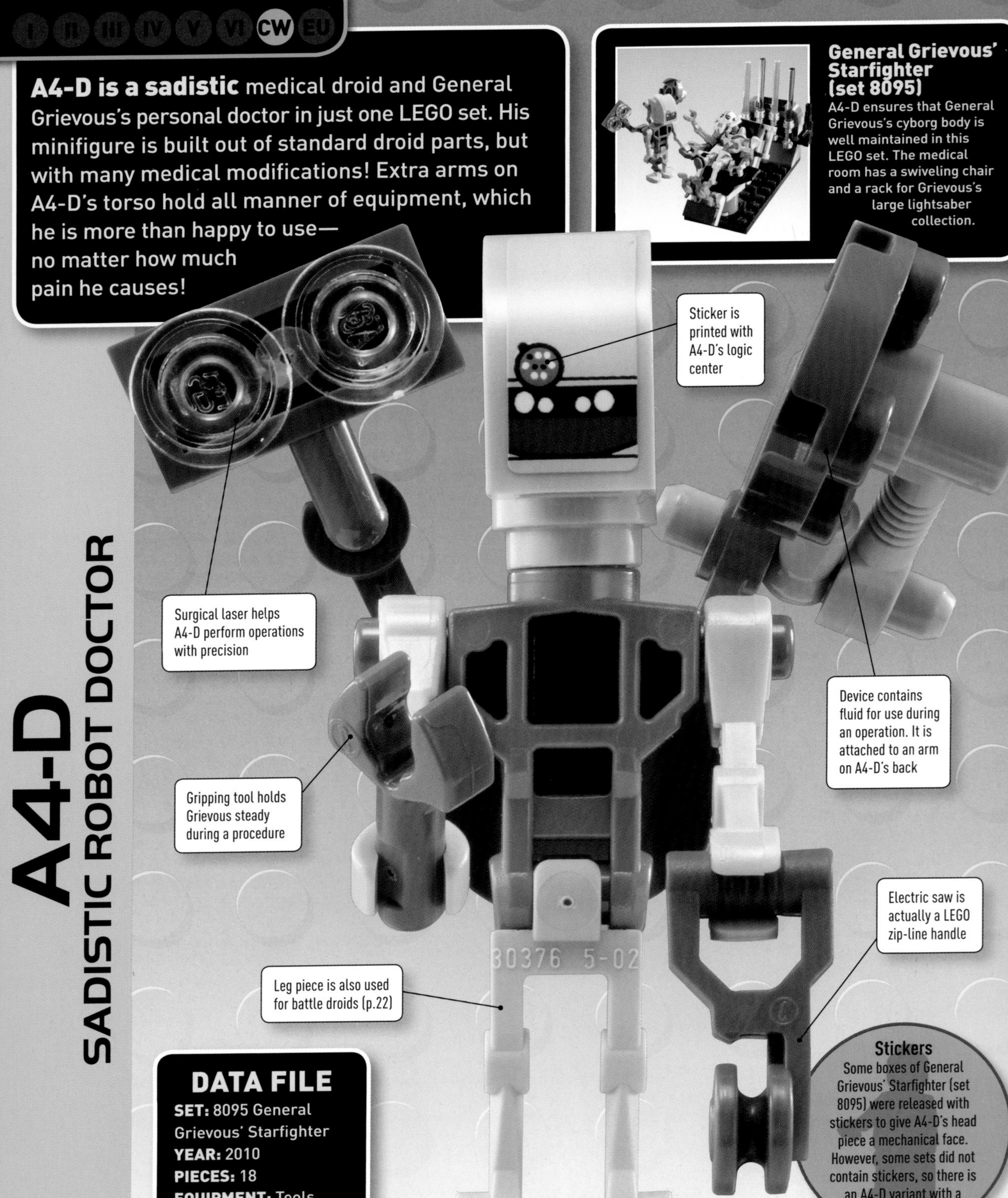

Sticker is printed with A4-D's logic center
Surgical laser helps A4-D perform operations with precision
Device contains fluid for use during an operation. It is attached to an arm on A4-D's back
Gripping tool holds Grievous steady during a procedure
Electric saw is actually a LEGO zip-line handle
Leg piece is also used for battle droids (p.22)
30376 5-02

Stickers
Some boxes of General Grievous' Starfighter (set 8095) were released with stickers to give A4-D's head piece a mechanical face. However, some sets did not contain stickers, so there is an A4-D variant with a plain head.

DATA FILE
SET: 8095 General Grievous' Starfighter
YEAR: 2010
PIECES: 18
EQUIPMENT: Tools
VARIANTS: 2

Hondo Ohnaka
WEEQUAY PIRATE

Hondo Ohnaka is the fearsome leader of a gang of Weequay pirates. His minifigure wears mismatched clothes, a black bandana, and green-eyed goggles—items he has scavenged on his many journeys. Hondo only appears in one LEGO set, but he and his pilfering gang are always plotting new ways to make a quick buck.

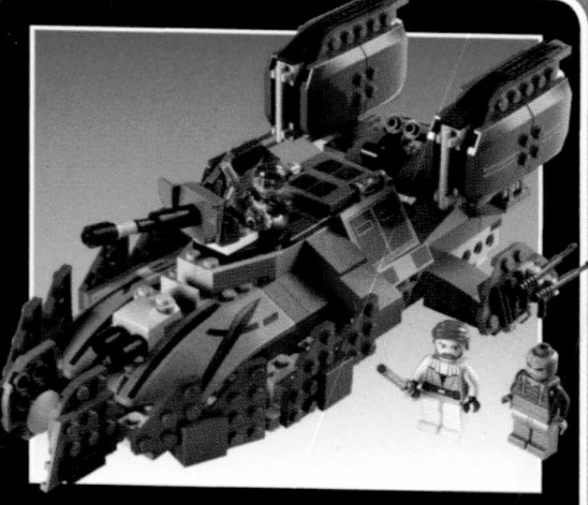

Pirate Tank (set 7753)
Hondo is the gunner on board the pirate tank in this set. The tank is equipped with flick-fire missiles and a huge blaster cannon. Hondo and his gang of pirates are on a mission to kidnap Obi-Wan—the Jedi Master will fetch a good ransom!

Black bandana is also worn by the Weequay bounty hunter Shahan Alama (p.183)

Hondo's unique head is printed with goggles and Weequay skin

Shoulder epaulets show all the other pirates who's in charge

Epaulet
The LEGO epaulet shoulder piece is worn by several minifigures across other LEGO themes, including pirates and soldiers. In LEGO *Star Wars*, however, only two minifigures wear epaulets, Hondo and Embo (p.193).

Torso is printed with an elaborate jacket, which Hondo wears over a ragged white shirt. Hondo thinks the jacket gives him a sense of grandeur

Only two other LEGO *Star Wars* minifigures have dark red arm pieces: Commander Fox (p.168) and Chancellor Palpatine (p.186)

DATA FILE
SET: 7753 Pirate Tank
YEAR: 2009
PIECES: 5
EQUIPMENT: Spear gun
VARIANTS: 1

Turk Falso
DANGEROUS PIRATE

Turk Falso is a tough Weequay criminal. His minifigure is second-in-command in Hondo Ohnaka's pirate gang, and he wears clothes suitable for a pirate's life of planet hopping and petty thieving. Turk searches for Jedi minifigures to hold for ransom, but he's also out to double-cross his fellow pirates. Luckily for everyone, this rotten pirate only appears in one set.

Pirate ponytail
Turk's black ponytail is printed on the back of his head—and continues down the back of his torso.

DATA FILE
SET: 7753 Pirate Tank
YEAR: 2009
PIECES: 3
EQUIPMENT: Cutlass, twin pistols
VARIANTS: 1

Unique head piece is printed with Turk's leathery Weequay face

Turk's headband wraps all the way round the head piece and ties up at the back

Turk is the only minifigure in the LEGO *Star Wars* theme with dark green arms

Unique torso is printed on both sides with Turk's tattered clothing and weapon harness

Turk carries a pair of ancient pistols. The same LEGO pistols are used for the 2007 destroyer droid (p.36)

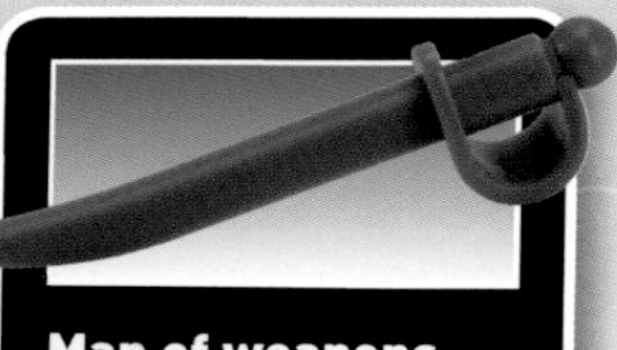

Man of weapons
Turk wields many weapons in his crime-filled life. He uses this dark bluish-gray cutlass to threaten Jedi hostages.

Aayla Secura
BLUE-SKINNED JEDI

Aayla Secura is a Twi'lek Jedi Knight. Her blue-skinned minifigure wears a brown Jedi costume and wields a blue lightsaber. Aayla only appears in one LEGO set, Clone Turbo Tank (set 8098), where she, Anakin, and Ahsoka lead their clone troopers against the ruthless bounty hunter Cad Bane.

Aayla prefers using her lightsaber for defense rather than attack
Unique head top clips onto Aayla's standard LEGO head to attach her brown helmet and blue Twi'lek tentacles
Twi'lek skin can be almost any color, but Aayla's blue skin tone is distinctive even among Twi'leks
Aayla's unique torso is printed with her Jedi costume: a cropped brown top with just one sleeve
Standard LEGO lightsaber hilt

Reverse Twi'lek
Aayla's tentacles hang down behind her minifigure's back. The back of her torso is printed with her Jedi clothes.

DATA FILE
SET: 8098 Clone Turbo Tank
YEAR: 2009
PIECES: 4
EQUIPMENT: Lightsaber
VARIANTS: 1

Anakin Skywalker

COLD WEATHER JEDI

Anakin Skywalker is seen in his snow gear in Freeco Speeder (set 8085). His fur-trimmed outfit equips him for icy planets like Orto Plutonia. His parka is similar to Han Solo's snow gear (p.92) but Anakin's is printed with Jedi insignia. This Anakin minifigure also has a reversible head.

Freeco Speeder (set 8085)
Anakin is on board his speeder, looking for a Separatist base. The cockpit is an awkward squeeze, but Anakin's piloting skills are second to none and he adapts to any situation in true Jedi fashion.

Anakin's face has heavy eyebrows, big blue eyes, and a burn scar caused by Asajj Ventress

Anakin's trademark blue lightsaber with chrome hilt

Anakin's removeable parka hood proudly displays his Jedi insignia

Face protection
The other side of Anakin's dual-sided head piece features goggles and a gray bandana to keep the cold out.

Unique torso piece with blue parka and brown utility belt

Light bluish-gray waterproof pants for snowy conditions

DATA FILE

SET: 8085 Freeco Speeder
YEAR: 2010
PIECES: 4
EQUIPMENT: Lightsaber
VARIANTS: 1

Thi-Sen
TALZ CHIEFTAIN

Thi-Sen is the chieftain of the secretive Talz tribe which lives on the ice planet Orto Plutonia. This unique minifigure has an elaborate dark bluish-gray extended head piece. He wears a distinctive armored shell and carries a spear for protection so that he can defend his tribe from any unfriendly visitors.

One piece
The detailing on Thi-Sen's sandwich-board head piece extends down the back of his torso to show his narglatch cape. The headdress is integrated into this piece, too.

Thi-Sen's fan-shaped tailbone headdress marks him out as the chieftain

Talz have four eyes; one set for day and a bigger set for night vision

Thi-Sen eats and communicates through this small, tube-like snout

A single LEGO piece combines Thi-Sen's head, narglatch tailbone headdress, cape made from narglatch hide, and fur body

Thi-Sen has a standard light bluish-gray LEGO torso piece beneath his extended head piece

Thi-Sen's sandwich-board piece is made from ABS plastic, like most LEGO pieces

Light pearl-colored spear appears in many LEGO sets for various themes, including LEGO Castle

DATA FILE
SET: 8085 Freeco Speeder
YEAR: 2010
PIECES: 3
EQUIPMENT: Spear
VARIANTS: 1

Mace Windu

CLONE WARS JEDI GENERAL

Wise Mace Windu is a Jedi General during the Clone Wars. His minifigure wields the same purple lightsaber as the classic Mace minifigure (p.18), but he now wears a tan Jedi tunic with no cape, and has new printed detail on his head piece. Mace fights for the Republic in three Clone Wars sets.

Republic Attack Shuttle (set 8019)

Mace Windu leads clone troopers into battle aboard this huge Republic attack shuttle. The Jedi General has his own LEGO seat inside the ship, which also has flick-fire missiles and deadly bombs to deploy!

Mace's Clone Wars head piece is printed with a lot of detail, including brown eyes and a determined expression

Mace is one of the top lightsaber duelists in the galaxy

Unique torso printed with tan tunic and white undershirt

Utility belt has a loop that Mace uses to hold his lightsaber

DATA FILE

SET: *7868* Mace Windu's *Jedi* Starfighter
YEAR: 2011
PIECES: 3
EQUIPMENT: Lightsaber
VARIANTS: 1

Cad Bane
FEARSOME BOUNTY HUNTER

Cad Bane is a bounty hunter like no other, so it is fitting that his minifigure is the same. Wearing a unique hat and torso, Cad's blue-skinned minifigure wears a specially designed breathing apparatus and wields the villain's trademark twin blasters. He plots, schemes, and attacks the Jedi in two LEGO sets.

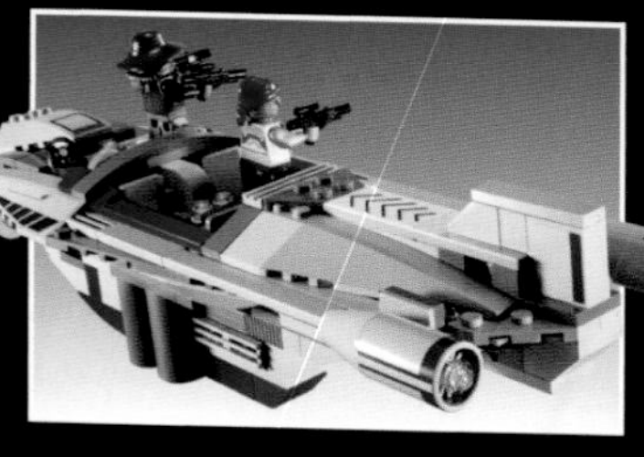

Cad Bane's Speeder (set 8128)
Cad Bane pilots a sleek speeder when he needs to make a quick getaway. The ship can fit six minifigures, including the pirate Shahan Alama (pictured)—and it has a secret compartment for contraband!

With his wide-brimmed hat, Cad thinks of himself as a space cowboy

Cad is a Duros, who all have blue skin and red eyes

Cad is prepared for any situation. He even wears a breathing apparatus just in case!

DATA FILE
SET: 8128 Cad Bane's Speeder
YEAR: 2010
PIECES: 5
EQUIPMENT: Breathing apparatus, twin blasters
VARIANTS: 1

Unique torso is printed with Cad's tattered brown jacket, under which he conceals a utility belt and lots of ammunition

Cad wears rocket boots so he can fly for short distances

Ruthless bounty hunter Aurra Sing will stop at nothing to get her prize. Her fearless minifigure is dressed in an orange jumpsuit laden with weapons, but wears no armor! Aurra appears in just one set and her minifigure is almost completely built out of unique pieces—only her arms and hands can be found on other minifigures.

Bounty Hunter Assault Gunship (set 7930)
Aurra Sing knows exactly what will fetch the highest ransom. In this set, she's managed to get hold of a LEGO Jedi holocron! Aurra's minifigure stores it in a secret chamber aboard the bounty hunter gunship.

Aurra Sing
RELENTLESS BOUNTY HUNTER

Weapons vest
The back of Aurra's unique torso is printed with her brown vest, in which she stores compact weapons and extra ammo.

Long brown hair is tied up, out of the way

Unique hairstyle
Aurra's long, brown LEGO hair piece was specially designed for her 2011 minifigure. It fits into the stud on top of Aurra's otherwise bald head piece and flows neatly down her back.

Unique head piece is printed with Aurra's bright green eyes and confident smile

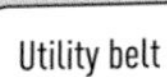

Utility belt

Aurra's orange jumpsuit is functional. It allows her to maneuver easily during combat

Unique leg pieces are printed with holsters for Aurra's twin pistols

DATA FILE

SET: 7930 Bounty Hunter Assault Gunship
YEAR: 2011
PIECES: 4
EQUIPMENT: Twin blaster pistols
VARIANTS: 1

Shahan Alama
PIRATE-TURNED-BOUNTY HUNTER

DATA FILE
SET: 8128 Cad Bane's Speeder
YEAR: 2010
PIECES: 4
EQUIPMENT: Blaster
VARIANTS: 1

Shahan Alama was a pirate—until he was kicked out of the gang for being too nasty! Now he is a bounty hunter who works with Cad Bane. His mismatched clothing and bandana point to his former life as a pirate, but his angry temper and willingness to use a blaster on innocent people suggest a more violent minifigure. Fortunately, Shahan wreaks havoc in just one LEGO set.

Dark red bandana hat piece is unique to Shahan. Hondo Ohnaka wears it in black (p.175)

Weequay skin
There are three Weequay minifigures: Shahan, Hondo Ohnaka (p.175), and Turk Falso (p.176). They all have faces printed with Weequay skin, but the patterns and colors vary between the three LEGO villains.

Shahan's unique head piece is printed with a murderous expression and a Weequay skin pattern, which continues on the back

Pearl gold arm was taken from a combat droid to replace Shahan's destroyed right arm

Protective chestplate worn around the neck

Belt was stolen from a Twi'lek nobleman

Shahan has a blaster—and is not afraid to use it!

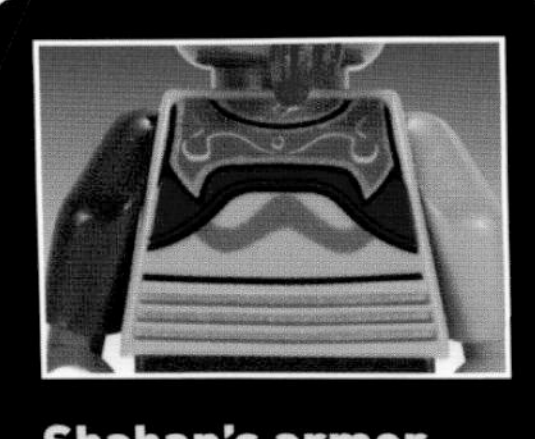

Shahan's armor
Shahan's chestplate is printed on the back of his torso, too. Working together with Cad Bane has its risks!

Senate Commando Captain

PALPATINE'S GUARD

The Senate commando captain leads an elite unit of senate commandos. They are Chancellor Palpatine's personal bodyguards on Coruscant. The captain is an intimidating minifigure in head-to-toe blue and white armor. He appears in just one LEGO set, although his expert commando troops appear in two.

Not a clone
The Senate commando captain's head piece is the same as that used for the clone trooper (p.152) and other clone minifigures, although Senate commandos and their captain are not actually clones.

Senate commando
The Senate commando minifigure (above) is identical to the Senate commando captain, but he has no white markings on his helmet and armor, as well as a wider visor.

White markings indicate the rank of captain

Unique torso has a similar armor design to clone trooper armor, but the blue coloring signifies the captain's elite commando unit

Black hip and blue leg combination is unique to senate commandos in LEGO *Star Wars*

DATA FILE

SET: 8128 Cad Bane's Speeder
YEAR: 2010
PIECES: 4
EQUIPMENT: Blaster rifle
VARIANTS: 1

ARF Trooper
SPECIALIST SCOUT

The Advanced Recon Force (ARF) trooper carries out recon missions and sometimes initiates surprise attacks. His minifigure is made up of the same LEGO pieces as the clone trooper, except for his unique ARF helmet with colored markings, which was designed specially for this minifigure.

Clone Trooper Battle Pack (set 7913)

The ARF trooper is exclusive to this Clone Wars set, where he is joined by a clone commander (p.153) and two bomb squad troopers (p.155). The set also includes a green and white BARC speeder, which is perfect for chasing enemies.

DATA FILE

SET: 7913 Clone Trooper Battle Pack
YEAR: 2011
PIECES: 4
EQUIPMENT: Blaster rifle
VARIANTS: 1

Specialized breathing apparatus adapts to new environments

Long-range comlink

ARF helmet

The ARF trooper's helmet is a unique mold for this minifigure. However, it shares some features with other scout trooper helmets, including the Kashyyyk trooper (p.52) and scout trooper (p.141) minifigures.

Armor is more lightweight than regular clone trooper armor

Rifle sight allows the ARF trooper to scout enemy locations

Energy pack

The back of the ARF trooper's armor is printed with an energy pack that generates air supply and battery power.

Chancellor Palpatine

SITH IN DISGUISE

The red-robed minifigure of Chancellor Palpatine looks stately and impressive in his all-red robes, but he has a dark secret. He is the Sith Lord Darth Sidious in disguise! His minifigure appears in one set, and it is the only time Palpatine is depicted as Chancellor, not as his alter ego, Darth Sidious (p.43).

Venator-Class Republic Attack Cruiser (set 8039)
Chancellor Palpatine's Clone Wars flagship is revealed in this set. The front of the ship opens up to reveal Palpatine's office, including his desk and swivel chair.

Death Star
Palpatine's hologram of the Death Star is actually a transparent red LEGO head piece with gold markings.

Palpatine is the only minifigure to have this hair piece in tan

Unique face is printed with sunken eyes and dark wrinkles. They are a sign that the Chancellor is on a path to the dark side

Palpatine's red Senatorial robes are printed on his unique torso

Dark red pauldron cloth pieces are unique to this minifigure

Palpatine wears bright, bold colors to assert his authority. Red is also a traditional Sith color, so it hints at his affiliation with the dark side!

DATA FILE

SET: 8039 *Venator*-Class Republic Attack Cruiser
YEAR: 2009
PIECES: 6
EQUIPMENT: Two pauldron cloths
VARIANTS: 1

Ki-Adi-Mundi
JEDI TACTICIAN

Ki-Adi-Mundi is a Jedi from the planet Cerea. Highly intelligent, his minifigure is a member of the Jedi Council and a top Jedi General. Ki-Adi-Mundi has a specially designed additional head piece to house his extremely large Cerean brain. His minifigure flies into battle over the planet Geonosis in just one 2011 Clone Wars set.

Ki-Adi-Mundi's large binary brain makes him extremely logical and a skilled tactician. He has a second heart just to support his brain
Unique head piece shows Ki-Adi-Mundi's white mustache and beard, and his pale Cerean eyes
Ki-Adi-Mundi favors a defensive form of lightsaber combat
Unique torso is printed with Ki-Adi-Mundi's Jedi robes. His long vest is styled after ancient Cerean clothing
Utility belt has a clip to hold lightsaber

Cerean head
Ki-Adi-Mundi's Cerean head is topped with a white ponytail. His binary brain piece has creases down the back, which are continued as printed lines on his head piece.

DATA FILE
SET: 7959 Geonosian Starfighter
YEAR: 2011
PIECES: 4
EQUIPMENT: Lightsaber
VARIANTS: 1

Eeth Koth
ZABRAK JEDI MASTER

Jedi Council member Eeth Koth is an Iridonian Zabrak. His minifigure wears traditional Jedi robes and wields a green lightsaber. A specially designed head attachment features Eeth's short Zabrak horns and long, dark hair. He appears in just one LEGO set, aboard a Republic Frigate (set 7964).

DATA FILE
SET: 7964 Republic Frigate
YEAR: 2011
PIECES: 4
EQUIPMENT: Lightsaber
VARIANTS: 1

Horned head and hair piece is made of rubber, not the usual ABS plastic

Unique face printing shows Eeth's simple tattoos

Eeth's hair is tied with traditional Iridonian rope. Two bunches hang over the front of Eeth's torso and a third hangs down the back

Torso is printed with a set of Jedi robes unique to Eeth

Eeth uses his strong connection to the Force to enhance his lightsaber skills

Zabrak horns
There are four Zabrak minifigures and their horned heads are all different. Darth Maul (p.16) and Savage Opress (p.198) share a head attachment but have different printing, Eeth's rubber head piece is unique, and Sugi's horns are printed on her standard LEGO head (p.192).

Quinlan Vos
JEDI TRACKER

Unisex hair piece
Quinlan's hair is unique to his minifigure in LEGO *Star Wars*. However, the same piece is used for female minifigures in other LEGO themes, including LEGO Harry Potter, where it adorns the heads of Hermione Granger and Molly Weasley.

DATA FILE
SET: 7964 Republic Frigate
YEAR: 2011
PIECES: 4
EQUIPMENT: Lightsaber
VARIANTS: 1

Quinlan Vos is an unconventional Jedi. He is an expert Force tracker, able to locate anybody by following their trail—but he has also teetered on the edge of the dark side. His unkempt minifigure has messy hair, a stubbled face, and wears a rusty chestplate over his Jedi tunic. He spends much time undercover, which may be why he appears only in one LEGO set.

Quinlan sometimes uses a lightsaber fighting style that taps into dark side energies

Printed hair braid

Quinlan uses the Force to read the "memories" of inanimate objects

Quinlan paints a yellow stripe across his face to help with camouflage while he is tracking someone

Quinlan's blaster-proof chestplate is part of his Jedi uniform because he finds himself in danger more often than most

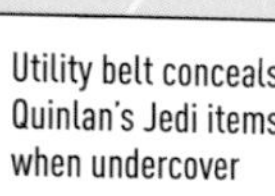

Utility belt conceals Quinlan's Jedi items when undercover

Torso printing
The unique printing on Quinlan's torso continues on the reverse, depicting the back of his tunic and armor.

Clone Commander Wolffe
LEADER OF THE PACK

Commander Wolffe is the tough leader of the elite Wolfpack clone trooper squad. His minifigure wears a helmet and armor printed with unique Wolfpack insignia and rank markings. Wolffe also has a unique face under his helmet, which sets him apart from the other clones in the LEGO *Star Wars* galaxy.

DATA FILE
SET: 7964 Republic Frigate
YEAR: 2011
PIECES: 6
EQUIPMENT: Twin blaster pistols
VARIANTS: 1

Rangefinder is connected to a display screen in Wolffe's visor

Red and yellow markings designate Wolffe as the unit commander

Stylized wolf design shows squad affiliation

Wolfpack armor is the same as regular clone trooper armor (p.152), but with sand-blue markings and sleeves

DC-17 hand blaster

Kama protects lower body from flying shrapnel

Wolffe's legs are sand-blue with white markings painted on top

Battle-scarred
Commander Wolffe has a face with unique scar and stubble printing. He lost his eye in a duel with Asajj Ventress (p160).

Wolffe's armor
Commander Wolffe's clone armor torso is identical to his squad member, the Wolfpack clone trooper (opposite).

Wolfpack Clone Trooper

READY FOR ACTION

The Wolfpack clone trooper is a battle-ready member of Commander Wolffe's fierce Wolfpack squadron. Although his armor-clad minifigure has the same torso and leg pieces as his commander, he has his own unique helmet and is equipped with a jetpack. He appears in one LEGO set, alongside his squad commander.

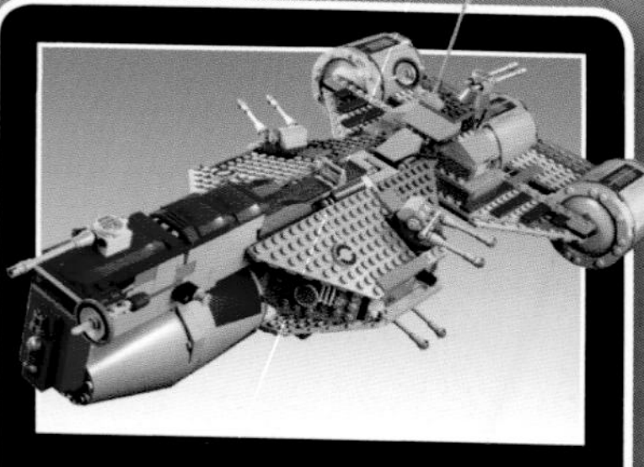

Republic Frigate (set 7964)
The Wolfpack trooper joins Eeth Koth, Quinlan Vos, and Yoda on board the Republic frigate. The frigate has four missile launchers on each side, and rotating front and rear cannons.

Wolf imagery shows squad affiliation

Unique helmet printing is similar to Commander Wolffe's (opposite), but is not identical

White jetpack fits around neck

The Wolfpack trooper wields the standard-issue clone trooper blaster

Under the Wolfpack trooper's helmet is a LEGO head piece printed with the standard clone trooper face (p.152)

Black combat gloves

Legs are unique to Wolfpack members

DATA FILE
SET: 7964 Republic Frigate
YEAR: 2011
PIECES: 5
EQUIPMENT: Jetpack, blaster
VARIANTS: 1

Sugi

HONORABLE BOUNTY HUNTER

Bounty hunter Sugi is honest but deadly. Whether she is sent to capture a Jedi Knight or protect a family of poor farmers, she will not give up until the mission is complete. Sugi's minifigure wears functional clothes that help her get the job done. She doesn't need anything else—apart from her weapons! Sugi carries out many missions, but she only appears in one set.

DATA FILE

SET: 7930 Bounty Hunter Assault Gunship
YEAR: 2011
PIECES: 3
EQUIPMENT: Blaster, vibroblade
VARIANTS: 1

Sugi is an Iridonian Zabrak. Her head piece has small printed horns and precise face tattoos

The back of Sugi's unique head piece is printed with two more horns and Sugi's purple hair. Her hair is pulled into a neat top knot, so it doesn't get in her minifigure's way during a mission

Sugi's unique torso is printed with her simple red vest and metal necklace—her most treasured possession

Vibroblade vibrates to make it more efficient than a regular blade

Sugi's weapon of choice is an EE-3 carbine rifle

Plain gray pants give Sugi ease of movement in combat

Embo
KYUZO BOUNTY HUNTER

Embo is a Kyuzo bounty hunter with sand-green, scaly skin and yellow eyes. He is part of Sugi's team of bounty hunters on board the Bounty Hunter Assault Gunship (set 7930). His minifigure carries a bowcaster and is made up of many unique pieces, including finely detailed hat, head, torso, and leg pieces.

Multifunctional
Embo's multi-purpose hat with traditional Kyuzo markings is a 3x3 inverted radar LEGO piece. The same piece (in black, without special printing) is also used for the Imperial probe droid (p.97).

Embo's metal hat can also be thrown as a weapon or used as a shield

Straps and armor
The back of Embo's torso contains more printed detail, which continues the pattern of his armor and ammo belt.

Epaulets piece is also worn by Hondo Ohnaka (p.175)

Embo wears a bronze breathing mask to filter moisture out of the air

Modified bowcaster

Unique torso is printed with Embo's sturdy armor and his ammunition strap

Utility belt printed on hip piece

Unique leg piece is printed with Embo's Kyuzo-patterned wrap

DATA FILE
SET: 7930 Bounty Hunter Assault Gunship
YEAR: 2011
PIECES: 5
EQUIPMENT: Bowcaster
VARIANTS: 1

Shaak Ti
JEDI GENERAL

Jedi Shaak Ti is a powerful Clone Wars general. She also trains new clone cadets. Shaak is renowned for her skill and intellect, even though she only appears in one LEGO set. Her minifigure has red Togruta skin and a unique detachable piece with blue and white head-tails that clips onto her head.

DATA FILE
SET: 7931 T-6 Jedi Shuttle
YEAR: 2011
PIECES: 5
EQUIPMENT: Lightsaber, cape
VARIANTS: 1

Hollow horns on top of Shaak's head are called montrals

Unique red head piece printed with white Togruta markings

Shaak Ti only fights with her lightsaber when all other options have been exhausted

Shaak Ti wears a traditional Togruta akul-tooth headdress

Unique torso printed with Shaak's brown Jedi robes and belt

The only other LEGO *Star Wars* minifigure with red hands is the Royal Guard (p.127)

Head-tails
This unique piece was specially made for Shaak Ti. She has two head-tails at the front and one at the back. Shaak is an adult so her head-tails are fully-grown, unlike Ahsoka's (p.150).

Saesee Tiin

JEDI WARRIOR

Telepathic Jedi Saesee Tiin is a celebrated pilot in the Republic fleet. He is from the planet Iktotch and his minifigure has a unique piece with down-turned horns that fits onto his head piece. Saesee is an integral member of the Jedi Council, as well as a brave soldier. He wears his Jedi robes and wields his lightsaber with pride.

Saesee's skin is very tough—able to withstand the strong winds of his home planet
Saesee's serious face can make him look quite intimidating sometimes!
Unique torso is printed with brown Jedi robes and a utility belt
Saesee's telepathic skills help during a lightsaber duel

T-6 Jedi Shuttle (set 7931)
Saesee Tiin is exclusive to this LEGO set. He and three other Jedi travel to a distant battlefield on the Jedi shuttle. The shuttle is armed with flick missiles, and the cockpit can become an escape pod—should trouble arise.

Iktotchi skin
Saesee Tiin's telepathic powers have transformed the skin on his head, resulting in symmetrical markings.

DATA FILE
SET: 7931 T-6 Jedi Shuttle
YEAR: 2011
PIECES: 4
EQUIPMENT: Lightsaber
VARIANTS: 1

CW EU

TX-20
TACTICAL DROID

Tactical Droid TX-20 is a strategic planner and supervisor of Separatist troops stationed in Ryloth City. His unique minifigure made his debut in the 2011 LEGO Clone Wars set Mace Windu's Jedi Starfighter (set 7876). He has an unusual combined head-and-torso piece that is exclusive to his minifigure.

DATA FILE

SET: 7868 Mace Windu's Jedi Starfighter
YEAR: 2011
PIECES: 4
EQUIPMENT: None
VARIANTS: 1

The TX-20 is much more intelligent than his battle droid counterpart

Unique Separatist symbol

Processing unit buried inside heavily armored torso to protect it when under fire from enemy forces

Dark blue mechanical arm exclusive to TX-20

Legs are also seen on the super battle droid (p.37) and MagnaGuard (p.163) minifigures

Mace Windu's Jedi Starfighter (set 7868)
The tactical droid zips around on his Separatist Flitknot speeder. He has a seat that allows him to comfortably perch and then jump out when he needs to.

R8-B7
METALLIC ASTROMECH

R8-B7 is Mace Windu's personal astromech droid and co-pilot during the Clone Wars. He has only appeared in one LEGO set: Mace Windu's Jedi Starfighter (set 7868) from 2011. The metallic gold printing on his cylindrical body and dome-shaped head makes R8-B7 a very special, unique astromech minifigure.

Mace Windu's Jedi Starfighter (set 7868)
R8-B7 sits inside the open cockpit with pilot Mace Windu, who has a canopy to cover his seat. R8-B7 navigates and is also on hand to repair the starfighter when it is damaged during battle.

DATA FILE
SET: 7868 Mace Windu's Jedi Starfighter
YEAR: 2011
PIECES: 4
EQUIPMENT: None
VARIANTS: 1

Good fit
R8-B7 is held in the cockpit of Mace Windu's Jedi starfighter with studs so he does not fall out during particularly dramatic battles. He can deploy flick-fire missiles from beneath the vehicle.

Unique metallic gold printing

Purple sensor for enhanced navigation

Acoustic signaler positioned above the system ventilation unit

Like all LEGO astromech droids, R8-B7's legs are secured with Technic pins

Recharge power coupling

Savage Opress
DARK APPRENTICE

Savage Opress is on a secret mission. Hired by Asajj Ventress to destroy Count Dooku, his minifigure poses as Dooku's new apprentice. Savage appears in just one LEGO set, where his horned, Dathomirian minifigure must decide who to attack: the Jedi Anakin Skywalker, or his two despised Sith masters?

Dathomir Speeder (set 7957)
Asajj Ventress, a Nightsister from Savage's home planet of Dathomir, pilots a Nightspeeder with Savage in this set.

LEGO spear piece with ax head attached

Enchanted blade is a weapon from a clan of witches called the Nightsisters

Savage's Zabrak head piece is the same mold as Darth Maul's horned head piece (p.16), but with yellow markings in a different pattern

Yellow Nightbrother tattoos

Savage's fellow Dathomirian, Darth Maul, is the only other minifigure to wield a double-bladed lightsaber

Unique armor piece fits over the minifigure's neck. The Dathomirian armor protects Savage's torso and shoulders

DATA FILE
SET: 7957 Dathomir Speeder
YEAR: 2011
PIECES: 5
EQUIPMENT: Double-bladed lightsaber, enchanted blade
VARIANTS: 1

Mandalorian
ARMORED WARRIOR

The Mandalorian is a deadly soldier from the planet Mandalore. He owns many weapons, but his distinctive blue and gray armor is his most treasured possession. Appearing in only one LEGO set, the Mandalorian's minifigure joins forces with the Separatists—even though his sturdy armor was the inspiration for clone trooper armor!

Mandalorian Battle Pack (set 7914)
Four armored Mandalorian minifigures attack the clone army in this LEGO set. They are equipped with a speeder and a variety of weapons, including a blaster turret, long-range rifle, and blasters.

DATA FILE
SET: 7914 Mandalorian Battle Pack
YEAR: 2011
PIECES: 5
EQUIPMENT: Jetpack, twin blaster pistols
VARIANTS: 1

Under the helmet
Beneath the Mandalorian's helmet is a unique LEGO head piece printed with blue eyes and pale features.

Helmet has similar markings to Jango Fett's helmet (p.30)

Jetpack fits around minifigure's neck

Mandalorians are trained to use a variety of weapons

Mandalorian armor is famous in the LEGO *Star Wars* galaxy. It is made from an almost indestructible metal, called beskar

Jetpack
The Mandalorian's armor is fitted with a jetpack. Jango Fett also wears a jetpack, but it is attached to his helmet (p.30).

V-Wing Pilot
IMPERIAL ACE

The Imperial V-wing pilot flies the high-speed starship during the Clone Wars, and his minifigure features elements from clone and Imperial trooper armor. He is built from the exact same pieces as the clone pilot (p.44), but with black Imperial coloring. His V-wing uniform is very similar to the TIE pilot's (p.88).

Imperial V-Wing Starfighter (set 7915)
The V-wing pilot takes control of this starfighter and begins to fight for the growing Empire. His minifigure is exclusive to this set. The vertical-opening cockpit has no controls, but that won't stop him!

Imperial symbols

Breathing apparatus in helmet is connected to the air supply by two tubes

Self-contained armor has a life support pack that enables breathing in space

Utility belt is attached to the parachute on the pilot's back

Flight mask
The V-wing pilot wears the same flight mask head piece as the clone pilot—but in black. Printed silver goggles cover his eyes.

Emergency!
A parachute and oxygen tank are printed on the back of the V-wing pilot's torso, so he is prepared for any emergency.

DATA FILE
SET: 7915 Imperial V-Wing Starfighter
YEAR: 2011
PIECES: 4
EQUIPMENT: Blaster
VARIANTS: 1

R2-Q2
IMPERIAL ASTROMECH

Imperial droid R2-Q2 helps the V-wing pilot navigate his starship. His minifigure is built from standard LEGO astromech droid pieces but they are a unique pearlescent gray color. R2-Q2 contains the data for one the most comprehensive maps of the LEGO *Star Wars* galaxy. The Imperial army wants to keep this valuable droid safe, so he only appears in one set.

Perfect fit
In the *Star Wars* galaxy, V-wing fighters are designed to carry Q7-series droids, but in the LEGO *Star Wars* galaxy, R2-Q2 fits perfectly into the V-wing model, which he helps to navigate and repair.

Imperial V-Wing Starfighter (set 7915)
R2-Q5 plugs into a socket on the V-wing starfighter. The starfighter has rotating wings and an opening cockpit with controls for the pilot.

DATA FILE
SET: 7915 Imperial V-Wing Starfighter
YEAR: 2011
PIECES: 4
EQUIPMENT: None
VARIANTS: 1

Compartment houses a periscope

R2-Q2 acquires all his data through his photoreceptor

R2-Q2 uses his computer interface arm to search the *Tantive IV* for Princess Leia's hidden Death Star plans

R2-Q2 can project a hologram of his galactic map from his holoprojector

Astromech body piece is printed with the same pattern as most LEGO *Star Wars* astromech droids

Pearl light-gray leg pieces are not found in any other LEGO sets

Darth Vader

SITH LORD

Battle-damaged Darth Vader appears in one LEGO set from 2008. Other than his damaged and normal helmets, every part of his minifigure is unique to this version. His torso and face have extensive battle damage printed on them.

Repurposed
Battle-damaged Darth Vader's helmet piece is also used as as a scuba diving mask or underwater visor in other LEGO themes, including Aquasharks and Hydronauts.

Normal helmet
The *Rogue Shadow* set includes Darth Vader's normal helmet as well as the battle-damaged version.

Head piece shows Vader's badly damaged face

Helmet was damaged during a fight with Galen Marek and Juno Eclipse

Darth Vader's metal suit has been ripped and broken in battle

Following a difficult battle, wires hang out of Darth Vader's torso

Red lightsaber with light bluish-gray hilt

This is the only *Star Wars* minifigure with one black leg and one white leg

DATA FILE
SET: 7672 *Rogue Shadow*
YEAR: 2008
PIECES: 4
EQUIPMENT: Lightsaber
VARIANTS: 1

Galen Marek
STARKILLER

***Rogue Shadow* (set 7672)**
Galen Marek is mysteriously named only as "Vader's Apprentice" on the packaging for this 2008 set.

Galen Marek is Darth Vader's secret apprentice, codename Starkiller. His real name has only been revealed to some and his minifigure is elusive, appearing in just one 2008 set. He cuts an untidy figure with his unique torso that is printed with his battle-damaged training gear.

Standard black LEGO hair piece

Tan head piece with worried expression is also used for the frowning Rebel commando (p.140)

Same lightsaber piece as Darth Vader's from the same set (opposite)

There are blood stains on the front of Galen's ripped shirt and he has different colored arms to represent a sleeve having been torn off in battle with Darth Vader

Standard black legs and hip piece have been used for many LEGO minifigures

All in a name
Galen Marek is named as "Vader's Apprentice" on the LEGO box because the video game *Star Wars: The Force Unleashed* had not yet been released and the LEGO Group didn't want to give too much away!

DATA FILE
SET: 7672 *Rogue Shadow*
YEAR: 2008
PIECES: 4
EQUIPMENT: Lightsaber
VARIANTS: 1

Juno Eclipse
IMPERIAL PILOT

Juno Eclipse is a high-ranking Imperial officer who works closely with Darth Vader and his secret apprentice on board the *Rogue Shadow* (set 7672). Her LEGO minifigure is distinctive, with unique torso and head pieces and interchangeable cap and hair for when she is piloting or on land.

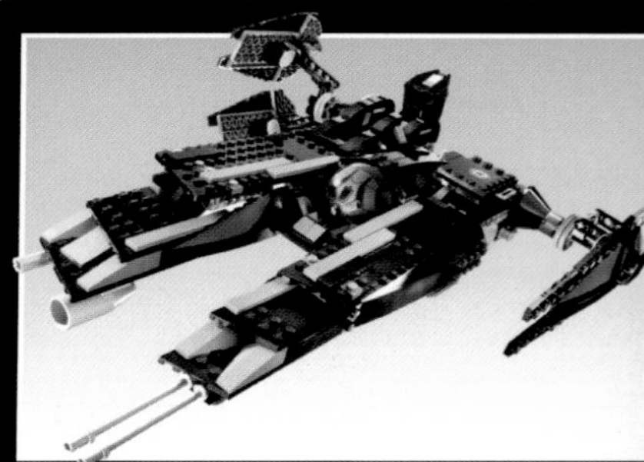

***Rogue Shadow* (set 7672)**
Juno Eclipse is the pilot of *Rogue Shadow*, which transports Darth Vader's apprentice across the LEGO *Star Wars* galaxy. It is a cumbersome ship to pilot, but Juno is a highly decorated pilot in the Imperial Navy and is more than capable.

Tan hair piece has a ponytail at the back

DATA FILE
SET: 7672 *Rogue Shadow*
YEAR: 2008
PIECES: 5
EQUIPMENT: Cap
VARIANTS: 1

Unique LEGO head is printed with peach lips and bangs so they can be seen when she is wearing her black cap

Code cylinders allow high-ranking officers access to high-security areas

Printed feminine curves, a unique red-and-yellow rank insignia, and a new belt design makes Juno's uniform differ from the Death Star guard and Imperial pilot (pp.125–126)

Kepi cap
As well as her ponytail head piece, Juno comes with a standard LEGO kepi cap in this set.

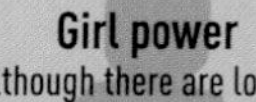

Girl power
Although there are lots of female minifigures in the LEGO *Star Wars* galaxy, Juno Eclipse is the only female Imperial minifigure to make an appearance.

Shadow Trooper

DARK STORMTROOPER

TIE Crawler (set 7664)
This is the first LEGO set to feature the shadow trooper. The 2007 set includes two shadow troopers, but only one can fit in the crawler's cockpit at any time. It is used for ground combat, so the other trooper can use his blaster to supplement the crawler's missiles.

The shadow trooper, also known as a Black Hole trooper, menaces in two LEGO sets. He made his debut in 2007 in the TIE Crawler (set 7664). Never before seen in the *Star Wars* movies, this shady minifigure's black head and torso pieces are not found on any other minifigure, and his mysterious name adds to his dark reputation.

Name game
In Imperial Dropship (set 7667), the shadow trooper is mistakenly named "Imperial Pilot" on the set box. In the *Star Wars* galaxy, shadow troopers have sophisticated stealth armor.

The shadow trooper has a plain black head underneath his black and blue helmet

Breathing apparatus adapts to different atmospheres

Shadow trooper armor is similar to the stormtrooper minifigure's (p.62), except it is black instead of white

Blaster gun for ground combat

DATA FILE
SET: 7667 Imperial Dropship
YEAR: 2008
PIECES: 4
EQUIPMENT: Blaster
VARIANTS: 1

Index of Minifigures

AN ALPHABETICAL LIST OF MINIFIGURES FEATURED IN THE BOOK, PLUS FULL DETAILS OF SETS

This index lists each minifigure featured in this book alphabetically, along with its page number to help you find your favorites. For super fans, we have also added the reference number of every LEGO set in which each minifigure has ever appeared. This includes all variants of the minifigures.

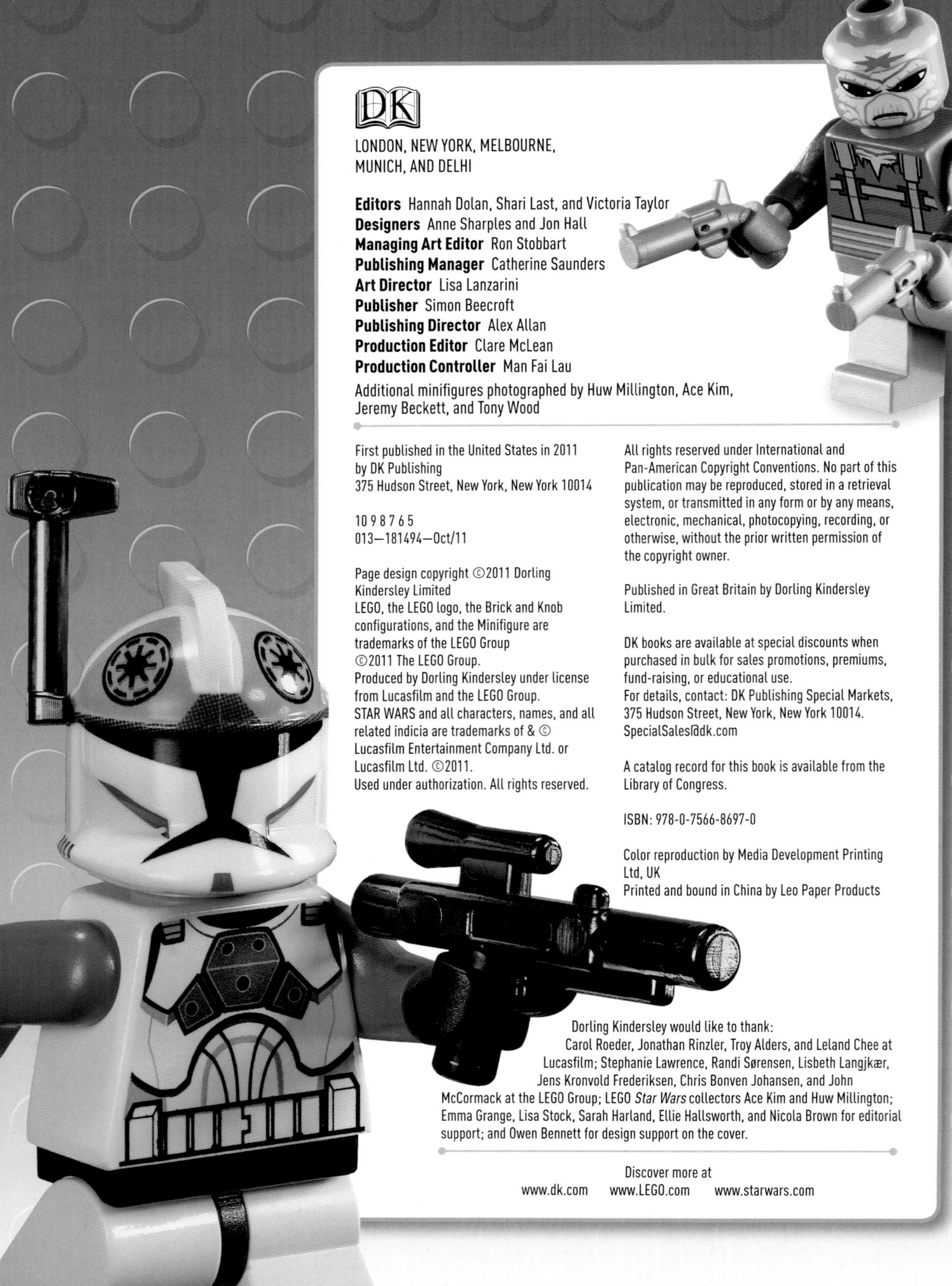

DK

LONDON, NEW YORK, MELBOURNE, MUNICH, AND DELHI

Editors Hannah Dolan, Shari Last, and Victoria Taylor
Designers Anne Sharples and Jon Hall
Managing Art Editor Ron Stobbart
Publishing Manager Catherine Saunders
Art Director Lisa Lanzarini
Publisher Simon Beecroft
Publishing Director Alex Allan
Production Editor Clare McLean
Production Controller Man Fai Lau

Additional minifigures photographed by Huw Millington, Ace Kim, Jeremy Beckett, and Tony Wood

First published in the United States in 2011 by DK Publishing
375 Hudson Street, New York, New York 10014

10 9 8 7 6 5
013—181494—Oct/11

Published in Great Britain by Dorling Kindersley Limited.

DK books are available at special discounts when purchased in bulk for sales promotions, premiums, fund-raising, or educational use.
For details, contact: DK Publishing Special Markets, 375 Hudson Street, New York, New York 10014.
SpecialSales@dk.com

A catalog record for this book is available from the Library of Congress.

ISBN: 978-0-7566-8697-0

Color reproduction by Media Development Printing Ltd, UK
Printed and bound in China by Leo Paper Products

Dorling Kindersley would like to thank:
Carol Roeder, Jonathan Rinzler, Troy Alders, and Leland Chee at Lucasfilm; Stephanie Lawrence, Randi Sørensen, Lisbeth Langjkær, Jens Kronvold Frederiksen, Chris Bonven Johansen, and John McCormack at the LEGO Group; LEGO *Star Wars* collectors Ace Kim and Huw Millington; Emma Grange, Lisa Stock, Sarah Harland, Ellie Hallsworth, and Nicola Brown for editorial support; and Owen Bennett for design support on the cover.

Discover more at
www.dk.com www.LEGO.com www.starwars.com